KNOCKOUT

by Peter Woodworth

Book III in the Dead Heroes Series

Based in the World of
Dystopia Rising

KNOCKOUT

ISBN-13:9781939785176

ESCHATON MEDIA PRODUCTIONS

www.EschatonMedia.com

For Trish

Thanks for believing in your dear Ben, always.

The Dystopian Future

Many generations have passed since the Fall of civilization. So much has been lost that no one can really say exactly how it came to pass, but the world's scars tell some of the story plainly enough. A terrible infection raged out of control - a fast-mutating disease capable of raising the dead and turning their insatiable hunger against the living. Nuclear weapons turned some cities to ashes while conventional weapons turned whole nations into battlegrounds. The world drowned in blood and fire as the living fought desperate battles, first against the dead, then later against each other as precious resources dwindled. In a flash, the time of culture and plenty was over, and the true test of survival began.

Most of the world's population perished in those early years, but against all odds some survivors held on, banding together for security as they carved out holdings in the burning wastelands and the ravaged cities. They soon discovered that the infection was not limited to the dead – everyone now carries it to some degree, and though it would raise their dead against them, it bestowed certain benefits too. Survivors healed far faster than their ancestors could imagine, and could tolerate levels of toxins and radiation that would have been fatal in days or even hours to humans of old. Divergent strains of humanity emerged as the virus continued to mutate within certain close-knit populations, creating brand new cultural and regional identities. A gifted few survivors even manifested powers humanity had never seen before, with fiery preachers calling down genuine miracles through the power of devotion and bizarre mutants known as psions displaying strange and terrifying powers of the mind.

Of course, just as the infection changed the survivors, so too did it warp the world around them. Strange plants flowered in the toxic fields, while bizarre new species stalk the wild places, many hungry for flesh and utterly unafraid of mankind Vicious raiders and feral degenerates are humans in name only, having been warped by generations of exposure to radiation, madness and brutality until they became little more than savage tribes of psychotic killers. Not that those savages are the only dangerous humans – rival groups of survivors are as great a menace to each other as humans have ever been, waging bloody wars over everything from faiths and borders to fresh food and the last box of bullets.

All of these threats pale in comparison to the constant struggle to hold out against not only the vast hordes of shambling corpses but also new and deadly breeds of the undead: predatory hunters, hulking goliaths, psionic toy boxes, vermin-infested animates and worse. Nowhere is safe from the hunger of the dead, from the tallest ruin to the depths of the oceans, and those that forget even for just a night most often pay with their lives. Worst of all, those daring and haunted few who study the shambling dead whisper about the terrible intelligence they call the Grave Mind, a dark and alien collective consciousness that forever drives the ravenous undead onward in search of flesh.

A survivor in this world grows up fast, with weapons in their hands as soon as they can hold them and hard truths told to them as soon as they can hear them. They not only grow accustomed to seeing loved ones die – from violence, illness, starvation or a host of other horrors – but also find it in themselves to face down the staggering ruin that rises up afterward. It is a brutal world, where every moment of peace comes in the shadow of violence and every bit of hope comes in defiance of horror.

Welcome to the world of Dystopia Rising.

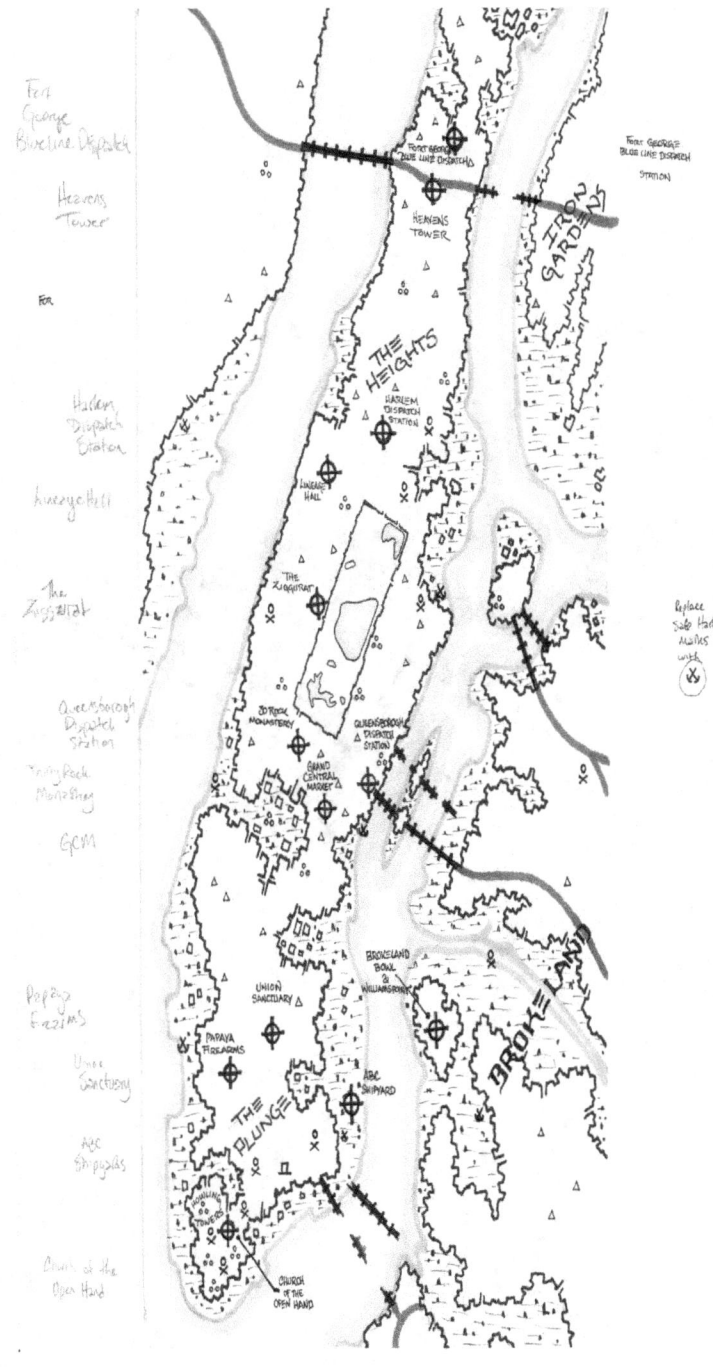

Fort
George
Blueline Dispatch

Heavens
Tower

Fort

Harlem
Dispatch
Station

Lunacy Hall

The
Ziggurat

Queensborough
Dispatch
Station

Tong Rock
Monastery

GRM

Papaya
Firearms

Union
Sanctuary

Abc
Shipyards

Church of the
Open Hand

FORT GEORGE
BLUE LINE DISPATCH
STATION

FORT GEORGE
BLUE LINE DISPATCH

HEAVENS
TOWER

THE
HEIGHTS

IRON GARDEN

HARLEM
DISPATCH
STATION

LUNACY HALL

THE
ZIGGURAT

Replace
Safe Harbor
marks
with
(X)

TO ROCK
MONASTERY

QUEENSBOROUGH
DISPATCH
STATION

GRAND
CENTRAL
MARKET

BROKELAND
BOWL
& WILLIAMSBRIDGE

BROKELAND

UNION
SANCTUARY

PAPAYA
FIREARMS

ABC
SHIPYARD

THE
PLUNGE

CHURCH
OF THE
OPEN HAND

Prologue

So no shit, there she was, Tribeca Verrazano Rockaway, hero of Old York, sniper turned runner, stuck out in the middle of nowhere with way too many fuckers out to kill her.

Tribeca Verrazano Rockaway, or just Rockaway as she was known, a sniper of the Dead Heroes gang of Old York. She got all this shit started when she agreed to be a runner for one Broadway Jack, a slippery bastard whose run turned out to be way more dangerous than advertised. Particularly when one item turned out to be half of the launch key set required to arm a nuclear missile left over before the Fall. So far it's taken her across the broken wastelands of York to a boat down the coast to the glittering cages of Aysea, and now inland into the Pine Barrens of Jersey en route to the Delphian Wastes and a hidden pre-Fall bunker codenamed "Domino."

She's only been killed once so far, so it's not too bad.

Then there's Jimmy Three Ex, another true child of York and one of the city's legendary bat men, as deadly with a humble baseball bat as most survivors are with a blade or a gun. He's a Dead Hero too, a couple of years older than Rockaway and fiercely protective of his fellow ganger. He's also in love with her, has been since he was her first some years back, but hasn't been able to tell her yet. Except once, but she was dead at the time, so it doesn't really count. Lately it seems like Jimmy's been manifesting some real miracles as a result of his devotion to the old music idols of the King's Court, but he's been a bit distracted by the fact that Doomsday has been making moves on Rockaway. That'll end well.

Speaking of Doomsday Dare, that's the current identity of one Dana Anderson, agent of the Federal Bonded Inquisition – or just G-Men, as the Yorkers call them – and sworn to protect what's left of the country from itself. She was undercover investigating a Darwinist sect that supposedly had gotten hold of a real missile from before the Fall when she crossed paths with Rockaway and Jimmy and realized they were the ones who'd actually stumbled onto the real deal, because sometimes life is just that fucking weird and cruel to all concerned. The agent joined up to make sure some crazy asshole doesn't get himself a live nuke to play with, which means keeping those keys out of the wrong fucking hands.

And there are a lot of goddamn hands reaching out for it. Back in York, Rockaway crossed paths with the Iron Cross, a gang of mercenaries who'd been hired to retrieve the shipment she was carrying and kill anyone who got in their way. Their leader, a psychotic body-snatching known as Red Hands, has made it a personal mission to track down Rockaway, even branding her with some kind of strange mark that seems to be triggering some strange changes in the Yorker. But nobody just turns psion, right?

Right?

As if that wasn't enough, Rockaway and her crew butted heads with the equally psychotic Big Playboy, boss of one of the biggest Aysea casinos and all-around fucking miserable prick. Big Playboy also turned out to be a Final Knight, a faith most for two things – worshipping demons and burning shit to the ground, because fuck you, that's why. He came after Rockaway too, tracking her down to the cult compound where they were trying to rescue a nice lady named Eve who was the other recipient of the original delivery order. When they finally beat him down, they had to cut him open to fucking kill him and found he'd been modified with zombie parts, giving him crazy regenerative powers as well as freak strength. So apparently that's a thing you can do, if you're fucked up enough to let some creepy fucking Grave Robber do some surgery on you.

Still, it might have all ended well at that point, except that it turned out Eve was in league with Big Playboy and some other Final Knights as well, and they wanted those arming keys as part of some plot to burn what was left of Old York to the ground. Rockaway shot the two-faced bitch when they found out she was in on the plot, but Eve still managed to make off with one of the keys, running fast in the direction of the city known as the Delphian Wastes.

Now the crew's in hot pursuit, not just to track down Eve but also to find out who's turned traitor in the Inquisition and tipped off the Final Knights to a real live nuke locked up inside "Domino." Of course, Eve's probably full of fucked up zed parts like Big Playboy, so who knows what crazy bullshit she has up her sleeve. Plus there's the Pine Barrens to get through on the way to the Wastes, a forest chock full of inbred Mericans, feral degenerates and who knows what sorts of crazy fucking animals.

And that's just the dangerous shit they know about. Let that sink in, right?

Fuck it. Here's how it all ended, and don't let anyone tell you fucking different.

Chapter One

"Fuck you say about York?" Rockaway said loudly, peering through the gloom of the hanging lanterns down to the end of the long wooden bar where three burly Mericans were gathered in a huddle, smirking back now that they had her full attention. The Yorker put down her chipped glass of hooch and pushed back from the bar, resisting the urge to reach for the hilt of the combat knife strapped to her thigh. Yet. "C'mon, fuckers, I don't hear you."

"Let it go," Doomsday said, putting a hand on her friend's elbow, but Rockaway shrugged it off irritably. A quick glance around the rundown bar told the story – it had gotten quiet, which wasn't good, but on the other hand none of the other patrons had gotten to their feet yet either, which meant that the three Mericans probably didn't have any close friends who'd be likely to jump in.

"Hey now, Dewey, we don't want any trouble," the bartender said mechanically, his tone indicating that he didn't really expect anyone to listen to him. The numerous blade gouges in the bar, the bullet holes in the knotted boards behind it and even the ugly throat slash scar the bartender sported seemed to affirm this conviction. He shook his shaved head as he stepped back from the trouble brewing. "I swear, every fucking bar I work …"

"Shut up, Johnny," one of the Mericans growled. He was tall and broad, with a salt and pepper beard and the sagging build of muscle mostly now gone to fat. His hat was black and broad-brimmed, with a number of long brown feathers struck through the band, so that when he moved his head it looked like a bird preening. He waggled a thick finger at Rockaway. "And you? You don't wanna go startin' trouble, missy. We're just drinkin' here."

"Drinking and talking shit, more like," Rockaway growled. A hand gripped her shoulder, but when she turned to yell at Doomsday to back off, she saw Jimmy standing there, the agent now a step behind him and taking in the room. He shook his head ever so slightly. The bat man wasn't quick to back down from a fight, so if he didn't think it was worth it … "Fuck," Rockaway swore, but without heat. She made eye contact with the big Merican and held her hands up high in the universal I'm fine, everything's cool gesture. He grunted and turned back to his drink, though the two other Mericans still had those irritating little smirks that made her grit her teeth. They were enjoying some joke at her expense, she was sure of it.

"Comes to it, we'll fuck 'em up." Jimmy said reassuringly as he let go of her shoulder.

"No fuckin' joke," Rockaway agreed. She put down a credit and gestured for another drink; after checking with the other end of the bar to see if violence was imminent, the bartender gave her a tight smile and poured her one. That was one thing she had to give this hick joint – the glasses were chipped and the bar looked like it would be improved by a fire, but the hooch was strong and surprisingly smooth.

In the few days since the shootout with Big Playboy and his goons, Doomsday had been filling in Rockaway and Jimmy about the local Mericans, these so-called Pineys, but she'd left out the skill of their distillers. Probably because she was busy covering the rumors about inbreeding, cannibalism and worse, but still, at the moment it seemed like a critical oversight. "How much longer do we have to wait?"

"I don't know. He should be here already,"

Doomsday said, biting her lower lip. It was one of her only tells, but it showed Rockaway that even she was getting anxious. Conversation in the bar was getting back to its previous level, though the other patrons were now sliding more glances in their direction than they had before. The agent pushed her dyed black hair out of her eyes, pulled it back into a tight ponytail she secured with a strip of leather. "It's not like a connect to be late."

"It's been two days since you did the, whatever it was," Jimmy said. Doomsday hadn't actually let them see what she was doing to get in touch with her connection; supposedly it was some sort of Inquisition secret. All the other two knew is that she had fussed with some of the rocks at the side of the road leading into this tired little town of Stillwater, and announced that an ally of the Inquisition would meet them in the Double Tap, the local saloon, in a day or two. What's more, this mysterious ally would be looking for the person with the white cloth tied around her left boot. It was a bit more gray than white, but she was still wearing it, three nights now.

"We really need to get on the fucking move again," Rockaway said quietly. "I mean, I'm all for some help, but Eve already had a couple days on us, and the gap's only gonna get wider. I don't know what shit she's got planned when she hits the Delphian Wastes, but it can't be good to let her get all set up, you know?"

"Yeah, except I don't know anything about the Delphian Wastes. Do you?" Doomsday didn't wait to hear from the two Yorkers – she already knew that they'd never been outside of Old York before this disastrous courier run gone bad. "It's a big place. Charging in blind isn't going to help us much, but getting a guide, or a map, that could be big for us."

"Aren't you part Delphian, or something?"

Jimmy asked.

"My mother was, but I didn't grow up there." Doomsday shrugged, brushing a few loose strands of long black hair behind her ears. "It's just a name to me."

"One more night?" Rockaway looked the agent in the eye.

"One more night," Doomsday agreed, relieved.

"Getting tired of this stuff anyway," Jimmy said. He picked up his glass of water and sniffed it experimentally. Supposedly it was from an untainted local aquifer – or as untainted as one could get these days, anyway – and it hadn't made him sick yet, but it just wasn't in a Yorker's nature to trust water that didn't need bleaching or boiling or both.

Across the bar, the bartender rolled his eyes at Jimmy – he hadn't wanted to serve water at all, and had insisted on charging the same as a glass of hooch for the trouble of the extra trips to the well. Perhaps to ward off others who might insist on a similar hassle, on the second night they'd come into the place a crude, hand-lettered sign appeared behind the bar: WE DON'T SERVE WATER, FISH FUCK IN IT. Jimmy took the hint and ordered it quietly after that.

"I think tonight's a bust anyway," Rockaway said, finishing her drink and dropping a couple credits on the bar. "We should probably get back to the caravan and get some sle—OK, fucker, you got something to say, fucking say it!" Rockaway caught the tail end of a comment and stormed to the end of the bar, the three Mericans immediately squaring off with her. Behind her, the sound of chairs scraping on floor and the rustling of clothing signaled most of the patrons getting clear of the danger area. Behind the bar, the publican sighed and ducked down, apparently intending to wait out the chaos.

"Yer a long way from the big city," the big

Merican the bartender had called Dewey said. He crossed his beefy arms against his chest and looked down at her. "I was you, I'd think on starting trouble 'round here."

"Oh yeah?" Rockaway said with mock sweetness, a savage grin on her face. Three days in a tiny town with nothing to do but sleep and drink had made her eager for a little excitement. And if smashing up some drunken Mericans didn't qualify, what did? "Why's that?"

"Because we're Baron's Boys, you dumb bitch," the shortest of the Mericans said. Like his friends, he was on the bigger side, though running far more to fat than muscle. There were grease stains on his faded white shirt the size of Rockaway's head, and from the look of it enough kernels of corn stuck in his beard to reassemble a whole cob. He tapped a badge on his hat, some sort of small animal skull mounted in front of a pair of crossed rifle cartridges. "We say git, you turn tail and fucking go!"

"Why?" Rockaway said, too sweetly. "'Fraid I might fuck your wife better than you, fat boy?" She smiled. Spy shit was one thing, but bar fights? Bar fights she knew.

"Here we go," Doomsday muttered, as the big Merican launched himself at Rockaway. His shorter friend put his head down and charged into Jimmy, while the third of the bunch – a tall, lanky sort with a bad scar on one cheek – came right at Doomsday with a wild haymaker swing. The agent ducked the punch and stepped inside his reach, striking his solar plexus with the side of her right hand in a brutal chop. He saw the hit coming and managed to turn aside just enough to keep the strike from laying him out completely, though even so it still staggered him and set him to coughing, waving his hands in front of his face to ward off more hits.

Next to her, the big Merican had used his reach and a lunge to get one arm around Rockaway's neck and was trying to pull her in close for a full headlock, but she slipped out from under his grip and stuck her foot out as his momentum carried him forward, tripping him up and sending him crashing into a table. The flimsy wood gave way under his weight, sending table legs skittering across the floor and breaking the two old glasses that had been resting on it. The big Merican gave a howl of pain as blood spurted from his nose, and Rockaway enjoyed a moment of vicious triumph before half-turning and delivering a full force kidney shot to Jimmy's attacker, who had gone low and managed to get the big Yorker a couple of feet off the ground despite the punches Jimmy was raining down on his back.

With a squeal of pain, the fat Merican dropped Jimmy back on his feet. The big Yorker took advantage of the opening to grab the back of the man's head and hold it in place as he brought his knee up three times in quick succession, battering his face repeatedly with his hard plastic knee guard. The squeal of pain quickly changed to a wet gurgling sound, and then trailed off entirely as the fat Merican went limp.

"Yub brug my noth, bith!" Dewey had rolled onto his back in the ruin of the table, one hand up to his nose to pinch off the flow of blood. The other reached into his vest, but Rockaway didn't give him time to find whatever weapon he had stashed there. With a few steps for a running start, the young sniper hauled off and kicked Dewey squarely between the legs. He howled like a half-skinned cat and doubled over on his side, both hands instinctively reaching between his legs; it seemed for a moment like he was trying to speak, curse her probably, but instead he simply vomited noisily and blacked out.

From behind her came the sound of a shot, and

Rockaway heard Jimmy cry out in pain and collapse, grabbing at his ankle. She spun, grabbing for her own holdout shooter, only to see Doomsday and the tall Merican backed up to the bar, wrestling over a pistol; it looked as though the agent had pulled the intended shot wide, but Jimmy was still down and Rockaway felt her anger boiling over. The bartender was shouting something but she wasn't hearing it – she charged forward, grabbed hold of one of the Merican's wrists and smashed her other hand down on his elbow, breaking it. He let go of the pistol and Doomsday pulled it free, but before the agent could get it pointed another pistol fired twice behind them.

"Enough of this shit! I declare this fucking over already!" The bartender slowly brought the barrel of the gun down from where it had been pointed at the ceiling, keeping it at a ready height but not pointing it at anyone in particular. "Am I fucking clear?"

Doomsday looked at Rockaway, who had frozen about three inches from taking out the man's eye with her thumb. Rockaway was breathing hard, but managed to nod slightly, then pulled back away from her target. "Clear," Doomsday said.

"I'm good with it," Jimmy said, his voice tight with pain. Doomsday looked to the bartender for permission, then walked over and knelt down by Jimmy's side to take a look at his wound.

"OK then." The bartender indicated the tall Merican. "Earl, you'd best collect Dewey and Fat Tommy and get out of here."

"But my arm, the bi – she broke my arm, Johnny!" Earl blubbered, holding up his stricken limb for emphasis. "An' they're out cold! How'm I gonna carry those two with my arm all broke?"

"Fine." Johnny looked at the small crowd gathered

at the door, singling people out as he spoke. "Tex, Bubba, you two give Earl a hand getting them back to Dewey's place. Virginia, you go on with them, make sure they get patched up. Tell them we'll settle up on damages later." He seemed to consider something and whistled for the waitress, a beautiful if bored-looking blonde in a battered straw hat. "Bessie, best to go with her, make sure she doesn't shoot off her mouth any. I'll cover in the meantime." The regulars obliged, Bessie herding them along and Earl shooting Rockaway and her friends dirty looks as he went, though snot from his blubbering was still running freely into his mustache and ruined the intimidating effect somewhat.

Rockaway barely fought down the impulse to give him more than a dirty look, but figured that being newcomers in these parts it was already pushing their luck far enough to get out of the bar without more trouble. There is an art to a good bar fight, and while she didn't have a lot of experience outside of a few trips to neutral places like the Grand Central Market back home, one thing you picked up on fast is that the crowd can turn on you quickly, especially if you're not a local.

It wasn't lost on Johnny either. "I'm gonna have to ask you folks to pay a share of the damages," he said, leaning across the bar to deliver the words in a conspiratorial murmur. "Nothing personal, just business – I can't be seen to be favoring out of towners in a dustup like this. You get how that is, right?"

"You don't look too local," Jimmy said, wincing as he tried to put weight on his injured leg. The loud print of the bartender's shirt and the gaudy jewelry did scream Vegasian, and the unpleasant memory of Broadway Jack swirled up in Rockaway's consciousness. There was a Yorker saying that Vegasians screwed everybody eventually; the trick was making sure you were the one who ended up on top. "How'd you wind up in this goddamn pit?"

"Two words, my friend," Johnny replied laconically. "Never. Franchise."

"Here," Doomsday said as Jimmy and Rockaway looked at each other, not following the joke (if it was one). She settled up by handing over a sum of about a half-dozen more credits than Rockaway would've dropped. "That about cover it?"

"Should do," Johnny said amiably, pocketing the stack. Rockaway could see him calculating how much of it he could direct his way and still make repairs, and she guessed the split of the take was one reason the place was so banged up. "Bit of friendly advice?"

"One more night here, tops," Doomsday responded, anticipating the sentiment.

"I'd say one night's pushing it," Johnny said, not sounding particularly interested whether they took his advice or not. "But hey, your call. In the meantime, I'd see to your water-loving friend over there. Looks like he caught a solid one."

"Yeah, we'll do that," Rockaway said, throwing Jimmy's arm over her shoulders and helping him to the door. "Nice fucking joint you got here," she said to no one particular, as the few remaining patrons parted to let them pass. "Classy."

"Like a double tap," the bartender agreed, and then they were outside. The night air was brisk despite the oilcan fires burning outside the bar, with no sign of the Mericans or anyone else hanging around looking to cause trouble. There was one guy apparently working his bike and a couple going off hand in hand in the direction of a beat up old caravan, but none of them seemed particularly interested in the trio of outsider leaving the bar. Doomsday closed the door behind them and fell in step on the other side of Jimmy. She tried to get his other arm across her shoulders but he waved her away, protesting that it wasn't as bad as it looked.

"You didn't have to do that, you know," Doomsday said quietly, when they'd gotten about halfway to their caravan.

"What, I'm supposed to let some inbred no-neck fuckwit talk shit on us and get away with it?" Rockaway turned and spat. "Fuck that. You don't stand up to that kind of bullshit, it gets out of hand real quick."

"What, you think the gangs back home are going to find out some asshole in the middle of the Pine Barrens talked shit on you? Please." Doomsday sounded disgusted. "You just wanted a fight, and you got one. Except that if they really are Baron's Boys, they could cause us a world of shit if we run into them before we get clear of the woods."

"Sorry if I fucking let you down," Rockaway muttered. Jimmy squeezed her shoulder sympathetically, letting her know he agreed with her despite Doomsday's words. "Just some shit don't stand, that's all."

"Yeah, well, big picture, you know what I'm saying?" Doomsday seemed about to boil over, but she took a deep breath and let it out slowly, and when she spoke again her voice was level as ever. "Sorry. I know you don't take shit, and that asshole certainly wasn't shy about pushing your buttons. I'm not sad we knocked them around – they had it coming. I'm just saying, it could screw us later, and we're already in a bad situation."

"We get it," Jimmy said quickly as Rockaway tensed up to reply. "Chill, alright?"

That might not have done much to cool off the two women on its own, but then the man who had apparently been wrenching on his motorcycle spoke, and just like that the final leg of their long journey began.

Chapter Two

"You people don't do 'subtle' all that well, do you?"

"Who's fuckin' askin'?" Rockaway turned and saw a slim man of slight build crouched facing away from her, apparently retrieving something from a lockbox chained to a beat up chopper. He was dressed in old jeans, a battered jacket that was some color between dull yellow and road dust, a broad-brimmed brown hat and an elaborately tooled leather gun belt that held one very shiny pistol. His movements were just a touch too precise to be as casual as his manner suggested, but compared to their loud and rather messy ejection from the bar it was a master class in discretion. "We know you?"

"Be easy," Doomsday replied, stepping out from under Jimmy's arm and leaving him to lean on Rockaway. "I got this. Just look like you're getting stuff from the caravan, or something," she muttered over her shoulder as she walked over to the biker.

"I am getting something," Jimmy protested sourly, his voice tight with pain as he hopped painfully into the cab of the caravan and lying across the seat to root around in his pack. "Something to wrap my shot up fucking ankle, f'instance."

"Wait, is this the guy?" Rockaway asked, not willing to turn her back on a stranger.

"Yes, it's the guy," Doomsday hissed impatiently. "Give me a second, OK?"

"Is it the guy?" Jimmy said, voice muffled by the cab but still far too loud.

"Apparently?" Rockaway answered evenly, still staring. Doomsday looked back at the two Yorkers, eyes wide with exasperation as she made a little gesture at the two Yorkers: Are you kidding me? Rockaway shrugged. This secret agent shit just wasn't her speed, and even though she'd come to trust Doomsday more than a bit for all the times she'd come through in the past week, they'd been fucked over by strangers with agendas on this run before. Way too much, in fact. Maybe throwing them off their game a little wasn't such a bad thing.

"Oh, Saints save us all," the man said wearily, shaking his head. To Doomsday, he said: "It's all right, I appreciate the effort. I don't think we're too exposed here anyway." He got up, dusted his hands on his thighs and sized up the group. In the orange light from the big oilcan fires outside of the bar, Doomsday saw fine features and a pair of glasses perched on a narrow nose, with a thick handlebar mustache which matched the red hair that fell out from under his hat almost down to his shoulders. A scratched and dented silver star was pinned to his jacket, right above the heart, the words "PONY EXPRESS" etched into it in simple letters. He held out a hand in an oiled leather fingerless glove. "If we can't be subtle, we can at least be friendly. Good to see you again, Doomsday. If that is still your name."

"At least a little longer, yeah." They shook, and Doomsday jerked her thumb back at the two Yorkers. "They're with me, obviously."

"Tribeca Verrazano Rockaway, of the Dead Heroes." Rockaway shook his hand. He had dirty nails and a surprisingly strong grip for such a lean guy, and she found her impression of him improving already. "That's Jimmy Three Ex back there, same crew. And you are?"

"Call me Heller." The man called Heller looked over at Doomsday, who gave Rockaway a final glare before waving him on. "Lucky for you guys I happened to be passing through on my way back up north."

"Wait, what?" Rockaway heard Jimmy sit up in the cab beside her. "You were just passing fucking through? The hell does that mean?"

"This place is too small to have an agent assigned to it – there's a lot of country to cover and not nearly enough of us," Doomsday explained. "But that doesn't mean we won't try to cover the ground if we can, so we set up spots where individuals friendly to the Inquisition can make contact if we need local help. It's a bit of a crap shoot, considering you never know if the friendly contacts are still around, but better than nothing. When I got went under with the Darwinists, I made an excuse to come out here a couple of times and make contact with the local connections, just in case. Heller included."

"How the hell did you know this place was one of them?"

"There are signs – kind of like gang tags but a little more subtle." Doomsday said. "A code. Plus during training we have to memorize where every one of these points are in a hundred mile radius. Heller here got the note." She smiled, a genuine one if a little stressed out all the same. "Good to see you again, believe me. How's that lunatic little town of yours? Still got you running to hell and back to keep their heads above water?" Heller let out a profound, long-suffering sigh, and then they both chuckled. Rockaway knew that kind of laugh. Usually it meant the people sharing it had fucked or spilled blood together, or maybe both.

"I expect it'll still be there, unless they started playing with the reactor while I was out."

"You'd think that something like that would be fairly self-evident, wouldn't you?" Doomsday said.

Heller allowed that he felt much the same way, but after a pointed cough from Rockaway the agent cut the rest of the pleasantries short. "We need a favor."

"A little free with operational security, aren't we?" Heller said, still smiling.

"It's been an intense week," Doomsday replied evenly. "I trust them."

"And how the fuck do you know we're not Inquisition?" Rockaway asked. "We could be undercover too, or some shit."

"Really?" Heller cocked his head slightly, one eyebrow arched.

"OK, OK," Doomsday said over the beginning of Rockaway's rather colorful response. "Like I said, I trust them. They could've cut and run but they didn't, and they kept watch while I was … in between lives. They're stand up."

"Thanks," Rockaway said. It seemed strange that they hadn't known the agent longer; this trip already felt like it was talking a lifetime. Most Yorkers had serious trust issues, but they weren't stupid either – once someone got your back often enough, it didn't matter how long you knew them, you just gave them some respect. It also didn't hurt that Doomsday's ass was on the line in this too. Self-preservation is a hell of a motivation for anyone.

"Hey, not my place to judge." Heller shrugged. "So what do you need?"

"We're heading into the Delphian Wastes. You been by that way lately?" Heller nodded. "Great. We'll take most anything you can give us that might help out in that regard."

"What, like a guide?" Heller took off his glasses and began polishing them with his shirttail. "Because, no offense, I don't know if I want to get mixed up in whatever you're looking into. Too many fires of my own to put out."

"Not a problem," Doomsday said smoothly. "You're a Postwalker, right?" She gestured to his badge, and he nodded. "Do you have any maps we could take off your hands? We've got the cred for them."

"Could use a bit of a low down in general," Rockaway added. "Faces, places, the big gangs and how they mesh, you know, the whole fucking show."

"Huh." Heller pushed his glasses back up the bridge of his nose. "How much can I say?"

"Like I said, I trust them." Doomsday nodded in the direction of the two Yorkers. "Consider them deputized. Give us everything."

"You got it." Heller pulled out a battered leather satchel and opened the clasps, revealing a stash of rolled papers in various sizes and colors. Jimmy whistled – it looked like the papers were fresh pulp, not bleached or endlessly copied over like most papers they saw. It was a difficult, time-consuming process, and most survivors considered far too much of a luxury to make the investment. Even when you forked over the credits for some new stock, it was often coarse, lumpy and discolored, barely better than writing on tree bark. Whoever Heller was, he was either one hell of a printer or knew someone who was, because that was fine stock indeed. She knew the Doc would've given up just about all he owned for a ream of that stuff, and considered it a bargain too. Heller thumbed through the stash, found the roll he wanted and gestured to the hood of the truck. "Mind if I lay it out?"

"Sure, go ahead," Rockaway said. Heller spread out a thin piece of fabric to act as a bottom sheet, and then unrolled the paper carefully, spreading it with practiced ease as Jimmy hobbled down from the cab to take a look. A finely drawn map was revealed as the paper unrolled, each line painstakingly inked by hand, a network of major roads, important monuments and known threats carefully inked in fine black lines.

Rockaway looked over at Jimmy and caught her own thoughts reflected back at her in his expression – if anyone had a map this good of Old York they'd make a killing selling it at the markets. Not that the territories weren't clearly marked, or for that matter zealously enforced, but due to a healthy level of paranoia among the gangs it wasn't exactly easy to make very good maps much beyond your own territory. Something like this would change the city – or start a war.

"OK, here's what you need to know." Heller went through the map methodically, emphasizing key points with pointed taps on the precious paper. "There's only one approach from this direction, and that's crossing at the Franklin Span. See? This is the Pale Horse Pike here – as you approach it gets re-routed north to feed into the approach to the bridge. The good news is the Span is held by Sainthood—" he nodded at Doomsday, "and a garrison of Fallow Hopes, so you don't have to worry about getting robbed or ripped there. So long as you don't cause trouble, they'll leave you be.

"Unfortunately it also means you have to pass through the Damned Den on the way in. It's not a long stretch, mile and a half or so, but it can get pretty rough. It's a wide open stretch without a lot of room to maneuver, especially since the Duponts tried to send a mercenary force around on a flanking maneuver."

"The who?" Jimmy asked.

"Pureblood family from further south," Doomsday answered immediately. The others stared at her. "What? The Inquisition works closely with the Lineage League. It pays to know the names of the big families, especially the ones on this coast."

"More on them in a moment, I promise," Heller said. "Right now the most relevant detail is that the bridge garrison has knocked out all secondary approaches and arranged switchbacks and roadblocks all along the two remaining roads leading into the bridge, to slow down any future assault forces. Over the strenuous objections of the Sainthood representatives, I might add, but in this case the Fallow Hopes followers overruled them. Losing almost fifty percent of your garrison and damn near losing the bridge made them … insistent."

"Fuckers took out half my gang, I'd get pretty loud about security too." Rockaway said. Jimmy grunted in agreement.

"Understandable," Doomsday allowed, "but that means we'll be really exposed on the way in. Is there any way to signal friendly as we approach? I assume they have spotters watching the approach."

"They watch, but after those nasty surprises they don't tend to ride out unless it's clear you're under attack by zed. That will always draw out Fallow Hopes – Sainthood too, for that matter – but they know it's the sort of thing that could be used against them, too, so … it's tough. Don't get me wrong, they're good people, but that attack has really ramped up their paranoia. I wouldn't expect a quick rescue if you get in trouble, much as it pains me to say so."

"Dumb fucking question – there another bridge?" Jimmy asked.

"Not dumb at all," Heller replied, "but damned inconvenient, especially if time is a factor. Franklin Span is the only crossing for miles – used to be a couple other bridges immediately north and south of it on the river, but the southern bridge got taken out during the

Fall and the northern crossing just sort of disintegrated over the years. Heck, the Franklin's only barely holding on in parts, and that's with a full-time crew of tinkers and scavengers dedicated to keeping it that way. There are other bridges still working, but one's really way out of your way to the north, and the next crossing to the south is deep in Dupont territory, so I'd recommend against those options."

"What about ferries? Boats? Any shit like that?" Rockaway didn't like boats much, but running through the Damned Den didn't sound like a much better option, so she figured it was worth putting everything on the table.

"Good thought, but no. Nothing that isn't about as far out of the way as making for one of the other bridges, anyway. The waterfront's mostly been collapsed and barricaded – too many zed making the crossing that way before. Only landings are pretty out of the way."

"So straight through Damned Den it is, I guess." Rockaway tapped it on the map. "With no hoping on the goddamn cavalry. You said it's pretty nasty – are we talking horde, raiders, warlords, what?"

"No organized raiding parties, but there are some odd scavenger clans that roll through from time to time, and the horde gets pretty thick there on a regular basis. The Fallow Hopes sends out patrols to keep the horde contained as best they can, but it's tough." Heller's brow wrinkled. "I don't know why, but something about the bridge really seems to draw them, and not just because it's the only way across for miles. The Sainthood has some theories on that, but I guess that's not really relevant at the moment."

"Let's stay in the practical for the time being," Doomsday agreed. "What's the toll?"

"Nothing," Heller replied.

"You're shitting me!" Rockaway exclaimed. "They hold a whole bridge and they don't charge anything for it? They're the most direct connect from the Delphian Wastes down to Aysea, and they just let people roll on by? Fuck's wrong with them?"

"Not everything boils down to credits," Heller said defensively. Both he and Doomsday were followers of the Sainthood of the Ashes, and obviously resented the slight against their fellow faithful. "Besides, they struck a deal with the big collectives in the city – so long as the major players provide some scrap and manpower, the garrison will keep the bridge open and as stable as possible. With that kind of backing, they don't need to charge the poor bastards who make it through the Damned Den hoping to find a safe place to sleep. Though they do take donations, I imagine."

"Fair enough. Guess we should be glad not everything's run like back home, sometimes," Jimmy said.

"As I remember, the Inquisition outpost is in the remains of the old rail station, at the border of the University Markets," Doomsday said, scanning the map until she found it. Her face fell a bit; the section marked University Markets was on the western side of the city, connected by a couple of narrow bridges from the look of it. "Oh. I was hoping it would be closer."

"Forget closer, try safer." Heller indicated the area immediately across the river from the Franklin Span, marked as Fort Independence. "This is the heart of the old city, goes back hundreds of years. It's pretty heavily dug in, lots of fortifications and trenchworks, but don't let looks fool you, the milita are mostly good folks. Lots of Mericans – I know what you're thinking, after nights like tonight the last thing you want to see are more Mericans – but this bunch is a bit of a different breed.

"They're still loud and proud as always, of course, but they're there to defend some of the oldest surviving ties to the founding of the country, and so they're a bit more driven and focused than usual. So long as you don't badmouth the flag or lip off to the Major, they'll generally treat you right. You might even be able to use the Inquisition thing to your advantage, if you really got backed into a corner, but I'd be careful about that. They've got plenty of love for the country, but the Inquisition's ties to the Purebloods could be a problem, since most of those fortifications are due to the Duponts attacking from down south."

"Again with those assholes," Rockaway said. "What's their fucking deal, anyway?"

"How much do you know about the world south of Aysea?" Heller asked. Rockaway and Jimmy looked back at him blankly, not responding. He turned to Doomsday. "Should I just assume that everything outside of York is one big question mark?"

"More like one big 'who gives a fuck'," Rockaway said, smiling pleasantly.

"Anyway," Heller said loudly, turning back to the map and pointing to the extreme southern end. "Most of the area south of the Delphian Wastes was low-lying land, and most of it went under during the Fall, taking a lot of industrial and manufacturing land with it as well. The Duponts control what's left, employing large mercenary forces to protect and expand their territory like Purebloods usually do. The Duponts will tell you that they have an old bloodline stretching back before the Fall, though I've heard some rumors to the contrary."

"True," Doomsday chimed in. "I know they've

applied for recognition by the Lineage League several times, but it's been refused. They're not the original family that went by that name, but a collection of smaller families who took over their lands and holdings during the Fall, so the League will not grant them true Pureblood status. They're pretty ticked off about it too, I remember that."

"Wait, you're not a Pureblood unless the League says so?" Jimmy asked. "I thought they were a strain like anyone else, not a social club?"

"It's a little of both," Doomsday said, slipping into that lecturing tone she got when reciting something from her training. "Yes, there is a so-called 'Pureblood' strain of the virus that's common to the descendants of the very wealthy, those who could shelter their families from the worst of the radiation and the infection in its early stages. That's genetics."

"But being a Pureblood is also about respect, about resources, and most of all about business connections. That's all social, and until the Lineage League recognizes a bloodline, a lot of the others won't do business with that family. Which effectively blocks them from the really big time, and makes them fair game for all the other families. There's a real animus – uh, hate – for upstarts among the Purebloods. They're a small club compared to the other strains, and they don't like letting in new members. It's part of how they stay so influential."

"And fuck the rest of us when they feel like it, don't forget," Rockaway added. Doomsday was a Remnant, half Delphian on her mother's side and a real mutt on her father's by her account, but she'd been raised in a Pureblood's household since her parents had been in his employ. That same Pureblood had arranged for her to get her post in the Federally Bonded

Inquisition, so she tended to look at the a bit more favorably than most. To most of the other inhabitants of Old York, the peacocks were a necessary evil at best, and outside of business it paid to avoid their attention altogether if you didn't want to get dragged into their endless family squabbles.

"Sure," Doomsday said, clearly swallowing an urge to argue about it. "Point is, they're a pretender family as far as the other Purebloods are concerned. That limits a lot of their options as far as really making it big time, but it also makes them dangerous. The other way to be recognized by the Lineage League is to make it impossible for them to ignore you. It's only worked a handful of times, but it has worked."

"Which explains what the Duponts are doing in the Delphian Wastes," Heller confirmed, bringing their attention back to the map. "Speaking as someone who just came up that way, they can't expand much to the south – they've got The District to contend with, another Pureblood bastion and basically a fortress, and the outlying lands worth a damn are heavily patrolled. It'd be suicide.

"As it is, they're lucky the families there haven't felt like pushing any further north. Pushing west quickly pits them against the Three Rivers syndicates, and the slavers would chew them up for every mile. East across the bay lands them in conflict with Aysea, and there's no way they're winning that one either, not with so many settlements relying on the business that goes through that harbor." He smoothed the corners of the map. "It really is go north and take the Delphian Wastes, or stay bottled up and go nowhere. Hence the attacks."

"How bad are we talking?" Rockaway asked.

"Well, it's not exactly a siege, but they've built

up some mercenary strongholds in the marshes at the outskirts of the city, and from there they regularly harass the southern edges of Fort Independence and the University Markets." Heller replayed common lines of attack on the map with his fingers. "Skirmishes mostly, with the occasional serious play for territory to keep the locals on their toes. Rumor has it that they've promised major territory and looting rights to any group that wins them their first big foothold in the city, so it gets pretty fierce."

"What are relations like between University Markets and Fort Independence?" Doomsday said, pointing at the border. "I remember my mom telling me that it was getting pretty factionalized when she left."

"Totally factionalized." Heller shook his head. "It's pretty tense. If it wasn't for the Duponts creating a common enemy I think there'd be open fighting. As it is, the last time I was in town they mostly keep to themselves except for the occasional supply deals and border flare ups. Johnny Rocket is the de facto leader of the University Markets gangs – skinny little Retrograde with a knack for making great shooters and using them on you before you use one on him. Met him once while I was negotiating some trade routes on my way south – he was charming to the point where you knew right off you couldn't trust him, you know what I mean?"

"I've met a few assholes like that, sure," Rockaway deadpanned. Doomsday punched her lightly on the arm.

"So he's the fucker we'll have to deal with?" Jimmy asked.

"Well, it'll get back to him no matter what, you can bet on it. Fortunately he's fairly mercenary, so as long as you pay the cover to enter the Markets he generally won't be too curious about why you're there. You're actually more likely to get questioned about your business by the Major in Fort Independence; I don't think they'd try to stop you, exactly, but tread carefully. If the border's been hot lately they're bound to be more suspicious."

"Are these are only options?" Doomsday pointed at an area north of Fort Independence, which was simply labeled "The Fishery" and accompanied by a skull and crossbones. "This doesn't look good, but exactly how bad are we talking here? Any chance we could skirt the edges, make our way to the north bridge?"

"No offense, I'm sure you're all very capable, but it's ... it's pretty damn bad." Heller looked over at her gravely. "Hence the warning label. They call it the Fishery because anyone who goes in there is basically bait. Lots of horde activity, plus enough raiders and bandits to make it a really pretty desperate option. They've actually fortified most of the area around the old bisecting highway that cut across the city there, in an effort to keep that trade route open, so even if you did make it through the Fishery the guards on the bridge might shoot you simply out of habit. It's grim."

"There any underground?" Rockaway swept her hand over the map in an encompassing gesture. "I dunno how the city was fixed for tunnels before the Fall, but York's full of 'em. Run by Lascarian clans mostly, apart from the odd section taken over by raiders. Still, you can pay your way through a lot of them, if there's no bad between your gang and the clan in charge."

"I hadn't considered that." Heller rubbed his chin, thinking. "Could work. There are some tunnels, yeah. Even a rumor of a working cart system in one of them. The city didn't have a huge underground system compared to some others, but there's still a Lascarian presence in what's left. From what I hear, it's run by a chieftain called the Underking, but that could be out of date – you know how fast they tend to go through leaders. No maps, either, and that means no guarantee they have a way to smuggle you to University Markets, if that's what you're after." He held up his hands. "I wish I could tell you more, but I don't have anything else on them. You'll have to find out more locally."

"You've told us plenty," Doomsday reassured him. "I've got no complaints."

"Yeah man, thanks," Jimmy echoed her sentiment. He flexed his leg a bit, seeing how far the healing had gotten. "Hope we didn't blow your profile or some shit like that."

"Folks around here know I'm a trader and a Jones." Heller shrugged, unconcerned. "As far as anyone who might be looking can tell, you wanted to buy a map and some route advice from me, and I obliged you." Evidently that was intended as a discreet request for compensation, as Doomsday pulled out a small stack of credits and handed it over. Heller tucked them away and shook hands all around. "Anything else, or are we done?"

"Stay on the Pale Horse until it redirects up through the Damned Den, run the gauntlet there to the Franklin Span garrison, cross over to Fort Independence and then either see the Underking or bargain with Johnny Rocket to make it to the rail station. Oh, and steer clear of the Fishery and the Duponts. I miss anything?" Doomsday looked at the others.

"You just came through the Wastes yourself, right?" Rockaway asked, and Heller nodded. "Fuckin' A. You didn't happen to run into a crazy blonde bitch in red leathers driving a beat up old red caravan on your way through, did you?" Rockaway asked. It was a long shot, but what the hell, why not?

"Actually, yes," Heller replied, looking at each of them in turn to see whether this was very good or very bad news. "She was at the Franklin Span garrison when I crossed, day and a half back or so. I was dropping off a load of bandages and counterseptic hooch from Fort Independence and one of their docs was treating her – bullet wound gone septic, I think. She was in pretty rough shape. I remembered because of the leathers, and the fact that it seemed odd a simple bullet wound could cause such a massive infection."

"I hope that fuckin' bitch chokes on her own blood and dies," Rockaway spat, feeling a bit of a vicious thrill at the idea of Eve laid out and feverish from the bullet she'd put in her. She'd been pissed it hadn't been a better shot, but apparently it had done the trick after all, or near enough. "Spare us a bit more travel at the fucking least."

"Too fuckin' right," Jimmy agreed, high-fiving her.

"I've seen plenty of wounds go toxic," Doomsday said, curious. "What caught your attention about this one?"

"The wound just looked strange," Heller explained. "There was this sticky white fluid coming out along with the blood – not pus, not anything normal. He wasn't taking any chances, though. Full mask, gloves, the whole bit. She's lucky she got a Sainthood doc, I'll tell you that – most medics don't screw around with strange cases like that, they just put a bullet in them and see if they come back better when everything restarts. Or skip waiting and burn them down, which is really just as likely."

"Luck of the fucking devil," Jimmy muttered. He balled one hand into a fist, then extended his index and pinky fingers while keeping his thumb laid across his middle and ring fingers, forming the sacred sign of the King's Court. It was an all-purpose sort of gesture, in this case a ward against the attention of powers behind the Final Knights, Rockaway knew. She made it herself, because she knew it would make him feel better, and anyway it never hurt to be too careful. She caught Doomsday crossing herself as well.

"I take it this is bad news?" Heller said, when no one spoke for a moment.

"Bad news that it sounds like she'll make it, good news that she's been slowed down. She had a couple of days on us, and even if she's not still there when we arrive, at least we'll have closed the gap a bit." Doomsday made a so-so gesture. "We'll take it."

"Shit, sounds good to me," Rockaway said.

"Take care of that crazy town," Doomsday said as Heller walked away. "If you ever get tired of running routes and taking shit for them, we could use someone like you in my outfit, full-time."

"Oh? Your name open a lot of doors?" Heller asked playfully, not looking back, but Doomsday just looked pained. "Thanks, but I'm going to see it through just a while longer."

"You said that last time," Doomsday bantered back, rallying a little.

"Well, you'll have to make sure to live long enough to ask again, then," Heller said, giving his chopper a last check before mounting up. He revved the engine to life, saluted. "Promises to keep, Doomsday."

"And miles to go before I sleep," Doomsday muttered as he drove off, a cloud of dust and thick black exhaust.

"You know where he's going?" Jimmy asked.

"Old poem by a guy named Jack Frost," Doomsday corrected. "My father taught it to me when I was a kid. The end of it goes: 'The woods are lovely, dark and deep, but I have promises to keep, and miles to go before I sleep, and miles to go before I sleep.'"

"Pretty," Jimmy said, impressed.

"Too fucking right, is what it is," Rockaway said. "We got miles to go ourselves. Let's get moving." She looked back at the shithole bar. "I've had enough of this hillbilly shit to last the rest of my fucking life. I could use another city, right about now."

"It won't be York," Doomsday cautioned.

"S'OK," Jimmy said philosophically. "Nothing is."

Chapter Three

Rockaway woke to the sound of Jimmy pounding frantically on the roof of the caravan. "We got company! C'mon! Get the fuck up!" There was some sort of high-pitched sound outside, but it was hard to make out exactly what it might be considering how muffled it was through the side of the caravan. Doomsday was already pulling her pants on, her pistol never out of reach.

"The fuck is it? Zed?" Rockaway hollered, skipping her pants and just tugging on her boots and her vest before grabbing up her rifle. She kicked open the rear hatch and immediately regretted her priorities a bit as a blast of chilly night air blew right up her boxer shorts and sent shivers up her bare arms. She pushed the discomfort aside and scanned the area – after the incident at the bar, they'd gone down the road a couple of miles before pulling off into the trees by the roadside. The idea had been to screen them at least a little bit from any night traffic, which had seemed good enough at the time, but now having the trees around wasn't doing anything for her nerves.

"Dunno, but it's some fucking thing. Maybe a couple of them. Listen!" Rockaway could hear the tension in Jimmy's voice, like a plucked guitar string, but it sounded like the noise stopped as soon as she opened the back of the caravan. Doomsday scooted up next to her, swinging her legs over the tailgate and pointing her pistol into the darkness. A moment passed with nothing but their excited breathing breaking up the silence.

Doomsday tapped Rockaway on the shoulder, gestured to the both of them and made a sweeping motion before pointing back to her eyes: Should we circle around and have a look? Rockaway nodded and they eased off the tailgate together and headed around opposite sides of the caravan, shooters up and ready. Rockaway was no stranger to moving quickly and quietly, but she was a stranger to the pine forest, and despite her best efforts the bed of dry needles at her feet crunched far more noisily than she'd liked. She was about halfway to the front of the caravan when Jimmy gave a short, soft whistle.

"Far side of the road," he muttered, barely audible. "On the right, one o'clock to my twelve." Rockaway heard Doomsday murmur something, but only Jimmy could make it out. He muttered back, then swore quietly. "Doomsday's got movement on her side too. At least two, big enough to be a problem."

"I see mine," Rockaway said, sighting down on a dark form that was slowly creeping around the trunk of a tree on the far side of the road. It was big but low to the ground, moving with predatory patience and barely making a sound, the movement so slow it would almost go unnoticed if you weren't looking right at it. "Fuck. Hunters, maybe?"

"Since when do hunters fucking screech?" Jimmy asked.

"I dunno, Jersey's backwards as fuck! Maybe their hunters howl or some shit. Maybe it's wolves. Fuck should I know?" The shape on the far side of the road had stopped at the edge of the deep shadow afforded by the trees. The moonlight made the road into something like a river of light, and whatever it was, it knew it would be exposed when it crossed. "Pass the word. Shoot when I do. We put out a lot of lead all at once, maybe it drops a couple and spooks the rest."

"Maybe it draws more," Jimmy countered.

"I say shoot," Rockaway said stubbornly. "Got it?"

"Yeah," Jimmy said, not happy. He could deal with it – she thought she saw another shape moving down the tree line. She heard the word get passed, and Jimmy tapped his bat on the roof of the caravan twice. Go time. "I hate these fucking woods," Rockaway said, steadying her hands against a shiver from the cold. Was it her imagination, or were there eyes glinting back at her in the darkness? Something to aim at, anyway. She took a breath, exhaled, and fired.

Whatever it was, apparently it took a bullet to the head like most anything else – there was a little puff of blood and brain matter and the shape slumped back into the shadows and out of sight. Rockaway racked another round and swung her rifle down the tree line where she'd seen the other shape lurking, hearing Doomsday's pistol crack three times in rapid succession as Jimmy scrambled to his feet, ready to drop down where he was needed. "One!" she heard Doomsday call out.

"Two!" Rockaway called back. So that was two down, whatever they were. Another shape burst out of the underbrush a few yards down from where she'd anticipated, but as Rockaway sighted down it rose from a loping quadrupedal gait to run upright, and when it hit the moonlight and she finally got a good look at it her finger hesitated on the trigger. "The fuck…" the Yorker heard herself say as the creature barreled toward her. Rockaway had seen a lot of fucked up shit in her life, and ended up shooting it without too much trouble most of the time, but whatever this thing was it was a whole new category of fucked.

In the moonlight it looked like a man, except instead of hair it had long, curled horns that rose from

43

its brow and swept back along the sides of its head. It howled as it came, a high, horribly keening sound, and its jaw hung open impossibly wide, revealing large, cracked teeth and letting ropes of thick, rabid slaver drool out as it shrieked. A thin tail whipped behind it, and aside from thick fur leggings of some kind it was naked from the waist up, its wiry body more heavily scarred and muscled than some pit fighters she'd seen.

There were some sort of strange symbol painted on its chest, but she didn't recognize it and didn't have much time to wonder besides. Its arms were long, too long, enough that it dropped down to a four-legged posture for a few strides as it came before bouncing back upright, powerful fists not so much as bleeding from the scrapes. The thing didn't have a weapon, but didn't look like it would need one. It was shockingly fast for something that size too, covering the ground at a pace that would put bursters to shame.

"Fuck it!" Rockaway recovered and fired, but the creature juked to the right and her round caught the thing in the shoulder instead of center mass. It spun all the way around with the impact and slowed its pace, hissing and yowling even as blood flowed freely down its body, but didn't stop coming. Rockaway took aim again as it finished crossing the road, dodging between trees to come at her. This time she feinted the shot, jerking the rifle up without firing, and the thing took the bait, juking as it had before. When it was fully committed, Rockaway fired, catching the thing in the throat and nearly taking its head off. The body crashed blindly into a tree and flopped to the ground, limbs twitching, but made no immediate indication that it was getting up again. "Fucking three!"

"They're fast!" Doomsday's voice was perfectly calm, as though she was simply talking over a loud party. Two more shots rang out, and another howl was cut off abruptly. "Four! And more out there!"

"Rock! Down!" Jimmy called out. Rockaway dropped flat, her bare legs scraping on the layer of dry needles. A large shape flew by above her, close enough that she could smell the rancid meat on its breath, crashing to the ground a few feet away and already rapidly scrabbling back to its feet. Rockaway fired point blank at the center of the shadowy shape, hoping to hit something vital; judging from the pained yelp it was a hit but not fatal.

"I got you! I'm – the fuck?!" Jimmy called out, followed by another monstrous shriek, cursing and the sound of heavy weight hitting metal. Rockaway couldn't spare a moment to help, though, as the creature was back on its feet and bearing down on her again. She dropped her rifle and snatched up her holdout pistol from its holster just as it readied itself to pounce, putting a shotgun round in its gut. In the flash from the shot she could see the hole her rifle round had already punched in its belly, and right after the shot she could smell the distinctive odor of a punctured bowel. Rockaway had a flash of a thought – fuck you, don't you jump and get me covered in shit – but the creature just pitched over backward, bleating weakly and clutching at its ruined belly.

"Five!" Doomsday called out, but the words were followed immediately by a loud clack. "Jammed! Shit! Shitshitshit!"

Rockaway opened her mouth to shout something about coming to help when she saw a huge shadow tumble off the top of the caravan toward her. A lifetime of ambush reflexes were all that let her roll away before the shape crashed down on top of her, and even so she got smacked across the face with something hard and leathery as it hit the ground and rolled into her. Whatever it was thrashed and snarled, lashing out as soon as it made contact with her, her armor turning aside what would have been a disemboweling claw strike so that it merely ripped some cloth and scratched the plate beneath.

"Fucker!" Rockaway said, unable to reach her combat knife with a leg half-pinned under the creature. Instead she reached out and took hold of one of horns on the thing's head and pulled back, hard, while she snaked her other arm around its neck and applied a chokehold as she pushed herself up into a sitting position. It was a messy move without much leverage, being as she was still half-buried under the thing and probably almost a hundred pounds lighter, but evidently it was a surprising one. The creature's growl guttered off into a startled gurgle as her grip tightened and she got her other hand around to secure her grip – it immediately tried a headbutt, but Rockaway jerked her head to one side and all it did was give her a fat lip with the side of one horn.

There was nothing like cutting off the air supply to make an enemy panic and forget all kinds of advantages. Angry Justin had taught her that when she just starting to learn how to throw down properly, and while he'd meant it more for rival gangs and raiders, it seemed to work just fine on fucked up Jersey forest monsters too. Massive clawed hands scratched and slashed at her, blindly seeking her eyes or her throat, anything to relax the hold, but Rockaway just screwed her eyes shut and put her chin to her chest as she tightened her grip even more. "Die, fucker, die, die, die…" she chanted through clenched teeth, wincing as she took a grazing scratch along her cheek perilously close to her eye.

The thing tried to regain its feet and she felt that leathery membrane slap against her face again, but she set her weight against the motion and gave it a few knee strikes with her free leg as it tried to rise. Her bare skin impacted against flesh under a coat of thick, oily fur, and something small and thin tried to twine around her leg as it came in for the second Rockaway couldn't put much power in them at this angle, though, and if the creature registered them it didn't give much sign. It tried another headbutt and this time it landed a rattling shot on her temple that caused an explosion of white stars behind her closed eyes. The Yorker choked back a fit of nausea and held on tighter, muscles straining, willing the thing to fucking die already.

"Hey! Ho!" Jimmy half-shouted, half-sang, followed by a sound like boots hitting sandy ground and the slide of aluminum against steel. "Let's go." The impact that followed jolted Rockaway painfully against the tree, but that was nothing compared to what the creature must have felt – she heard the sickly snapping of ribs breaking badly, and the flailing hands in her face slackened almost immediately. A few more blows followed in rapid succession, and from the sound of it at least one arm was broken, not to mention more ribs. Something that might have wanted to be a howl wheezed out of the creature, and she felt it trying to kick at Jimmy, but a lot of its power was already gone.

"Don't move, Rock." The sniper held as still as she could with a thrashing monster in her arms, and she could hear the bat whistling as it came down. There was a dull crack as creature's head jerked and she felt hot blood spray across her face as its body went limp. She let go and pulled herself free of the body, took Jimmy's offered hand and got to her feet. Movement at the front of the caravan caught her eye but before she could grab for the combat knife she saw it was Doomsday. The agent had a ripped sleeve with some blood on it, but otherwise looked unharmed.

"You OK?" Rockaway asked, touching the cut on her cheek and wincing at the sting.

Doomsday nodded. "I think I drove one off. Wounded it before the gun jammed, though." She looked at the big creature sprawled out at their feet, goggled a little as she took it in. "Saints, what is that thing?"

"Fucking, crazy, bullshit," Jimmy said, punctuating each word with another smash to the monster's ruined head, his bat dark with blood and tufts of hair. Apart from the horned skull, or what was left of it anyway, what remained of the creature seemed to bear up his verdict: a heavily muscled torso, furred legs that ending in jagged looking hooves, muscular arms ending in wicked clawed hands and a long curl of entirely hairless tail. Even stranger, spread out beneath it on the ground were huge, leathery wings.

"Degenerates, maybe?" Doomsday ventured. Rockaway grunted a cautious agreement. Degenerates were a bit like raiders, too many generations in the wastelands, except they went feral and animalistic instead of mindlessly aggressive. Some of the really far gone ones looked more like animals than people, or just as likely some fucked-up combination of the two. Not too many of them back in York, though she'd heard enough from the Ghost Station crew about the tribes of rat degenerates in the deep sewers to know that they were real and not a myth. And if there were rat-people living in the city, who could say what crazy shit was possible in deep woods like these?

"Fuck, I don't know," Rockaway said, wondering why she was shivering until she remembered she'd

48

skipped her pants in her rush to exit the caravan. Now her legs were cut and bruised in a dozen different places, not to mention streaked with dirt and blood. Now she'd have to wipe down with a rag before she could put her pants back on – she wasn't shy about dirty, but still, there was a line. The sniper slid her rifle out from under the body, along with her holdout piece. "This whole shitty state is deeply, deeply fucked."

"No argument," Doomsday said, pressing a scrap of her ripped sleeve to the cut on her forearm, then pulling it back to examine the bleeding. Apparently satisfied it wasn't a dangerous wound, she knelt down to look closer at the body. "This one is a lot more mutated than the others, though. It has fur on its legs, real fur, but the ones I got just had fur leggings. Plus, none of them had-" she gestured to the wings and the tail "-all of this. Worshippers?"

"Kids?" Rockaway offered. For a moment nobody spoke as that ugly thought sank in.

"Fucker dropped out of the fucking sky on me," Jimmy said darkly, not taking his eyes off the body. A fresh bruise of impressive size was blooming on one cheek and his lip was split in two places, but he twitched away when Rockaway tried to examine him. "I'm fine," he muttered, fingers curling and uncurling around the handle of his bat. "Dropped on me right out of the damn trees, just floated down on those fucking wings. I hadn't heard it start howling right before it hit, who fucking knows, you know?"

"But you're dead now, arentcha, fucker!" Jimmy shouted with sudden fury, then spat on the corpse and wiped his bloody lips with the back of his fist. He looked over at the two women and smiled a tight smile that was just a little bit unnerving with so much blood on his teeth. "Let's burn these assholes and get the fuck up out of here." At that he kicked an area of clear ground around the body, to keep the fire from spreading, then turned and walked to where their spare fuel tin hung on the side of the caravan.

"I don't know how much we can spare," Doomsday said carefully. Her eyes flicked to Rockaway, asking what was going on. Rockaway gave a shrug and a small gesture of indifference: He'll get over it, leave him be. This was what he was like when he was rattled, and Kings knew that it would rattle most anyone to have that fucked up monster drop on them out of nowhere. Shit, the more she looked at it the more it creeped her out that she'd even been touching it, let alone put it in a chokehold. She never thought she'd prefer a zed come calling in the night, but looking down at that mess of creature made her wonder.

"Then we burn this fucker, at least," Jimmy said calmly, taking down the fuel can and sloshing out some over the body. "We burn him, we drive down the road a couple miles and we leave these freaks way the fuck behind us. Plan?"

Doomsday and Rockaway nodded, the agent leaning against the Yorker as she did so. Rockaway rested her hand in the small of Doomsday's back reassuringly, not quite sure what inspired her to do it but knowing it was right all the same.

"Cool," Jimmy said, and if the fuel can shook a little in his hands as he put it back on the caravan, he hid it well. He rummaged through his pockets until he came up with his striking set and methodically worked it until he nursed a usable spark and the body was well ablaze. He scattered a few handfuls of dry needles on it, just to make sure the fire well and truly caught, then stood back and watched it burn, absently chewing at his bloody lip. Doomsday started to say something after a minute but Rockaway just tapped her back and shook her head.

They watched the monster burn until it was well on its way to being a lump of greasy bones and ashes in the woods, Rockaway not even bothering to retrieve her pants as they stood by the fire. At last, Jimmy looked at them with an expression closer to the one Rockaway was more familiar with. "Ready?" he asked lightly, as if they'd been watching a cooking fire burn down instead of torching some hideous backwoods creature.

"Fuck, been waiting on you, Thirteen," Rockaway said, smiling tiredly. Jimmy returned it and gestured to the caravan. Doomsday and Rockaway crawled into the back, making clumsy efforts to clean off their new cuts and bruises and generally feeling twice as exhausted as they had before they'd gone to sleep earlier.

"This place smells like shit and monsters," Jimmy said with some finality, hauling himself into the cab and coaxing the old engine to life. "Let's get the fuck out of here." He eased them out of the trees and back onto the road, from the sound of it driving over at least one of the degenerates in the process.

Despite the bumps in the road and the fresh aches in her body, Rockaway started nodding off almost immediately, head on her pack and curled into her much-mended blanket, Doomsday spooned up against her as comfortably as they could manage with their injuries. She was out of it so fast that Doomsday had to repeat her question. "He OK? Really?"

"Sure," Rockaway murmured sleepily, wincing as she shifted and put her weight on a fresh scrape. "He's cool. Just not used to backwoods monsters 'n shit."

"Yeah," Doomsday agreed, a far-off note in her voice. A moment later, even fainter, she whispered, "I hate this place."

"No shit," Rockaway said, jabbing at Doomsday playfully and getting a gentle elbow in return. "Kings, I get home, I'm never leaving fucking York again."

"Me neither," Doomsday said softly. "Me neither."

Chapter Four

They started up again around dawn, and almost made it to noon before the Baron's Boys showed up.

At first, it didn't look like anything too out of the ordinary: Doomsday had warned them that the Baron's Boys put up roadblocks along the Pale Horse Pike from time to time, collecting "protection" tolls from travelers or simply robbing the less defended ones and sending them on their way. So when they saw the two armored trucks blocking the road up ahead, with a dozen armed individuals in rugged clothes lounging around the vehicles waiting for them, it was cause for tension but not outright panic. Yet.

Jimmy was in the back, resting his ankle – despite the fight a few hours earlier, the wound had mended clean, it was just tender – so Rockaway was riding shotgun up front. As they slowed down, she scanned the roadblock for Dewey and his friends but didn't spot them. Mostly it looked to be other Mericans in worn jeans and heavy dusters or denim jackets to ward off the morning chill, a few with the skull over crossed cartridges symbol visible as painted decorations or actual badges. A couple of Retrogrades were mixed in too, bandannas pulled up over their faces, their grayish skin still betraying their mutated ancestry.

Most of the crew was smoking, little trails of gray vapor mixing in with their breath clouds, and while their manner might have looked casual they were watching the caravan approaching just as carefully as Rockaway was studying them. The trucks had been painted black at some point a long time back, though from the look of it the paint had badly flaked since then, not to mention been scratched and shot up besides.

"What's going on?" Jimmy asked as the caravan started slowing down.

"Baron's Boys have a roadblock up ahead," Rockaway said, turning to talk to him though the little window to the bed of the truck. In response, Jimmy pulled his bat out from under his blanket and dragged his shield within reach. They wouldn't do much good in the cramped confines of the caravan bed, but it was better than nothing.

"You want me out there when we stop?" Jimmy cracked his knuckles.

"Are we getting out?" Rockaway asked Doomsday.

"Not if we don't have to," the agent replied. "I've been through a couple of these before. It shouldn't be a problem, so long as we don't rile them." By now they were slowed to almost a complete stop, and a few of the men started ambling their way.

"Lotta guns if they turn ugly," Rockaway noted. She'd been through too many fights to rule out anything, but being boxed up in the caravan would make them easy targets, and she doubted Doomsday would be able to get up to enough speed to make it through before the caravan was completely shot up. "Ex, what do you think?"

"Hand me your holdout," Jimmy said, which reinforced just how dire the situation looked. As a Yorker bat man of the old school, Jimmy hated shooters and preferred not to use them unless he didn't really have a choice. Rockaway slid her backup out of its ankle holster and passed it back to him. "You see any sign of the assholes we tangled with last night?"

"Not yet," Rockaway said, taking in the crowd more carefully. Then she caught a strong resemblance in one of the group – he looked like a smaller, more in shape version of the big Dewey they'd seen the night before. "Aw, fuck. Green ball cap looks just like the big fucker, what was his name? Dewey. Could be a brother, and that could be a fucking problem."

"Saints," Doomsday breathed, when she'd had a look for herself. "Well, no other way but through it now. Keep it cool." She rolled the window down as they rolled up, and over top of the pine scent of the woods and the burned oil of their exhaust Rockaway could smell of something fragrant and floral, like really good weed but not quite the same. She hoped that's what it was – it might help make the men a bit less inclined to violence.

"Hey now!" The lead, a pretty young lady with smiling blue eyes and bushy blonde hair sticking out from under her straw hat, held up a hand in greeting as she walked up. A buck knife was strapped to the outside of her right thigh and the stock of a rifle or a shotgun was sticking past her shoulder, while the others all had their shooters and weapons ready in hand. It was a pretty standard setup, similar to ones Rockaway had seen back in York during meet-ups with other gangs – send out an attractive and more importantly less threatening member to do the talking, with the others standing by the remind anyone who didn't get it how serious the situation could become. Evidently she got to do the talking; the other Mericans just held back and watched, faces neutral. "How y'all doing on this fine morning?"

"Well, yourself?" Doomsday gave the young blonde her best smile back. Her hands were in her lap almost primly, though Rockaway could see the twitch that signaled her desire to have them on her pistols. Rockaway had her rifle out in the open – the agent had been clear on showing some strength. Too little and they were asking for a whole different kind of trouble, and besides the Baron's Boys would think it more suspicious to find an unarmed caravan rolling through the Pine Barrens.

"Can't complain, no ma'am." The girl seemed inclined to lean down and rest her elbows on the window frame, then saw Rockaway's rifle across her lap and thought the better of it. Instead she stepped back and whistled appreciatively. "Now that is one fine shootin' iron," she exclaimed. "What's her name?"

"It don't got one," Rockaway said, keeping her tone as pleasant as she could. It was an old question, though, and one she was long familiar with – soon as folks learned she was a sniper they assumed she had some sort of weird relationship with her shooter, like she'd named it and put little hats on it for holidays and gave it birthday presents or something. Make no mistake, she loved her rifle like nothing else in the world, knew every line and every curve like her own body or better, but it was a rifle, end of story. Too much got taken away from you in York – you didn't get too attached to anything if you could avoid it. Rockaway saw Doomsday looking at her. "Thanks for the kind words, though, motherfu – man."

If the kid caught the near-profanity, she gave no sign. "Nice piece, and no mistake. I'm partial to the shotgun, m'self – got shot for long range and shells for short, solves most any problem, I tell you that!" She grinned but the threat was unmistakable, especially as she patted the stock of the shotgun sticking out from behind her shoulder.

"Versatile weapon," Doomsday agreed amiably. The kid looked at her blankly. "Means good in most any situation," the agent amended.

"Oh! We got some eddicated ladies here, fellas!"

The girl turned back to her companions, laughing. Rockaway was sure some sign was passed to the other Baron's Boys while the girl's back was turned, but evidently it wasn't open fire, and so they'd have to wait and see what sort of less obvious command it might be. The blonde faced them again, still beaming. "Where y'all headed, anyhow?"

"Out to the Delphian, running for the Roman down in Aysea." The ploy was Doomsday's calculation – saying you were on your own meant it wasn't likely anyone would miss you, but saying you were on errands for some bigshot improved your odds, even if only slightly. The agent maintained that dazzling smile. "Believe me, not my choice of duties."

"No, I can't imagine it is," the blonde agreed, chuckling.

"Hold on. Ain't you one of the compound folk of a few miles over?" One of the men spoke up, a tall, gangly Retrograde in a wool cap and a painted denim jacket. He was covering most of his disfigured face with a red, white and blue bandanna, but his eyes were sharp despite the early morning sun. He gestured at the truck. "This caravan sure looks familiar."

"Well, sure," Doomsday said, not missing a beat. "I'm with the Darwinists, but we got a deal going with the Roman – we bring 'em scrap we turn up, they keep us in credits to buy provisions and whatnot."

"What's so special about your compound's scrap makes it worth their while?" The Retrograde wasn't backing down, even though his tone was still neutral. He was setting snares and waiting for Doomsday to fall in one so he could pounce, like a bully asking questions whose every answer would provide some provocation for a fight.

"You do know what we Darwinists gather 'round,

right?" Doomsday answered easily, giving the word just enough emphasis to make it clear she was putting him in his place but not so much he'd have to answer the slight directly. There is a fine art to taunting an armed man, after all. "Rads? Hot stuff? Cozy green glow?"

"Sure I do," the Retrograde muttered, while some of his buddies snickered.

"Well, we pass along some to the Roman, they use it for special gladiator fights – nice glowing weapons for the crowd to cheer on at night, that sort of stuff." Doomsday gave an elaborate shrug. "We don't really care what they use them for, to be honest, just that they pay us real well for it. That fine by you?"

"Nobody's gettin' mad," the blonde said reassuringly.

"Well, uh, she don't look like no Darwinist," the Retrograde protested, pointing at Rockaway, but one of his own comrades dismissed him with a rather pointed question about what Darwinists were supposed to look like in the first place, exactly.

"It's OK, we get that all the time," Doomsday said. "Folks believe what they want, that's fine by us. But if it's all the same to you, we'd like to be on our way. Sooner begun is sooner done, you know how they say."

"I do indeed," the blonde said. She looked back over her shoulder and caught some sign that Rockaway didn't. "One last thing an y'all can be on yer way. Whatcha haulin'?"

"Oh, c'mon," Doomsday protested, playing the overworked messenger to the hilt. "I respect you all plenty, make no mistake, but you know I'm not supposed to tell anyone that. What if you turn out to be bandits?" The last part was delivered as a joke, and got a round of low laughter from the Baron's Boys standing nearby, though off at the barricade the others remained

58

as impassive as ever. Aside from toking and spitting, anyway.

"Sorry, sugar, but we gotta insist." Nothing about the blonde's attitude had changed, but suddenly the air was taut with tension, almost an audible hum like someone had strummed a single string on a guitar.

"We're not hauling anything, I promise." The agent held up one hand like a promise. "Just order information for a contact up Delphian way, that's all. No hard goods except our packs, bedrolls and ammo."

"All the same, we'd like a quick look-see," the blonde said, and for the first time her smile died by a degree or two. Rockaway scanned the men standing nearby and noticed a few of them giving hard stares back, neutral expressions forgotten. "Y'all mind?"

For a moment she and Doomsday stared each other down, then the agent let her shoulders slumped and appeared to break, though the look she shot Rockaway as she turned to take the keys out of the ignition was anything but defeated. Be ready, it said. "We got a man in back, just so you don't get alarmed. He's friendly enough."

"Sure," the blonde said, with a little giggle. "I bet he is."

Rockaway choked back her response and moved to unbuckle her rigging strap, but Doomsday stopped her. A few of the Mericans had detached and were walking around to the back of the caravan. "Stay close to the truck and leave your door open," the agent said softly. "If this goes bad, we'll have to move fast."

"Fuckers looking for trouble?" Rockaway muttered back.

"Can't tell yet. This isn't normal but if they were just going to start shooting they'd have opened up by now. They might just be throwing their weight around, so for now we'll have to ride it out."

"If you fucking say so," Jimmy growled from the back.

"Be easy, Ex." Rockaway got out slowly, rifle away from her body so as not to offer any excuse for some twitchy redneck to start shooting. The Retrograde who'd given Doomsday a hard time seemed a bit more agitated now, and kept whispering something to the potbellied fellow next to him. It was impossible to make out what he was saying at that distance and with a mask on besides, but judging from the smile the fat boy had, it probably wasn't good. "How you boys doing today?" She waved. They didn't answer.

The blonde led a few of the Baron's Boys around to the back of the caravan, while Doomsday popped the back hatch. Rockaway could hear a few short sentences exchanged – the blonde made some indistinct noises, Jimmy said a couple short phrases, and she heard Doomsday say something that got a laugh from all concerned. Before Rockaway could relax at all, however, the blonde said something else, and she heard Jimmy climbing out of the back of the caravan. He came around to her side, Doomsday next to him, the Mericans coming up behind. Jimmy flashed her a quick gang sign: Trouble, and Doomsday's eyes read much the same way. Nobody had their weapons pointed, but it wasn't far off, she could tell.

"Something wrong?" Rockaway asked the blonde as the Baron's Boys lined up across from them. That put them between two groups, with a third group still by the roadblock. Shit odds and shit angles. Rockaway tapped two fingers against the outside of Jimmy's leg, pointing a "v" shape at the group across from them, and he nodded almost imperceptibly. Push came to shove, he'd take the two in the middle, splitting the group for

Doomsday and Rockaway to take out the ends. She wished the agent knew their code, then realized that was the first time she'd ever even considered teaching an outsider any of the Dead Heroes' codes, the first time it had even crossed her mind as a remote possibility. There was no time to explore that thought now, though, so Rockaway pushed it aside and focused on the moment.

"Just a few words we was asked to pass on to folks fittin' your description," the blonde said. She gestured and the potbellied Merican stepped forward and produced a crumpled note from his vest pocket. He unfolded it and read it, slowly and laboriously: "'You hurt me and mine, but now I'll kill you and everyone you care about." He frowned. "Retrey, retruh, retrab —"

"Retribution?" Doomsday guessed, unable to help herself.

"'Retribution will be terrible,'" the potbellied man said, with a small nod of thanks. "Your city will burn and your friends will die screaming.'" He folded the paper back up and offered it to them; after a slight hesitation, Doomsday took it and tucked it away in a pocket. "Weren't no name on it, but it was a pretty blonde lady in red what was shot up some. She come through and left it for y'all, said you'd know who it were from."

"Oh, we do," Rockaway said, and spat off to the side. Doomsday tensed but the Mericans seemed to find the gesture an appropriate response to a maniacal death threat, or at least gave no sign if they thought otherwise.

"She leave any other messages?" Jimmy asked warily.

"Naw, just the one," the blonde said, apparently taking over the conversation now that it had no further literacy requirements. "You kin go on yer way now. Our apologies fer the delay, but y'all know how it is. Get paid, do the job, ain't that right?"

"Too fuckin' right," Rockaway agreed. Jimmy started for the back of the caravan as the Mericans drifted back in the direction of their roadblock and Doomsday crossed the front of the truck to get to the driver's side.

The blonde hung back as the others walked away, tugged on Rockaway's arm. "Some sorta feud?" She asked quietly, looking around as if she didn't want to be overheard.

"Something like that, yeah," Rockaway said, pulling away and plopping back down in her seat. One of the Baron's Boys whistled and the group sitting on the caravans began to load up, though the small detachment that had come to meet them stayed a short distance away, watching warily. Rockaway heard Jimmy fumbling with the latch and swearing.

"Gonna be trouble out here, you reckon?"

"Prolly not," Rockaway said, pulling the door shut but leaving the window down. "Would you go help Ex with the lock?" she asked Doomsday, who rolled her eyes and got back out of the cab. Rockaway kept her eyes on the Retrograde, who had his rifle out and was looking even more agitated as the roadblock began to break up. "No harm in delivering a fucking message, anyway. I got no beef with that."

"Oh, good," the blonde said, and as she heard the sound of metal sliding against leather Rockaway knew she'd made a huge mistake. The Retrograde had been a distraction, but as she turned to bring her rifle up on the blonde, all she saw was a black, gaping barrel pointed at her.

Chapter Five

Rockaway sat up suddenly, feeling cool sand running between her fingers and a cold wind blowing across her face. A few yards ahead of her the ocean was dark and churning, waves scratching gouges into the shore like icy fingers, while out to sea the island was a black shape on the horizon already getting closer. Behind her, she heard the whispering starting up, the overlapping babble getting louder as the island got closer, threatening to make sense.

She had died again.

"Fuck, no. Not like that," Rockaway thought. Had the blonde really fucking killed her? The last few moments before dying were always a little hazy, but she didn't remember hitting the ground or bleeding out, so between Doomsday's medical training and Jimmy's newfound ability to lay on hands it would have had to been a cherry shot, something that killed her outright. She ran her hands through her hair, checking the back of her head almost reflexively to find the injury -- she didn't feel anything, but then again she never did while she was here.

"Oh, fuck. Jimmy." If the girl had killed her back at the roadblock, then nothing short getting killed too would have stopped Jimmy from smearing the contents of the Merican's head across the blacktop, and all her friends he could reach too. Rockaway looked up and down the beach, half-expecting to see Jimmy there, maybe Doomsday too. That wasn't how the dead space worked, but she couldn't help it. The first of the cold waves reached her toes, and she wished that she didn't always lose her boots somewhere between living and dying. A wall of water was building in front of the island as it approached the shore, and she braced herself as the wind picked up and the whispering got louder and louder –

"Fascinating." Rockaway jumped as the man stepped up from behind to stand next to her. He was tall and powerfully built, wearing utilitarian black pants of a military design and a simple white shirt that looked to be homemade from some rough fabric. His short brown hair was parted in the middle and he sported heavy stubble that hadn't quite organized into a beard. He turned his head ever so slightly in her direction to acknowledge her, the corners of his lips turning up in a faint smile.

"Who – who the fuck are you?" Even though she knew she wasn't in her body, not exactly anyway, Rockaway felt her stomach drop and her heart begin to pound. She was always alone in her dead space – there were voices, sure, but never anyone else, and certainly never anyone she could see, much less that interacted with her.

In response, the man held his hands out in front of himself and turned them over, palms up. Two large crosses were burned into his palms. As Rockaway watched, the scars opened up and began to bleed, the edges smoldering slightly. Her own hands twitched in reply, and with the certainty of a nightmare Rockaway knew what would be revealed even as she turned them over – her wounds were slightly smaller, but otherwise almost identical. They looked like they had when the grenade had gone off in her hand during her desperate fight with the lunatic Final Knight, Big Playboy, a few days earlier. She'd been unhurt, but the wounds had smoldered just like this. "Oh fuck no," she said, angry and frightened in equal measure.

"I'm afraid so," Red Hands said, his voice

carrying a friendly tone that did not quite match his eyes. The Iron Cross captain who had chased her across Old York and – she thought – been devoured by a persistent hunter as she escaped to Aysea might have looked different than last she saw him, but then he'd done that before as well. Red Hands was a psion, one of the rare few who received strange mental powers from the infection, and had already demonstrated the eerie ability to move from one body to another when one was destroyed. He'd made some cryptic remarks right before his last death, cutting into her palms to "mark" her, but Rockaway had chalked it up to a sign of the sort of notoriously unstable mind most psions possessed and not given it much more thought. Compared to the torture and massacres he'd perpetuated trying to get at her, it seemed little more than an odd detail.

At least, it had seemed that way until a few days ago, when the scars started to itch and then re-open spontaneously, strange enough experiences on their own but even moreso when they were accompanied by strange flashes of insight, like a voice warning her of danger that always turned out to be right. Then came her experience coming away unharmed after handling the exploding grenade, followed shortly after by the passage of what seemed to have been some kind of aircraft on its way and the absolute, utter certainty that Red Hands had been aboard. Rockaway had kept as much of it to herself as possible, but she knew Jimmy had noticed something was going on – the Dead Heroes didn't tend to keep secrets from each other as a rule, and he didn't miss much in general.

It wasn't that Rockaway was afraid of psions, exactly. Well, she was, but no more than it was reasonable to be when considering they were survivors who could read minds, light things on fire with a gesture, move things without touching them and all sorts of other creepy tricks. The Dead Heroes even had a psion in their number, Winter. She wasn't especially close to anyone else in the gang, mostly due to her unfortunate habit of casually talking about what other people were only thinking, but she was true York otherwise, and had gotten Rockaway's back when it counted too many times to count. Winter's talents were useful, no doubt, and aside from the mind-reading she kept them under control.

But deep down, Rockaway gave thanks to the Kings or whoever else was listening that she wasn't born that way. There was different, and then there was different, and she saw how the rest of the gang never completely relaxed around Winter and yet never let her totally out of their sight for long either. In the close knit world of Yorker gangs, that level of alienation would've driven Rockaway right out of her mind. Maybe Winter didn't care, because it was all she had ever known, but if something was happening to Rockaway – if Red Hands had changed her, somehow, imprinted his damaged mind on hers – she wasn't sure if she could survive a transformation like that. Not so much the trauma of psion powers, but of losing her place in the gang, of becoming an outsider within the group. It was too much to think about.

"Is this really how you see your world?" Red Hands looked out at the approaching island, which seemed to have slowed somewhat, as if confused; now that she listened, the voices had died down too, though she still didn't dare look behind her. "So bleak. I was not exactly expecting a carnival, but this …" He made a sweeping gesture that took in the island, the ocean, the beach, everything. "And if that's Old York, why are you here, so far away? Are you really that lonely?"

"Fuck you, tryin' to head shrink me!" Rockaway drew back a fist to hit him, then wavered, the desire to hurt him warring with the revulsion at the thought of touching him. "Get out of my fucking head, asshole!"

"Is that where you think we are?" Red Hands caught her discomfort and his smile widened. He reached up and tapped his temple with one blood-streaked finger, drops falling to the sand at his feet. "Sure. Let's go with that, then. No matter what you think, though, you're not going to get rid of me. I'll outlive you, though you probably won't see it that way."

"How the fuck are you even here?" Rockaway demanded.

"You know how." He turned one hand toward her, letting the blood run down his palm to drip on the floor. "I marked you. That's what I do with all my hosts. And once I do that, I can go just about anywhere. You're becoming more like me all the time, or haven't you noticed?"

"Bullshit. You can't make someone a psion. You've gotta be born that way." That was the truth, or at least it was as far as Rockaway had ever heard. Psions developed their talents young, which was another reason for their poor reputation; those few that she'd heard of who "suddenly" displayed abilities later in life invariably turned out to have been hiding them, often by moving from settlement to settlement.

"I'm not making you a true psion, Tribeca." Red Hands shook his head almost sadly. "Don't you think if it was that easy we would have converted the rest of you already? But I can't promise it might not … knock some things loose."

"Converted? The fuck does that mean?"

"You really don't have any idea, do you?"

67

67

Abruptly Red Hands turned and fixed her with a intense stare, as though he was examining a particularly interesting bug that he'd found crawling through his camp one morning. What's worse, it reminded her of a particular expression that she'd seen Winter use before, usually from the edge of the circle around the fire. She would often sit just outside the group, adding the occasional comment here and there but mostly just listening to the rest of the gang bullshit, tell jokes, argue about who was taking the next shift of civic duty at the lookout posts and otherwise do their day-to-day. "What's it like to live in a mind that small? It must be so … limiting."

This time Rockaway did hit him. Nothing complex, just a right cross to the jaw, but it hit with a satisfying crunch, and for the first time ever in her dead space she felt real warmth and heat. Her pulse raced in her ears, drowning out the whispers, and when Red Hands staggered backward, hands up to defend his face, she punched him in the gut. The Iron Cross doubled over with a whuff of expelled air, and Rockaway interlaced her fingers and brought down a hammer blow on the back of his head, feeling the hot blood of her open wounds running down her arms along with the strike. Red Hands collapsed at her feet, and Rockaway realized that she was smiling, another first ever in this cold, desolate place.

"Listen up, asshole." Rockaway dropped down into the sand next to Red Hands, who had turned on his side and was choking on mouthfuls of sand. "You're a big shit mindfucker. I get it. But only idiots idiot fuck with a Yorker on their own turf, and the way I see it, this shit is about as personal as it gets, you feel me?" She made a show of studying her hands while he regained the ability to speak. "Plus, it looks like you can feel pain just fine, whatever you are, and as it turns out I could really use a fucking distraction while I'm here. Thanks for that." Red Hands glared at her venomously but said nothing. "So cut the fucking crap and answer my goddamn questions. Starting with what the fuck are you?"

"I'm a shard." Rockaway leaned over and rapped his forehead with her knuckles, hard enough to make him flinch. The glare intensified and he answered sullenly, "I'm not really Red Hands. Not yet, anyway. Think of me like a bit of shrapnel left behind in a wound, the kind that'll turn the wound septic if you don't remove it. When I marked you, I passed a little piece of me to you through the blood. That little piece has been growing this whole time, and eventually it'll be ready to take over the whole works. When the body I'm currently inhabiting dies, anyway." He gave her a wolfish grin. "Call it insurance."

"So that's how you came back before?" Rockaway spat. Around her the wind and the whispering started picking up again, as though the dead space was trying to remind her of its presence. "Jeter and the MPYRE Dogs burned you down, so you just jacked another Iron Cross and kept going? You spread yourself like a fucking disease?"

"It beats the alternative," Red Hands said. "I've been doing this a while. A long while." He gave her a significant look. "Only one I know who does, so far as I can tell."

"So how many you got out there?"

"A couple. It's taxing to have too many. I wasn't going to do you, but what can I say? You're impressive." He gave her a lascivious looking over, but the leer died when she failed to react. "I have to say, you're taking this really well. Most people fight it harder. Doesn't work, but they fight it just the same."

"Oh, I'll fucking fight you, believe me. Just wouldn't settle anything here, am I right?" When Red Hands didn't answer, she took it as a yes and kept going. "I mean, aside from whupping your ass." Rockaway thought something over. "I do owe you, though. Until now, every time I came here, I was like, I dunno, hypnotized or something. I just stared at that fucking island—" she gestured at the black mass gliding towards them across the slate gray sea, an angry wall of water gathering ahead of it, "and listened to the whispering until I woke up again. But now? Fuck it." Rockaway took a deep breath, let it out, and looked over her shoulder in the direction where the whispering was coming from.

The first thing that struck her was how endless it seemed, a stretch of white sand dunes that seemed to go on forever under a dirty gray sky, so that the only difference was a slight change in hue at the horizon. It looked vaguely like the dunes at the Aysea shoreline, but on an entirely different scale. Even sitting down, Rockaway felt a sudden rush of vertigo, as though she was perched on the edge of a very high place and might fall off into the landscape at any given moment. Not that she would be alone, judging by the shuffling gray figures that filled the landscape, like a cloud of mist barely separated into vaguely human figures.

At first Rockaway couldn't make out any features in the crowd, but gradually her eyes adjusted – or perhaps they began to solidify, she wasn't entirely sure – and Jimmy was there, front and center, looking at her with an expression of great pity and longing in equal measure. As she watched, he smiled at her sadly, raised a hand and slowly waved at her.

Jimmy had done that exact gesture years ago, when

they parted company the morning after they'd slept together, the memory lurching back to the front of her mind with almost painful clarity. For a time Rockaway had worried if he'd be weird about it after – he'd gotten very quiet, during, and very sweet – but it had passed and she'd let it slip from her mind. He had other lovers, though not too many, and so did she, perhaps a few more than him, though never for the kind of time that he did. Jimmy was with most of them for months, and one girl – Black Eye Suzie, who'd been lost in a horde rush two years back – for almost three years, off and on. Whereas the longest Rockaway ever went with someone was, well, shit. Offhand, she couldn't think of anything longer than two months. Whatever it was that made people want to be together in a romantic way, for the long term, she just didn't have it.

Sometimes she used to wonder if it was some kind of a character flaw, that she would sleep with someone a couple of times and then move on, but considering she didn't hook up all that often either, it didn't really matter to her either way. Most of the time the closeness of the gang was enough; when it wasn't, she found somebody to take the edge off. It was as simple as that, and she wasn't shy about saying so to those she approached. She supposed she'd hurt some feelings here and there, but she hadn't lost any friends over it – the relationships weren't that serious to start, so it was hard to wring serious feelings out of them.

Except.

"Hey, Ex." Rockaway wasn't exactly sure why she was addressing the grayish specter of Jimmy standing in front of her. If Red Hands was telling the truth – admittedly, not necessarily a solid bet – then chances were that she was just addressing herself, some part of her mind that wanted to talk to her best friend.

Next to her, the Iron Cross mercenary fell silent and watched intently, as if trying to memorize every word and gesture. As soon as she spoke to him, the phantom Jimmy stopped waving, his arm lowering to his side.

"Hey, Rock." The voice was barely more than a whisper, and she had to strain to pick it out above the overlapping whispers of the shades standing behind him. "You finally noticed me." It sounded like a joke, but only barely. There was real pain there.

"You're hard to miss, asshole," Rockaway bantered, refusing to take the emotional bait. "Six and a half feet tall in boots and bright green hair? I'd be a pretty shit sniper if I didn't notice something like that."

"C'mon, you know what I mean." Phantom Jimmy was still smiling at her, though it looked a bit more strained. "I'm right in front of you, always have been, but you never notice me. Do you really not see it? Or don't you care?"

"The fuck is this bullshit?" Rockaway felt her temper spark, even as the cold waters lapped at her feet. She turned away from the spectral Jimmy and shot Red Hands a glare, as if he was personally responsible. "You stir this up, mindfucker?"

"This isn't me." Red Hands shook his head. "Anything here is your doing, I'm just along for the ride." He shrugged. "For now, anyway. Promise."

"Yeah, well, we'll be back on that in a minute." Rockaway turned back to phantom Jimmy, who was looking at her with so much pain in his eyes that she had to bite her lip to keep from apologizing. "Look, I don't know what this shit is here –"

"It's me, you know it's –"

"—but I don't have time to dick around. Maybe I ain't treated the real Jimmy exactly right, that's on me. I'll square it when I get back. But really? You're trying

72

to tell me that the real Jimmy's been all messed up with love and shit for years, and that I should feel bad because, I don't know, I've been a bitch or something?" Rockaway spat through her teeth, then looked the phantom Jimmy in the eye. "Fuck you. You're no Dead Hero and you're no friend of mine, just a fake-ass copy." She raised one hand in a mocking variation of his plaintive gesture, extending her middle finger with pointed slowness. "Fuck. Off."

Phantom Jimmy's face twisted up in an expression of such raw, unexpected hate that Rockaway nearly took a step back just from its intensity. Jimmy Three Ex had a temper, no doubt, and she'd seen him lose it during some pretty awful, fucked up times before, but this, this was a whole other level. It didn't even look like him anymore, more like someone had made a bad mask of his face and put it on hastily. She expected him to say something, but he just stepped back into the milling shades and faded into the crowd.

"Feel better?" Red Hands asked, a faint note of mockery in his voice.

"Fuck you." Rockaway said, the thrill of telling off the apparition of Jimmy fading somewhat as she started really counting all the other phantoms milling about in the wasteland. They didn't have faces, not yet anyway, but she knew in her gut it was just a matter of time before someone else stepped forward and busted her balls about something. "You've been here before, right? Like, someone's dead space?"

"Many times," Red Hands answered smoothly. "Though each one is different, as I suspect you already knew. This one's actually almost pleasant, compared to some. There was one Accensorite fellow I knew whose time inbetween was spent in a collapsing cathedral. Can you imagine what that must have been like, to have tons and tons of stone falling on your head on top of all the stress of struggling with your own death?" He made a chilly sound. "Unpleasant in the extreme."

"Are they always here? I mean, these spirit fucking goddamn phantom things?"

"Oh, yes. Though not always like this. Yours are fairly straightforward, it seems, but then you are a Yorker. Everyone sees it differently, in my experience, but everyone sees it."

"Sees what?" Rockaway said, though she had a decent guess what he would say.

"All of this is a reflection of the Grave Mind as much as it is your own," Red Hands said. "Right now, somewhere in the wilds of Jersey your friends are watching as the infection works its dark little miracles on your body, scraping bones and flesh together, finding bits of a body where there rightfully should never be one again, and they're praying that you've got enough left in you for your mind to take over when it all kicks back into gear. But they only know half of the story. Right now you're as close as you've ever been the Grave Mind, and it's getting a good, long look." Red Hands sounded closer to her now, but she didn't take her eyes off the gray, indistinct mass. "It wants you, like it wants all of us. Always has, always will. So every time you die, it reaches out and hooks you a little deeper, brings you a little closer. And now you're very, very close."

"You know an awful fucking lot about it."

"I should. I've been staying one step ahead of it for a long time now, but I wouldn't be able to if I didn't learn how it worked, what it wanted. It doesn't just mindlessly devour." The mercenary's voice got a bit distant. "That's just what its children do. They hear it telling them to consume, and so they consume, but they're too crude to carry out what it really wants."

"Don't keep me in fucking suspense, here," Rockaway said, when he didn't speak for a moment. "Fucking out with it already."

"It wants us, every bit of us. Not just our bodies, but our lives. Our stories."

Rockaway laughed, and she could practically hear Red Hands grinding his teeth at her disrespect for his big revelatory moment. "Yeah, right. I've had zeds fucking chasing me up and down buildings my whole life in York because they just couldn't wait to find out how I learned to shoot a fucking gun or what it was like to get inked into the gang. I could just fucking tell." She shook her head, still chuckling. "Kings, that's fucking stupid."

"You don't get it!" Red Hands hissed, grabbing Rockaway's shoulder and spinning her around to face him. "You –"

The rest of whatever he was going to say was lost as Rockaway drove two fingers into his throat, a choking blow that dropped him gasping to the sand. Out of the corner of her eye she could see the island barreling down on the beach, a wall of gray surf ahead of it, and she knew her time was short. "Hey. Dipshit. Remember I can hurt you here?"

Rockaway kicked Red Hands in the side for good measure, then toed him onto his back and knelt down on his chest. She clamped a bleeding hand over his mouth and he writhed, trying to get away from the blood flowing freely from her palm, but she had him solidly pinned, and when she vised his face between her thumb and middle finger, he stopped struggling. "Listen up, asshole, because this is the last time we're fucking meeting like this, I promise you that. Yeah, yeah, you're a big dick mindfucker, but you try to take this body, I will fucking make you pay blood for every goddamn inch, you hear me?"

Rockaway gestured at the oncoming island and its wall of water. "This is what I bring to the party, motherfucker! Old York may kill me yet, but try and take me and I'll make damn sure it brings you down too. You get that? You fucking get that?!" She saw the shadow of the wave fall across them, heard the roar like an oncoming truck barreling down on them, watched his eyes get huge and white as he renewed his struggles. Calmly, patiently, Rockaway held him down and waited for the end. There was none of the dread that usually accompanied the impending crash, none of the bitter chill sinking down into her bones she felt as her time in the dead space came to a close.

The whispering stopped, or maybe it was just drowned out by the roar, but Rockaway looked up and saw the gray faces staring back at her, little more than eyes and shadows in the mist, dozens of them, hundreds of them. Maybe it was the Grave Mind, maybe it was her mind, maybe it was somewhere in between, or maybe Red Hands had just been fucking with her the entire time, but right then it didn't seem to matter. She knew the score now, and it didn't matter whether it was in her own head or shouted throughout the horde.

"Fuck alla you monsters." Rockaway raised a single finger in salute to the scores of watching figures, and even when the wave came crashing down, she let them have a good, long look at it.

Chapter Six

"Welcome back, Rock," Jimmy said, looking down at her with a smile. The look quickly changed to one of alarm, though, as Rockaway sat up abruptly, trying to get her bearings. They were in the back of the caravan, that much was clear, and it was sometime during the day. The caravan bounced and rattled along, but when Jimmy spoke she could feel it start slowing down. She grabbed a canteen and chugged most of it, her mouth desperately dry and not exactly appetizing in taste either. Up front, Doomsday was saying something, but Rockaway didn't catch it.

She was too busy kissing Jimmy.

At first he pulled back, trying to say something about how he didn't feel right considering she'd just come back and might not be quite in her right mind, but she pulled him down by his necklace and shut him up with more kisses until he stopped protesting and returned them, first slowly, then with more intensity. His lips were cracked and the stubble on his cheeks burned her as they kissed, but she didn't care. It was what needed to happen, and so she went with it, kissing as if she'd just discovered it and wanted to share it with the world.

A distant part of her registered the fact that the caravan had come to a halt, that Doomsday had made some sort of comment and then exited the cab, slamming the door behind her, but otherwise the world was the back of the caravan, the cozy heat of two bodies in a small space, the kiss of a friend who'd obviously been dreaming about it for a very long time.

"I was so scared," Jimmy murmured in her ear as she nuzzled his neck before coming back up for a lazy kiss. He pulled back after a moment and she let him; she could feel the need to share what was on his mind rattling around inside him like a cartridge in a coffee can. His eyes were desperate with love and fear, and the scary thing was how closely the two resembled each other when you put them side by side. "You went green vein as you were coming back, and I thought – I thought …" He gripped her as though he was afraid she might vanish at any moment and let the terrible implication hang between them. If she came back zed, he would put her down. No question.

"It's OK, I know," Rockaway said. From outside the caravan she could smell a cigarette; Doomsday was evidently going to give them some privacy, though the slammed door indicated how she felt about it. One thing at a time, Rockaway figured. "Ex, I remember this time. I know what happened in my dead space, every fucking moment of it."

Jimmy caught his breath. "No shit?"

"No shit." Rockaway brushed his cheek with her fingertips. "I learned some things. Or more like, admitted some stuff I already knew, deep down. Like, you've been all about me for what, ten years now?"

"I wouldn't say all about you," Jimmy said, smiling without denial. He reached out and brushed a few wisps of hair out of her eyes. "There's been a few others, but … yeah, it always comes back to you." He sighed, a surprisingly sweet sound. "That probably sounds pretty pussy to you, doesn't it?"

"Just a little." Rockaway punched him lightly on the arm. "But mostly, I like it."

"I can kinda tell," Jimmy said, leaning in for another kiss. They kept it up for a long time, neither one terribly interested in stopping, just stretching out the moment for as long as they could. "Careful. A guy could get to like this."

"Yeah." Rockaway looked in his eyes and struggled to find a way to say the next few words as carefully as possible. "About that. I mean, you're great, and this is great, but still – you know I'm not … fuck, you know I'm not that like that, right?"

"Like what? The kind who goes with someone long term, maybe has a preacher say some words over them to make it official?" Jimmy laughed, and there was nothing mean about it, though it might have been just a little bittersweet. "Fuck, you do know I know you, right? I didn't have any big ideas about making you my girl."

"And why not, asshole?" She slugged him playfully in the ribs. "I'm fucking awesome."

"Too fucking right," he said, jabbing back. "But for real, Rock, I know the score. Why did you think I never said anything? I know how you are, so I didn't want to make things, you know, fucking complicated and shit."

"Am I that bad?" The implication of his statement surprised her with how much it stung. Rockaway knew the rest of the gang regarded her as a bit distant most of the time, and she was cool with that, but she didn't think she really scared people off. Well, she figured she scared some people, but not like this exactly.

"Nah," Jimmy said reassuringly. "You're just you, and I'm not fucking stupid enough to think that you're gonna change just because I have the hots for you." He ruffled her hair a little. "Though I gotta admit, it's nice to kiss you again."

"I'm sorry," Rockaway said, not quite sure what she was apologizing for but fairly sure she needed to regardless.

"Don't be," Jimmy said, a bit more forcefully. "Just enjoy this, whatever the hell it is." They kissed a little more, and it was sweet despite her chapped lips.

"Sure, but we do much more and I think we're really gonna piss off Doomsday."

"No joke." Jimmy shrugged. Rockaway hadn't talked to Jimmy about Doomsday hitting on her, but she knew that he'd noticed. She just figured Ex had been stewing about it, like he often did with big decisions, and she'd just beaten him to the punch with making a move before he said something. "She likes you too. I get it."

"She just wants to fucking jump me, you mean," Rockaway corrected him.

Jimmy laughed. "Maybe, maybe, but I can't blame her, right?" He ran his fingers down the side of her face, down her neck, and ever so lightly across her chest. Considering the fact that they'd kept her armor vest on while she was dead, it was more symbolic than anything else, but it got the point across just fine.

"You're not ticked?"

"Did you miss the part where I explain that I've fucking known you for your entire life?" Jimmy shook her shoulder gently. "You can fuck whoever you want, I'm not gonna fucking stop you." He leaned in and gave her a long, lingering kiss. "I'll take what I can and call it fucking victory."

"I just wish you'd said something sooner, because now …" She held up her hands, with the scars Red Hands had left on the palms and her greenish veins on the other. "I'm fucked no matter which way this thing goes, looks like."

"Don't say that!" Jimmy propped himself up on his elbow and glared down at her. "You're not dead until it's a fucking done deal, you hear me? We both know plenty of people live years after they go green. It's not a fucking death sentence, not on its own. Anyway, what do you know about those scars? What, like you didn't think I'd notice you kept itching your palms? Or that you'd had a fucking grenade go off in your hand and didn't even chip a nail?"

"If you noticed so damn much, how come you didn't say anything?"

"Because I know you!" Jimmy insisted. "You get things in your head sometimes, and you just need to chew on 'em for a while. Anyone comes around asking just pisses you off, so I give you your space when you need it. Just how you are, is all." He put his own hand up, pressed his palm to hers. "Besides, it's not like I haven't had weird shit happening with me lately too, what with the laying on hands bit. Who the fuck am I to judge?"

"We're turning into a fucking freakshow," Rockaway agreed, twining her fingers in his.

"You still haven't said what's up with the scars, though," Jimmy said, squeezing her hand slightly. "What'd you see that's got you so messed up?"

"Red Hands was in my dead space, Ex." The words felt leaden, heavy, like even speaking them was an effort.

"So?" Jimmy shrugged. "I've seen all sorts of people in my dead space. Mostly it's Heroes who got got years ago, like Ruby or Spider Jack, sometimes it's people I don't even know. I guess my mind makes 'em up, or something. Point is, it's not that weird."

"Well, I don't normally see anyone in between, so yeah, it was pretty fucking weird to me, but you're not hearing how it was – he was in my dead space," Rockaway stressed. "Like, the man himself. Not a dream, not a memory, but right there and talking to me just like we're here talking now."

Jimmy's mouth fell open. "Bullshit. How the fuck could he even do that?"

"It's some sort of mindfucker thing he does – he breaks off a piece of himself and plants it in your brain, like a seed. Then when it's ready, or he gets capped, he just jumps right in and takes over." She snapped her fingers. "And your body's jacked, just like that."

"What … what happens to you? Are you, like, still in there, or are you just gone?"

Rockaway pulled away from Jimmy, though she didn't let go of his hand. "Shit, Ex, I don't know! I'm not sure which is worse, either – getting snuffed or watching him wear my body like a pair of boots. Either way I'm fucked if it happens, so really, what's it matter?"

"Sorry, I didn't mean to – you're right, that wasn't cool. Kings." Jimmy reached out tentatively as though he might stroke her hair, then thought better of it, and settled for squeezing her hand again instead. "So was that what he did? Just stand there and tell you what he was going to do?"

"I think the sick fucker gets off on watching people squirm. I kind of lost it a little, at first, I'm not gonna lie, but then I figured, if he's in here with me," she tapped her temple, "then that means I can affect what's he put there. So I beat the shit out of him. Felt a lot better after."

Jimmy snorted. "That's a Dead Hero for you. Never gloat anywhere near where we can still get our fucking hands on you. I hope you fucking killed him."

Rockaway shook her head. "I wish, but it doesn't work that way. I don't know how I fucking know that, but I do. He's still here, somewhere, just buried deep again. Bastard. I probably wouldn't have even fucking known except that it came to the surface when I was, you know, killed."

Just like that, the reality of the last situation she'd remembered reasserted itself. She sat up, looking at him warily. "Wait a goddamn minute – who killed me? And how the fuck did you two get away from those assholes?"

"It was the blonde. She just pulled out her shotgun and," Jimmy made a gun with the fingers of his free hand, pointed it at her and fired, "put a shot through the back of your head." His eyes wandered across her forehead, tracing the lines of the injury the infection had repaired before bringing her back, and he shuddered involuntarily. "It was back, Rock. I mean, real bad. Everything north of your eyebrows was pretty much gone. Loudest damn blast I've ever heard."

Rockaway brushed her forehead with her hand self-consciously. "Probably a mule kick load. Wreck the shit out of your barrel after a couple shots, but until it gives they put serious holes in things." Amateur ordnance, mostly for grandstanding types who loved the big loud bang, but that didn't mean it didn't do its job. Explained her headache too, most likely.

"Anyway, she shot, and about a second later Doomsday dropped her, and then they all had their guns up, and it looked like we were about to get shot to pieces when … something happened." Jimmy looked away, embarrassed.

"The fuck do you mean, something happened?" Rockaway demanded. At that moment she heard the driver's door open and Doomsday ducked into to cab, muttering something about needing to get another smoke, but before she could pull back out again Rockaway called out to her to hold up. "What happened at the roadblock?" She asked the agent.

"Oh, are we done with kissing now?" Doomsday said, sticking her head in the little window to the back. She didn't wait for an answer, but just jerked her chin in Jimmy's direction. "He happened, that's what. Well, his Kings happened, anyway. I've heard of preachers doing some amazing things, but that was unbelievable. Do you want to tell her, or should I do it?"

"No, I'll do it," Jimmy said, still blushing. He let go of Rockaway's hand and sat back, trying to find the words. "It's hard to explain, though."

"I'd say the guys you blasted would disagree," Doomsday said. "Pretty simple to them."

"Blasted?" Rockaway looked at Jimmy for confirmation, but he was studying his hands, wringing them slowly in his lap.

"It's just – fuck," he began, then ran out of words, the frustration he was prone to when he couldn't say what was on his mind clearly growing. Finally he composed himself. "I just saw you on the ground, alright?" Jimmy said, very quietly, still not looking at her. "I saw the blood, and the brains, and knew you were fucking gone, and in another second they were gonna gun us down and probably burn us up after, and it just wasn't fair, you know? It couldn't end like that. I – I couldn't let that happen. So I prayed for, I dunno, justice? Whatever you want to call it, it just felt right."

"What he means to say is that he started to sing, pretty loudly, and I think they were actually too confused to shoot for a second. Then he just pointed at them and boom boom boom, there were these flashes of light and three of the Baron's Boys were on their asses, chests popped open and smoldering like sausages dropped on a grill. Not dead, judging from the moans, but badly hurt for sure. There was this music in the air, too, just for a second, instruments and voices and

84

everything. One of the others took a shot then, and your boy just sort of … avoided it." Doomsday shook her head. "Damndest thing."

"I had the rhythm, I could just feel where I was supposed to be," Jimmy said, his hand gestures getting more agitated as he tried to get across what he was saying. "You know how it gets, sometimes, when you're in a fight and it's like everything is going just the way you want it to? Like you can't do anything wrong, even if you tried? It was like that. I saw him pointing the gun and just knew if I moved like this-" Jimmy twitched his upper body to the side, "—that he'd miss and I'd be fine. I just knew, Rock." His voice sounded small, and a little scared.

Doomsday looked at Jimmy with genuine concern in her eyes, and when he didn't pick up the tale again, she finished it for him. "Then he pointed again, and bam bam bam, the shooter and two of her friends went down, and that was pretty much it. The ones left got out of our way in a big damn hurry and we got the hell out of there."

"Well, shit. This is something different, Ex," Rockaway said quietly, after a moment of silence had passed in the cramped confines of the caravan. She reached over tentatively and touched his hands; no sooner had she slipped her hand in his than Jimmy gripped it like the bottom rung of a ladder hanging above a forty story fall.

"I know," Jimmy replied, sounding almost sick. It was not all that uncommon for devout preachers to work a little faith healing, but calling down wrath like that was a whole other category of thing. They'd heard of a handful of priests in Old York who could call down wrath like that, and all of them were dangerous to be around – not just because of that powerful talent, but also because their blessings tended to increase their devotion to levels of zealousness that even some of their fellow faithful found hard to be around. Being a conduit to the raw, visceral power of your faith didn't lend to feelings of moderation and tolerance, after all. It wasn't a guarantee, but she knew the thought must be weighing heavily on Jimmy's heart; he had barely had time to process the fact that he had a faith healer's touch, and now this.

"Look at me. Look at me!" Rockaway repeated, tugging on Jimmy's hand until he met her eyes. "It's all good, you hear me? You hadn't called down some wrath, we'd probably be burned down in a ditch somewhere in these fucking woods, you got me? You're my fucking hero, Ex, and not for the first time either. Fucking believe that!" She took his chin with her other hand, forced him to keep eye contact. "Do I look like I'm kidding, asshole?"

"Kings, no!" Jimmy said, and the faintest hint of a smile appeared at the corners of his mouth. "You can let go of my face, though, that'd be fucking great." She pinched his cheek and he swatted at her playfully, then gave a little rueful laugh. "Aren't I the one's supposed to be putting your head back together right now?"

"Fuck, it's as together as it's gonna get. No, wait, don't go," Rockaway said as Doomsday started to pull back. "You're gonna want to hear this."

"What is it?" Doomsday looked at the two Yorkers curiously.

"Nothing shady," Rockaway said. She looked at Jimmy, gave his hand a squeeze. He looked confused, then caught on, and he grinned like she'd just told the Dead Heroes had found a stash of brand new steel baseball bats. "You like me, right?"

"What do you mean?" Doomsday's eyes flicked to

Jimmy and back to Rockaway.

"Simple fucking question," Rockaway said. "No fucking trick to it." She nodded down at her body. "You think I'm hot, right?"

"You know I do." Doomsday still sounded as though she was waiting for a follow-up shot to the gut. "What's going on?"

Rockaway held up her hand, and Doomsday sucked in her breath at the sight of the green veins. She'd almost certainly see that happening to Rockaway when they loaded her into the back of the caravan, but it was a different thing to see it up close, especially combined with her the blood slowly seeping from her palms. "If I'm not on my last go, I'm real fucking close." Pain flashed across Jimmy's face at the thought, but she saw him push it away with a supreme effort. Doomsday tried to object, but Rockaway shushed her. "And this run has been one long fucking disaster, so I'm inclined to take what I can get, when I can get it. You feel me?"

"Oh." Doomsday seemed about to say something, swallowed it, and said very carefully, each word handled like a fragile piece of glass: "You sure about this?" It was clearly a question for both of them, though she was looking at Rockaway when she said it.

"You good, I'm good," Jimmy said. "I mostly plan on just sitting here real fucking quiet-like and hope you two forget I'm here, know what I'm saying?" He grinned.

"Dick." Rockaway kicked Jimmy. She turned back to Doomsday, who was still waiting, caution and enthusiasm warring in her expression. "Fuck I ever said shit I don't mean?" Rockaway said. Jimmy pointed at her, mock-serious. "You trynna make me beg, G-Man? Or just not interested no more?"

Doomsday answered by making it out of the cab, around the side of the caravan and into the back with the two Yorkers in less than five seconds.

Chapter Seven

"Fuck, it doesn't look like much," Jimmy said as he hopped out of the cab. They were parked on top of a half-crumbled overpass, staring down at a stretch of road with nothing but barely standing brick ruins scattered on one side and a long overgrown patch of scrub brush and a few hunched over trees on the other. In the distance, a tall bridge watched over the forlorn expanse like a lonely sentinel waiting for relief that wasn't ever going to arrive.

"Does it ever?" Doomsday replied, shading her eyes against the late afternoon sun as she looked down the wreckage of the run. "You know what they say: Looks like an ambush, probably is. Doesn't look like an ambush, it definitely is."

"Damn straight," Rockaway said. She had her rifle up and was slowly scanning the wrecked road ahead of them through her scope. Rusted out hulks were spaced at regular intervals across the lanes of traffic, many with crushed bodywork indicating serious collisions. Their placement was standard enough to be deliberate – Rockaway had seen that sort of arrangement before in the caravan lanes in Old York.

"What do you see?" Doomsday asked. Click-click. Click-click. From the sound of it, she was playing with the safety on her pistol again. It was the other anxious tell that Rockaway and Jimmy had picked up on so far, but it was a sure sign. Even with Heller's directions – and his warnings – the agent was feeling the nerves. Click-click.

"No sign of zed. No sign of recent feedings either. Not even any goddamn bones. The horde's been through here recently, they were quiet about it." Rockaway swept the caravans again. "No sign of movement in the caravans either, but then we're pretty fucking exposed up here. Anyone's down there, they probably went to ground soon as we cleared the rise."

"You figure?" Doomsday said. Click-click.

"S'what I'd do, I was trying to cap some people coming through." Having exhausted everything worth scoping, Rockaway lowered her rifle. Her palms were itching, but she didn't want to take off her gloves. Her veins were still green, and much as she played it off earlier, it made her skin crawl to see it up close. It usually took a day or two for the blood to go back to normal. She focused on the task at hand instead.

"Driving that's gonna be slow, no other way to do it. Whoever set all that up doesn't like surprises. We'll be target practice for anyone nearby who wants to try." Click-click. "Plus we'll be going right into the sun, which doesn't help. I'll go as fast as I can, but we need to have a plan if things go bad."

"Rock up front on the rifle, I'll ride in back and be ready to drop out and fuck up anyone gets in close." Jimmy spun his bat a bit unnecessarily. "Sound good?"

"Solid," Rockaway agreed. "I hope Heller was right, I really fucking do. 'Cause if it's not Sainthood up on that bridge, if it's been taken by raiders or whatever, we're absolutely fucked." Doomsday looked at her, a little exasperated, and she shrugged. "I call it like I see it."

"Well, let's do it then." They got back into the caravan, and Doomsday put it into drive. It lurched and rumbled down the overpass and into the gauntlet of rusted metal, Rockaway scanning the wreckage intently for any sign of movement. The rifle was unwieldy in the cab of the caravan, but wouldn't be use at all in the back, and so she managed as best she could.

"Anything?" Jimmy called from the back. Rockaway could hear him drumming his fingers on the shield he'd picked up back at the Darwinist compound. Patience wasn't a common Yorker virtue; Rockaway had cultivated a kind of it in order to be any good as a sniper, but Jimmy had no such training. Not that anyone ever has a particularly easy time waiting to get rushed or shot at, especially cooped up in the back of a rattling caravan.

"Yeah, the Iron Cross is riding a herd of goliaths straight at us." That got a tense laugh from the others. "Anything fucking shows, I'll shout. Now shut up, I'm concentrating." They turned through another set of switchbacks, and as they passed a burnt out husk of a caravan, Rockaway tapped Doomsday on the arm and pointed silently. A row of shotgun blasts stitched the side of the vehicle at about waist height, accompanied by a messy smear of long-dried blood and a few gory tatters. A handprint slid down the side of the caravan, weathered in so deeply it looked like it had been engraved. Whatever happened here had been some time back now, but it had been brutal when it did. Doomsday maneuvered the truck through the switchbacks, a pistol across her lap and her mouth set in a tight line of concentration, not talking at all.

A feeling down the back of her neck caused Rockaway to glance up and spot a rifle pointing down at them from the window of one of the buildings lining the street. The barrel was slowly tracking them, and a moment later she caught the glint of optics. "Shooter, red building, upper right window," Rockaway said casually.

"Problem or lookout?" Doomsday asked.

"Don't know. Fucker's tracking us though." Rockaway thought about bringing her own rifle up and

91 91

pointing it right back at the bastard, but whoever it was had the drop on her already, and besides it would mean not watching the rest of their surroundings. As much as it pissed her off to know that some other sniper had her in their sights, watching the road was the smarter play overall. Not that being responsible would matter much if she got a round through her head, but it was something at least.

The next five minutes were some of the worst of Rockaway's life, worse than a lot of the actual fights she'd been in even. At least then something was happening. Or when she staked out a target, she knew that she had the initiative, that things were going forward on her schedule. But inching forward in a crawling caravan, moving a few feet at a time through a maze of rusted-out hulks, waiting for zeds or raiders or who knows what to leap out from hiding and attack, and knowing someone else had crosshairs on her the entire time besides? That was the worst. She caught herself itching her palms through her gloves and forced herself to stop. She kept re-opening the wounds, and every time she did she thought about Red Hands again, and wondered what was in her blood.

Another comforting thought.

Chapter Eight

"Saints, I think we made it through," Doomsday said as they cleared the last switchback. Up ahead was an old toll plaza with most of its lanes blocked by concrete barriers and screens of reinforced fencing, forcing travelers to take one of a few manned entry points. A large sign atop the booths read "FRANKLIN SPAN OUTPOST – ALL WELCOME – NO VIOLENCE" accompanied by large symbols of the Sainthood of the Ashes and the Fallow Hopes. Smaller signs hanging off of it bore crude pictographs indicating the availability of food, shelter, and medical attention, as well as a Post Walker collection point for mail delivery.

Immediately beyond the toll plaza and to the right was a fenced off parking area with a number of caravans, bikes, wagons and even a couple of horses, as well as what appeared to be a machine shop with several caravans in various states of disassembly. To the left of the bridge was a fenced off corridor that appeared to lead to several buildings that still stood in the shadow of the structure. Several neatly lettered wooden signs identified the fenced path as leading to the Fallow Hopes' barracks and armory as well as a lodging house, chapel and medical center run by the Sainthood.

At first glance it might seem odd to some that the Cult of Fallow Hopes and the Sainthood of the Ashes would could live and work in such close quarters, but Rockaway had seen the pairing before back in York and wasn't all that surprised. The Cult was intensely hierarchical by organization and militaristic in outlook, with a dogmatic approach to its teachings. By contrast, the Sainthood was more of a movement than a true organization, with each practitioner largely left to find their own path to faith, often by combining bits and pieces of pre-Fall religions as well as insights from the modern world. The Cult was soldiers struggling to pry the world from the grip of damnation; the Sainthood saw their role as teachers and caregivers, passing from town to town and leaving wisdom in their wake. It would seem like a perfect recipe for disaster to put them both together, on the face of it.

And yet both religions had a key belief they shared right down to the core: the undead are an enemy that must be burned from the face of the world. Rockaway supposed most all survivors felt that way, of course, but these two faiths made it a central part of their doctrine – and expected their followers to uphold it zealously. Wherever the horde attacked in strength, Fallow Hopes followers would be found in the thick of the fighting, and the Sainthood's wanderers were famous for their ability to track and destroy particularly dangerous zed.

Rockaway's personal experience was with a small mercenary crew called the Old Guard that operated in some of the worst parts of the Broke Lands, offering caravan escorts and community support for some of the most dangerous areas of that already shitty part of town. The Old Guard was about half Sainthood and half Fallow Hopes, at least judging from the decorations on their gear, and they had been posted to the settlement she'd been visiting for a big gang sit down when a major horde attack came rolling in. Watching those professionals work over the course of the next three days had banished any doubts she might have about their compatibility, much less their effectiveness under fire. An entire outpost likely wouldn't be terribly luxurious, as neither faith had much truck with unnecessary material possessions, but it would be clean, hospitable and well-defended. She hoped, anyway.

A stocky young woman with strawberry hair poking out from under her compact military cap and dressed in the black and red of the Fallow Hopes stepped out from one of the reinforced toll booths as they rolled up. A heavy duty rebreather covered the lower half of her face, and she signaled them to come to a stop well shy of the plaza. As she approached, her counterpart eyed them warily from inside his pillbox. Rockaway felt a shiver at the parallel to roadblock the Baron's Boys had set for them, but pushed the anxiety aside.

"Nobody here has any problems with the Fallow Hopes, right?" Doomsday asked.

"Not really," Rockaway said.

"Except that the whole damn Iron Cross is in the Cult," Jimmy pointed out. He was peering out warily from the back of the caravan.

"Shit, there is that," Rockaway allowed.

"That doesn't mean anything," Doomsday said. "It's a big faith, no reason they all know each other."

"Just fucking keep it in mind, all right?" Jimmy replied as the guard came around to the driver's side. "They're all about ranks and shit, so if they get orders from a higher-up—"

"Noted, now fucking shut it," Rockaway cut in.

Doomsday started to roll down her window, but the guard gestured for her to stop and roll it back up. "What's going on?" Doomsday said, raising her voice to be heard through the glass.

"Quarantine." The Cultist's voice was muffled two different ways, but there was no mistaking that grim tone. "Do you have face protection?"

"We do." Doomsday looked at Rockaway

questioningly, but Jimmy was already fishing theirs out of their bags. Back in the Heights, the Doc soaked strips of cloth in counterseptics and herbal remedies, then bound them tight in plastic to seal in the effect until they were needed. It might not be as effective as a genuine rebreather, but so far it hadn't let them down. Of course, Doomsday had the real deal in her travel pack, and fixed it in place as Jimmy and Rockaway were tying their cloths across the lower halves of their faces. The guard raised an eyebrow at the bandit look the two Yorkers were sporting but didn't comment. "What kind of outbreak?" Doomsday asked.

"Unknown," the Cultist said, shaking her head. "The patient fled before our medical team could finish examining her. Nasty, though. Knocked out a whole floor and anyone she came near on her way out. Some are still pretty out of it."

"Fuck," Jimmy muttered, pounding the back of the seat in frustration.

"Was it a blonde woman? Tall, red leathers?" Rockaway leaned over.

"Yeah," the guard narrowed her eyes warily. "How'd you know?"

"I'm with the Federal Bonded Inquisition," Doomsday said, holding her identification up to the glass for the guard to see. "That woman is an extremely dangerous fugitive. We've been tracking here since Aysea."

"You're with the Inquisition?" The Cultist sounded skeptical, but she inspected the credentials anyway, her lips moving faintly as she read the words. "I thought you people were made up. No offense," she added hastily.

"None taken," Doomsday said, clearly trying for a friendly tone, though the lightness of her comment was lost somewhat between her rebreather and the glass. "There aren't that many of us to go around."

"What about her? She with the Inquisition too?" The look in her eyes told Rockaway exactly how likely the guard considered that possibility.

"She's been, ah, deputized, you could say. As has our friend in the back." Jimmy waved and the Cultist returned it. She lowered her weapon a few more degrees as well; either the girl was one sloppy guard, which Rockaway doubted if only due to the Cult's known insistence on discipline and drill, or this official business stuff meant they were going to make it through the roadblock without anyone getting shot. Rockaway clicked her safety back into place. A lot of Yorkers called pussy on anyone who put a safety on their shooter, but then again, Rockaway never had to live down blowing off part of her own tit fucking up holstering a pistol in a shoulder rig like Suzie Jacks from the Red Runners. She figured that made up for taking some extra shit now and then.

"We heard she was wounded?" Doomsday asked.

The guard nodded, apparently eager to help now that she knew it was Inquisition business. "Rifle round to the chest. She drove right up to the checkpoint and collapsed. The doctor said it was a miracle that she had managed to drive at all, her wound was so infected. They were draining some awful pus, I know that. A few people even passed out, but the tough ones managed until they could get it cleaned and dressed. Touch and go for a little while, but our doc's a bit of a medical genius, so she pulled through." The look of pride faded when she realized the implications of that statement. "Not that we know who she was, of course."

"It's fine," Doomsday said reassuringly. "This is important, though – can you tell me exactly what happened to make the outpost call for the quarantine?"

"As far as I know, she was spotted heading for the bridge late last night. When one of the sentries approached to ask how she was doing, he just keeled over a few feet from her. Out cold. She didn't even touch him. One of the others went to help him and he went over too, just down and out. There was another woman on post who saw it all happen from the spotter's nest. She was going to put a round in the woman, but on the other hand, she hadn't seen your fugitive so much as lift a finger, and she didn't seem interested in eating or robbing them, so she hesitated on the trigger. By the time she got the nerve, the fugitive had vanished into the gardens on the span." She shook her head. "In the wind, now, I expect."

"That's it?" Rockaway splayed her hands. "She just knocked out two sentries?"

"That's what it looked like, until they went to the medical center and found a trail of unconscious people going all the way back to her room. Just like what happened during the surgery when they opened up that wound, only all over the place. Out cold, close to comatose for some of them. We had a real hard time waking them up too. Some of them still aren't quite normal – bad headaches, numbness in their hands and feet, that kind of thing. Plus there was the smell. Hence the precautions." The Cultist tapped the front of her rebreather.

"What do you mean, the smell?" Jimmy spoke up from the back.

"There was this scent, like rotting fruit or decomposing flowers, so sweet it would make you sick. It was everywhere she'd been. That, and this trail of thick white pus. So as soon as they could, they locked everyone down. The outpost's closed to visitors right now."

"Understood," Doomsday said. "Other than this incident, did you notice anything else unusual in the past few days?"

"What, that not strange enough for you?" The guard shook her head. "Well, sure. There was something strange a few nights back. Weird sounds in the sky. Thought it was thunder at first, or maybe some of the big guns across the river, but it was too regular for that. It was like a real deep whump whump whump." She shook her head. "Damndest thing. It sounded like it passed by overhead and then it was gone."

"I'll bet," Rockaway muttered. Confirmation that the aircraft they'd heard back at the Darwinist compound really was heading to the Wastes, at least, though she wasn't sure if she should be happy or depressed about it.

"What about our caravan?" Doomsday was asking.

"You can leave the caravan here and move through, but I'm afraid our facilities are off-limits until this thing is worked out."

"Wait, leave our caravan?" Jimmy asked incredulously.

"It'll be perfectly safe here," the guard said stiffly, as if insulted that they would imply anything to the contrary. "We're not thieves."

"No, I think he's wondering why the fuck we can't cross the bridge with it?" Rockaway said, trying not to let her frustration creep in too much. The caravan was a battered heap that bounced terribly on the slightest bumps and it was sweltering and cramped at the best of times in the back, but it still beat the hell out of walking when it came to covering straight up distance. Growing up in York, caravans were a vanity at best, and aside from the traders who rolled down the few cleared routes on their way through the city, nobody in their right mind tried to get around in something as big and loud and obvious. So she'd never seen the appeal until the last few days, but it was definitely growing on her.

"You've never been across Franklin Span, have you?" The guard gestured to the rusted green structure rising ahead of them. "Whole sections have fallen out. They keep saying they'll repair it, make it better, but for all their big talk about forging the future, it's all the engineers can do to keep it from degrading further. I don't think there's enough structure left for your truck to not pitch down through a hole at some point or another. Sorry."

"What the hell good is a bridge that can't take caravan traffic?" Jimmy exclaimed.

"Plenty," the guard said hotly, and Doomsday shot Jimmy a warning look. "We're the only crossing that doesn't charge a toll, and has medical and lodging for little to no cost besides. We're not affiliated with any of the Delphian factions, and we won't let their petty feuding cut off the one safe way out of the city for anyone who needs it."

"Look, my boy here meant no offense—" Doomsday began, but the guard just talked right over her, growing more animated as she spoke. Evidently Jimmy had touched a nerve.

"We're the reason they can keep their guns pointed at each other or those heathen Duponts from downriver and not have to worry about the horde biting them in the back. We are the reason the Post Walkers don't simply route around the city most of the time. We are the wall that keeps the raiders out. Do you understand?"

"Understood," Rockaway said, holding her hands up, palms open.

"Sorry," Jimmy added, looking down contritely.

"It's been a long trip, and she's slipped away from us twice already," Doomsday explained. "I hope you understand we mean no disrespect. It's just that time is of the essence, and we need to stay as mobile as possible. Are there other crossings that will take caravans?"

"There are," the guard said, her body language easing up a bit. "There's the Taconic ferry a few miles upriver, and the scrappers sometimes hire out at the shipyards downriver."

"How far?" Doomsday asked.

"Day or two, either way." The guard looked at the sun, which had nearly set behind the buildings of the Delphian landscape across the river. "A little longer, as I wouldn't advise leaving now. You're welcome to camp in our caravan area – it's secure, we just ask that you maintain coverage discipline, do not mingle with the others staying there and do not try to enter the quarantined buildings."

"Thank you. One moment, OK?" Doomsday gave the guard a thumbs up, and she stepped back a few feet to let them talk. The agent lowered her voice anyway, just to be on the safe side. "We can't wait another couple of days, agreed?"

"Too fucking right," Rockaway said emphatically. "Sounds like the bitch is already healing. We gotta catch her and put her the fuck down."

"Fuck healing, what's this all this stuff about her bleeding white pus and shit?" Jimmy asked, eyes wide. "What the hell is she? Because that shit ain't natural, no way."

"What? What is it?" Doomsday said, looking over at Rockaway, who had slumped back in her seat and was rubbing her brow with the back of her hand. "What are you thinking?""

"Ever hear of a white lady?" Rockaway said, hoping she was wrong but knowing with the terrible certainty of the terminally screwed that she was probably right. After all, it was only the worst, most terrible possibility she could think of – why wouldn't it be right?"

"Oh, fuck," Jimmy said.

"You mean the zed?" Doomsday asked, and then the logic caught up to her as well. "Big Playboy and his tank heart. Saints. This is getting to be a whole lot of too damn much."

White ladies were actually something of a misnomer – they could be male or female. According to Winter, who was the Dead Heroes' expert on the horde, they got their name from a similarity to old legends about ghost women in white who wandered lonely roads at night, luring unwary travelers to their doom. Their zed equivalents weren't any less terrifying, either. White ladies rotted strangely, almost entirely internally, leaving them almost human-looking on the outside, at least until you got real close. The strange reaction fueled by their rot sweated from their skin, bleaching whatever clothing they were wearing a pale white, and creating a sickly-sweet haze that accompanied them wherever they went. That was one of the warning signs, at least, that was supposed to keep travelers from approaching them.

Rockaway had never seen a white lady herself, but the way Winter told it anyone who got too close and breathed the shit in got really calm and happy, like a strong pot high. Pretty soon the skin went numb and the victim fell asleep, so drugged and fucked up that they didn't even notice as the white lady started peeling strips of skin off, devouring them slowly.

Supposedly other zed found the scent attractive as well, so some white ladies would be surrounded by packs of shamblers, shuffling along at the head of a macabre parade.

If a Grave Robber could implant a fast-regenerating tank heart in a psycho like Big Playboy, then it stood to reason that Eve might have some unholy modifications as well, particularly since she was his superior in the Final Knights hierarchy. Of course, Rockaway putting a bullet in whatever had been implanted couldn't have been good for such arcane and delicate surgery, and there was a certain joy in knowing that Eve might be getting poisoned by the very thing she had added to give her an advantage.

But apparently some genius had put her back together, and now they risked losing her again.

"Fuck the ferry, we're going in on foot," Rockaway announced. "We gotta get this bitch."

"You know I'm fucking all about that," Jimmy added emphatically.

"Agreed," Doomsday nodded.

"What, not gonna ask if I have a plan or something?" Rockaway said, mildly surprised.

Doomsday shook her head. "Not at this point. Besides, we're getting close to Domino – if she links up with whoever's gone traitor everything gets a whole lot worse, even if she doesn't have the missile keys. We get her now, we might get her to name her accomplice, then maybe we get to Domino and take that asshole out too. Before they get any sort of warning and go to ground." Doomsday looked at the two Yorkers, who exchanged sidelong glances as she spoke. "What? I curse, you've heard it before."

"Yeah, no, it's not that, it's just … those are your own people you're talking about, you know?" Jimmy said after a moment's hesitation. "You gonna be able to just walk up and cap one, comes to it?"

Doomsday didn't even blink. "One of yours betrayed the Dead Heroes, how hard would it be to put them down?"

"Fuck 'em, I'm with you on that." Rockaway held Doomsday's gaze. "I'm more concerned with whether you know how to get it out of her. Hurt or not, she ain't likely to crack easy – and if she does, how the fuck will we know she's not just naming names as a last fuck you, you know?"

"I know how to interrogate someone," Doomsday said firmly.

"Interrogate?" Jimmy sounded dubious.

"OK, fine, torture. We know how to make sure someone's telling the truth, believe me. I mean, we are the Inquisition, right?" At that they had to admit she had a point. "Just make sure we take her alive so I have something to question, got it?"

"Fuck it. Kill her, wait out her dead time, then torture the shit out of her. Make a fucking statement, know what I'm saying?" Rockaway patted her rifle.

"I see the merit," Doomsday said as Jimmy gave Rockaway an enthusiastic high five, "but we can't chance her not making it back. She might have green veined already, or even if she's not, busting what those Grave Robbers put in her might have jumpstarted her endgame. Much as I want to say she's burn on sight, if we put her down and she doesn't come back usable we lose out big."

"Fucking G-Men," Jimmy swore, "being all logical and shit." It was delivered so deadpan that Doomsday actually hesitated a moment, then all three of them laughed. "Screw it, I was sick of sitting in this ass-smelling caravan all day anyway."

"Too right," Rockaway agreed. "Let's park this, grab our gear and get the fuck on outta here before we lose all the light."

Doomsday signaled for the guard to approach again. "We're going to park and head across on foot."

"Not what I'd advise, but you seem like you can handle yourselves." The guard pointed to the left of the bridge. "When you're across, follow the markers for Fort Independence. Their trenches don't start far from the base of the bridge, and they're your best bet for shelter tonight once you're across. Just watch out – they've been getting hit pretty hard by the Duponts the last week or so, so their sentries are bound to be a bit jumpy."

"Thank you," Doomsday answered sincerely.

"Just park off to the far right there. We'll keep an eye on the caravan, but I have to tell you, if it goes unclaimed for more than a month, we'll sell it or break it for parts. It's nothing personal, we just can't spare the space indefinitely."

"Fair enough," Doomsday said. She started to pull forward, but Rockaway tapped her on the arm, stopping her.

"Can you get a message to York from here?"

"Soon as the quarantine lifts, sure. There's a Post Walker already on site. What do you want to send?"

"'Almost done with the bastards. Back soon. Tell Mercy she can have her fucking job back.' Goes to the Dead Heroes in the Heights. Got all that?" The Cultist repeated it back, twice, word for word. "Cool, thanks. There a charge on that?"

"Nah," the guard said dismissively. "We'll get it written down and pack it for their next run, I promise." She looked past them, and Rockaway turned to see in the mirror that another caravan that was approaching through the switchbacks. "Anything else?"

"We're good. Thanks again for all the help." Doomsday pulled past her through the toll plaza and parked the caravan. There wasn't much to do in terms of gathering their possessions; none of them traveled with much more than a pack. For a moment Rockaway considered chucking the tank heart they'd cut out of Big Playboy, which was still glowing a faint green even days later, but in the end she pushed the wrapped bundle to the bottom of her backpack. The ladies also took the opportunity to clean their shooters as the last of the light began to fade, while Jimmy said a quiet prayer, turning his bat over slowly in his hands as he mouthed the words. One last check on ammo and provisions – plenty of the former, a tight but manageable supply of the latter – and it was time to go.

"Journey to the end," Jimmy said as they shut the caravan, his tone philosophical.

"What'd you say?" Doomsday asked. She tossed the keys to one of the Franklin Span mechanics, who was already eyeing their ride from a distance.

"Old verse. Not my Kings, but heard it once, seems right." Jimmy pulled his cap on tight, straightened it twice with a decisive tug each time. It was one of his little pre-battle rituals, like Angry Justin bouncing on the balls of his feet or Winter humming tunelessly to herself, and when he caught her noticing he smiled the same sort of smile he'd had in the back of the caravan not too long ago. Tourists often said Yorkers liked to fight, and there was some truth to that, but the reality of it was that Yorkers liked things simple.

Living day to day in the ruins was hard enough, moving from building to building, staying off the street, collecting water, scrounging scrap; having a clear objective ahead, a definite enemy to take down, well, that was a nice change of pace. You can't shoot starvation, but you can sure as hell put a bullet in some asshole trying to run off with a case of your canned vegetables. It might not be much comfort, but they say the little things are what make life worth living, even in the wasteland. And right now, she could go for some simple.

"To the end," Rockaway said, clasping his hand in hers and pulling them together for a rough embrace. Jimmy clapped her on the back, reached out a hand and pulled Doomsday in. Rockaway was about to say something about it when she realized she didn't mind, and the three of them stood there for a few minutes.

Not much time compared to the journey they'd had and the distance still left to cover, but sometimes a moment of rest makes an hour of travel easier.

Chapter Nine

Rockaway never thought she'd feel anything like it so far from York, but she had to admit, crossing the Franklin Span felt a little like coming home. Wind whipped against them, high and cold with altitude, carrying clouds of rust from the tarnished metal and putting a faint coppery taste in her mouth despite her protective bandanna. Ahead of them the Delphian Wastes sprawled out like a cheap date on a dirty mattress, and despite the feeling of relief at getting out of the sticks and back into a city, Rockaway could see what Red Ed was always saying about Delphians having a chip on their shoulder about being compared to Yorkers.

Even nuked to shit, York still had more skyscrapers in a block than the whole of the Delphian Wastes. While the Wastes did stretch impressively far toward the horizon, even the dim light it was clear whole sections had been burned out, probably during the Fall, and never really rebuilt, leaving long blackened scars through the rows of shabby buildings. Gunfire rattled and popped in the distance, nothing close enough to be any cause for real concern, but enough to let them know the neighborhood was lively. The comforting scent of rust and the feeling of heights quickly drained into a feeling of mild disappointment.

"Yep," Jimmy said when they crested the top of bridge, capturing Rockaway's thoughts exactly, "this place sucks."

"Fuck is this even a city?" Rockaway shook her head.

"I warned you." Doomsday said. "York isn't like anywhere else."

"Too fucking right," Rockaway said, turning her

108

head to the side to spit.

When they reached the base of the bridge, they found a strange metal statue in a weird zigzag shape on a platform, and hand-lettered signs pointing in different directions. FORT INDEPENDENCE was marked with a particularly large sign, and they struck off in that direction. By now it was full dark, but the moon was mostly full and the sky was clear, so the way was easy enough to follow. Once they'd gone a short distance, there were strings of lights hanging from threadbare wires over some of the sections of the street, adding a harsh fluorescent light that cast surprisingly dark shadows in the night.

It quickly became evident what the guard had been talking about when she mentioned trenches – the residents of Fort Independence, unwilling or unable to dig fortifications, had built their trenches up from street level instead. Everything from caravans to concrete barriers to carefully stacked piles of logs had been placed to either side of the path, funneling foot traffic into narrow passageways with walls as high as eight or nine feet to either side. Small metal-sided sheds were placed at regular intervals, often reinforced with bags of dirt or sand, and here and there they could see wood-roofed passageways branching off from the main trenchworks. At every intersection more large signs directed them toward Fort Independence, with smaller ones indicating field medical centers, armory supplies and other military

"Check this shit out." Rockaway pointed to regular cut-outs in the walls, a foot or two above street level. "Firing steps. These are some hardcore fuckers."

"Looks like they need to be," Doomsday said, nodding down a side street. It looked like repairs were underway to fix a gaping hole in the street, the telltale burns of an explosion all around it. They'd noticed bullet holes, dents and the occasional claw mark in the trench fortifications as they walked, but this was something else entirely.

"Fuck, what did that?" Jimmy asked. "Grenade?"

"Too big for a grenade," Rockaway and Doomsday said simultaneously; Doomsday smiled and deferred to the sniper for the rest of the answer. "Looks more like a mortar. Damn. That's fucked up. Last time I saw heavy incoming like that …" Rockaway trailed off, remembering the Iron Cross ambush on top of the Green Eyes' building back in York. For a sick moment her mind connected the two, expecting the Iron Cross to burst out and attack, but she pushed the thought away. They weren't the only crazy assholes in the world with artillery. She fought down the urge to scratch the scars on her palms. "Last time I saw ordnance like that, shit got bad in a hurry."

"Something else bothers me more," Doomsday said quietly.

"Little fucking deserted, isn't it?" Rockaway finished.

"Seen at least two sentry shacks with no one in 'em," Jimmy added. He had his heavy metal shield on one arm and his bat in hand, and was spinning the bat as he walked. If straightening his cap was his pre-battle ritual, spinning his bat was a sign that his blood was already hot. "Something's fucked."

"Eve?" Doomsday said. She clicked her safety once, then caught herself doing it and very consciously put a stop to the nervous tic.

"Fucking has to be," Rockaway said, and spat. "Look." A bloody handprint was smeared at the corner of one of the trench intersections. When the sniper ventured up for a closer look, she saw a thick, viscous white fluid mixed in with the blood. "Looks she's still fucking leaking the good stuff too."

"Kings, this is bad." Jimmy pointed at a small side passage off the main trenchway. A pair of bodies in loose fatigues and combat gear had been hastily dragged there and dumped, face down, but there was no mystery about had happened to them – the backs of their fatigues were practically shredded from close range gunfire. "Eve's a blade fighter and she's hurt besides – how the fuck did she do this?"

"Blood's still fresh, too," Doomsday said, kneeling down to take a closer look. "We might have heard this on the way over."

"Heads up, locals," Rockaway said, as another pair of soldiers rounded the corner twenty yards ahead of them, a heavyset young man with a straw cowboy hat adorned with old bottlecaps and bald Retrograde with one of the most heavily rotted faces Rockaway had ever seen on one of the living. It was hard to tell in the light, but it looked like they had something smeared on their faces, though whether it was blood or warpaint Rockaway couldn't say. They might have been mistaken for zombies except that they carried their weapons with obvious purpose. Like the two bodies in the alley, they wore bulky scrap-reinforced jackets and carried rugged looking carbines, which they immediately leveled at the trio. "Hey there, look, this isn't on us, we just— down!"

Rockaway dove to the side as the soldiers opened fire, the noise thunderous in the narrow confines of the trench. She pressed herself into narrow dugout in the wall, feeling the impact of rounds thudding into the trench next to her, flinching as hot splinters of wood and shaved metal sprayed past her. It was enough cover to survive an initial burst or two, but she was barely covered at best, and even a small flanking move would leave her totally vulnerable. Not only that, but her rifle was too long to easily bring to bear in such narrow confines – by the time she got it aimed they'd already have her targeted. "Fuckin' pinned!" Rockaway called out.

Caught in an awkward kneeling position when the enemy opened up, Doomsday likely would've caught a burst if Jimmy hadn't interfered, bowling her over with his momentum and knocking her into the cover of the side passage. He grunted as a round creased his left arm just above the elbow, ripping open his old military jacket with a spray of blood, but managed to bounce the round after it off his shield, leaving a tremendous dent in the metal but sparing him a rifle round to the torso. Jimmy staggered into cover behind Doomsday, barely sparing a second glance at his arm once he judged the wound superficial.

"Not hostile! Not hostile!" Doomsday screamed. She tried to lean out and wave to the soldiers but jerked her head back into cover as another burst smacked into the trenches next to her. "Stop firing! We are not hostile! Repeat: We are not hostile!"

Rockaway glanced around cover with a quick, practiced motion, saw one of the soldiers covering as the other reloaded. "Hey! Assholes! Stop fucking shooting! We're not here to hurt you!" Her reply came in another carbine burst, putting a hot splinter in her cheek as one of the wooden struts lost a chunk in the barrage. "Fuckin' quit it!"

"What do we do, Rock?" Jimmy Three Ex called between bursts. Next to him Doomsday had taken up a fire position at the mouth of the side passage, pistol ready, but she hadn't fired yet. Mistake or not, they all knew once they returned fire that changed the equation considerably, much less if they actually took out one of the Fort Independence soldiers.

"Got a miracle?" Rockaway yelled back, as another withering volley smashed into the trench wall. Most of the beam was vanishing quickly. "'Cause I'm gonna fuckin' need one!"

"I got you," Doomsday said calmly. The next time there was a break in the enemy fire, she ducked out and targeted fast, loosing two shots less than a second apart. Rockaway heard a couple muted cries of pain and glanced out to see the two soldiers clutching at wounded hands, carbines scattered at their feet.

"What the fuck? Why are you shooting at us?" The young man in the cowboy hat looked honestly confused. He bent down as if to pick up his carbine, but his friend elbowed him and they both put their hands up, blood and all.

"Maybe because you were fucking shooting at us?" Rockaway fired back.

"Look! Everyone take it easy!" Doomsday called out before things escalated again. The agent leaned a bit more out of cover now that the enemy guns were safely on the ground. "We're law enforcement, OK?"

"Never gonna get used to that," Rockaway muttered to herself.

"We don't have any quarrel with you, and we're not trying to infringe on your territory," Doomsday continued. If there was any kind of adrenaline tremor in her voice, she masked it well. "We're chasing a fugitive, and we know she came this way."

"You mean the lady in red?" The bald one said.

"Yes. When did you see her last?"

"Not half an hour ago," Cowboy Hat replied. "She's been with us since this morning. She told us to guard this intersection, make sure no one came after her. Said there were bounty hunters after her, and that we needed to protect her."

"What, and you pricks just fucking believed her?" Jimmy called out incredulously. "What kind of sentries are you? Kings!"

The two soldiers looked at each other, as if seeking confirmation. "She was hurt," Baldy said finally, as if that explained everything.

"And she smelled nice," Cowboy Hat added.

"Wait, what?" Doomsday asked, signaling for Rockaway and Jimmy to ease off a bit. "What do you mean, she smelled nice?"

Cowboy Hat looked down at the ground like a kid caught with his first bottle of hooch. "I dunno, she just smelled like … momma, I guess."

Baldy snorted. "She didn't smell like your mother, idiot, she smelled like the Gallery tunnels where I grew up. And I don't remember your pretty faces down there when I was a kid, I'll tell you that."

"This shit just gets better and better," Rockaway said across the trench. "I thought she just knocked people the fuck out and kept moving?"

"Maybe it's more controlled than that, at least until someone punches a big hole in the works," Doomsday said. "They did say that the doc at the Franklin Span is some kind of genius. Maybe he patched her back into working condition?"

"Yeah, well, thanks for nothing, asshole," Rockaway spat.

"Bigger fucking concerns," Jimmy said. He raised his voice to address the two soldiers. "Hey! You gonna try and kill us some more, or you done with that?"

"You're the ones with the guns, you tell us," Baldy replied.

"We're coming out now, just don't pick up the shooters and everything will be fine." Doomsday gestured and Rockaway came out of cover, rifle leading, not exacting aiming at the men but not at ease either. Jimmy brought up the rear as Doomsday fell in next to Rockaway. "I can bandage those hands, if you like. Call it a goodwill gesture." Cowboy Hat nodded at her, but before Doomsday could even unroll a length of bandage, however, she stopped up short. "What's that white stuff on your face? How did it get there?" Mixed in with the streaks of blood on their faces were a few gobs of smeared white goop.

"What white stuff?" Baldy asked suspiciously.

"When we found her, she reached out for help. I got smeared across here," Cowboy Hat said, twitching his chin to indicate the streak of blood and pus across his face. "Him too. I didn't think anything of it – she was hurt and kind of flailing, you know?"

"This about the time you figured it would be such a great fucking idea to do what she said?" Rockaway rolled her eyes.

"Well, yeah, I guess." Cowboy Hat thought about that a moment, then hung his head. "Shit."

"Are you saying she drugged us?" Baldy demanded.

"Something like that," Doomsday said, before Rockaway could really warm to her reply. "After she touched you with that … stuff, she just told you to wait here and shoot at anyone who came this way?"

"Not exactly," Cowboy Hat said sheepishly. "She asked us to take her back to the barracks first."

"Oh, fuck," Jimmy swore.

"How many others would that put her contact with?" Doomsday asked.

"At our barracks? About thirty," Baldy said. "You figure she drugged all of them?"

"Our fucking luck, sure." Rockaway spat again. "And she's just, what, fucking hanging out at the barracks now? Or she move on?"

"She was gonna move on, but she damn near collapsed when she tried. Opened a bunch of fresh stitches. She looked like she was in a lot of pain, I felt bad for her." Cowboy Hat looked around defensively. "What? I was drugged!"

"At least we know where she's at," Jimmy said placatingly. "That's not nothing." From somewhere nearby, a whistle sounded, high and sharp, three short blasts. Baldy cursed and fumbled with a chain around his neck, but his wounded hand was making it clumsy work.

"What's that fucking signal?" Rockaway asked, the barrel of her rifle lifting just slightly. The three blasts repeated, sounding slightly more urgent this time.

"I have to send back or they'll know something's up!" Baldy hissed.

"Do it fast!" Doomsday urged.

"Where the fuck is it?" Baldy said, near desperate now. Cowboy Hat urged him to check his pockets as the three blasts sounded again, and with drops of blood flying freely from his wounded hand he patted himself down in a parody of security that might've struck Rockaway as funny if it hadn't been such a desperate moment. Doomsday clearly wanted to help but was wary of getting too close to the white goop.

"Got it!" Baldy retrieved the whistle from a vest pocket, awkwardly extracting it cross-body with his good hand. Before he could get it to his lips, however, there was one long, high blast. Several others echoed it, further off. "Fuck. Fuck fuck fuck fuck!"

"What's that mean?" Doomsday asked.

"Means let us pick up our goddamn guns, we're about to have company!" Cowboy Hat said. "C'mon! They'll be here in under a minute, tops!"

Chapter Ten

"How are we working this?" Doomsday asked as she quickly wrapped the hands of the wounded men. Both wiped off their faces with rags they quickly tossed afterward, handling the cloths like a Pureblood dandy might handle live rats.

"We're not killing anyone," growled Baldy. "If they're mindfucked like we were, it's not their fault, whatever they do." Cowboy Hat didn't add anything to that thought, but the look of grim resolve on his face said enough. It was tense enough, trying to cover an intersection, but Rockaway's suggestion that they fall back to a different spot had immediately lost its appeal when whistles sounded from two other directions as well, and close by at that.

"Mindfucked or not, I'm not taking a goddamned bullet to be fucking polite," Rockaway answered, getting her sights settled on the intersection. There could be worse spots to weather an ambush, Rockaway reflected, though not many came to mind – siting at the juncture of a "T" intersection with little cover and no fallback route didn't do much her confidence.

"Pain seems to break the control." Doomsday re-checked her clip. "Shoot to wound."

"Are you serious?" Rockaway said, her rhythmic breathing giving her an artificial calm.

"Aren't you some badass sniper?" Doomsday teased. "Bullets go where you put them?"

"Yeah, like their fucking foreheads," Rockaway countered. Cowboy Hat growled something at her; she didn't catch the words but the tone was clear enough. "I'll fucking try, all right? But comes down to it—"

"They get it," Jimmy said quietly, patting her

lightly on the back. Rockaway hushed.

They didn't have long to wait. These soldiers moved with more of a purpose and knew their cornering better – the point man peeked out fast, catching a glimpse of Rockaway without giving her much of a target (at least not to wound), and then firing off a blind burst from his carbine as his partner launched herself around the corner hard and fast, moving to the opposite wall to get a better angle on the sniper's position and firing as she came.

Rockaway weathered the storm of bullets with patience born of too many firefights and put a round in the woman's left shoulder as neatly as if she'd been popping bottles on a ledge. The impact spun the soldier around hard, sending her crashing into the wall and sliding down it as she fell, clutching her wounded shoulder in pain and surprise. It took a real effort of will not to put a follow-up round right between her eyes when she stopped moving, but Rockaway managed. The point man fired a few more blind shots that ricocheted off the trench walls ineffectively and then retreated completely out of sight, reloading by the sound of it.

"Darla?" Cowboy Hat called out. The injured soldier, Darla apparently, looked up at the sound of her name, face contorted with pain. "Darla! It's me, Gunner!"

"What the hell is going on?" Darla croaked, blood welling up between her fingers as she clamped down on her wound.

"It's the red woman! She's fucked with our heads!"

"No, don't say that now, asshole—" Rockaway hissed, but it was too late. There was the briefest of pauses as Darla looked over at whatever forces were gathered around the corner, and she had just enough

118

time to raise one hand in a warding gestured before the enemy opened up. It only lasted a few seconds, but Rockaway counted at least six guns in the onslaught; Darla wasn't so much shot as pulped.

Gunner's cry of outrage was drowned out as more gunfire erupted down at the other end of the trench corridor – evidently some signal had been given, because the rush was immediate. There was nothing else to be done but trust Doomsday and Baldy to hold the far intersection as Rockaway and Gunner held this one. "Watch my fucking back!" Rockaway yelled as more blind fire came her way; behind her Gunner yelped. "You hit?"

"Caught a ricochet, I'm fine," Gunner answered, voice tight with pain.

"Fucking focus then!" Rockaway was starting to learn the timing of the blind bursts, and so when the next one came she concentrated past the noise and the muzzle flash and saw the grenade whip out into the corridor, bouncing off the far wall and rolling towards her. "Grenade!" She yelled, pulling back from the corner and hunching up against the blast, seeing Gunner do likewise. Whoever had tossed it had enough sense to cook it first – the blast was almost immediate, and powerful enough to set her ears ringing.

That wasn't a homemade grenade like some of the gangs cooked up back home – or if it was, Fort Independence had one hell of a black powder cook working for them. Angry Justin would've traded his left nut – well, somebody's left nut anyway – for a crate of grenades like that, but there was no time to dwell on that now.

Rockaway knew the rush would follow the blast and rolled back into her firing position, muscle memory locking her in place and putting an advancing soldier right in her sights. He fired first, spraying as he came, but the shots went high. Hers didn't, though once again she had to twitch off a perfect center mass shot at the last second. It still wasn't a particularly kind wound – right into the meat of the thigh – but unless it clipped the artery he'd probably live long enough to sort this shit out. It also took his leg out from under him, dropping him on his face where he banged his head on the ground, hard.

"Contact!" She could barely hear Gunner over the tone in her ears, and figured out what he'd said more from the sound of his carbine opening up than anything else. More rounds twanged past her, this time from behind, as whoever Gunner was engaging fired back. She felt horribly exposed, her back to incoming fire, but gritted her teeth and fired past her fallen target at the next form rounding the corner. Her attempt at a leg shot missed as her target vaulted over her fallen comrade, the oncoming attacker howling an eerie, keening war cry as she came.

Another soldier, this was one was wiry and moving fast, a pair of hatchets in her hands as she came. She had a wild mane of dark brown hair that was teased into spikes and fierce blue and red warpaint streaked across her deeply tanned skin, though the designs were marred by thick gobs of white goop like the other two. Her fatigues were adorned with a number of primitive black designs, and strips of leather hung from her belt, each with more designs burned into them. Rockaway noted all of these details with a sniper's clarity in the split second before firing, feeling a momentary surge of respect for her attacker when she realized that the charging warrior clearly wasn't wearing body armor, right before she decided to put a bullet in her chest. She knew Gunner and Baldy would be pissed, but she was coming on too fast and there wasn't time to dick around with another shot to wound. Rockaway adjusted her aim and took the shot on reflex, aiming to take Warpaint down before she could get any closer.

Sure enough, the bullet soared right through her target's center mass – or at least where it should have been, if her target hadn't pulled off an incredible feat of agility to avoid it. Rather than landing on her feet, Warpaint had seen the shot coming and landed on her kneepads instead of her feet, sliding forward on the asphalt even as she dropped her body backward out of the line of fire. The bullet whipped past less than an inch above her chin, and when Warpaint snapped her head back up, she gave Rockaway a look of absolute savage pride and triumph. Hell, Rockaway would've agreed – she'd never seen someone avoid taking a bullet so perfectly, especially at close range – except that she knew Warpaint intended to bury those weapons in her skull in a matter of seconds.

"Damn, bitch," Rockaway snarled, resisting the reflex to rack another round. She knew there wouldn't be time before Warpaint was on her, and so she backed up out of her firing crouch instead, bringing the butt of her rifle up to block as the assault trooper closed the distance and started swinging. Rockaway knocked the first swing aside by the flat of the blade, but almost got gutted when she bought a feint from her attacker's offhand weapon and nearly caught a backhand swipe from the first weapon. As it was, the hatchet ripped a line across the front of Rockaway's armored vest, scraping against the metal underneath.

"Bloody Thirteen!" Rockaway heard Jimmy shouting over the sound of gunfire. She spared a glance as she dodged backward from another hatchet flurry and saw him engaged in furious close combat with two soldiers. Evidently they had jumped over the trench wall somewhere along its length, but whatever flanking maneuver they'd hoped to pull off had been blocked by six feet of angry Yorker and forty-two inches of flashing aluminum. She put her trust in him keeping those threats contained and focused on not getting dismembered by Warpaint, who was quickly proving that her incredible agility had not been a one-time fluke.

Rockaway would have preferred to pull her combat knife for close work like this, but Warpaint was too fast to give her an opening. Instead the sniper tried a feint of her own and left herself open for an overhand chop; when it came she shifted her weight and intercepted it, thrusting the butt of her rifle into the oncoming strike as hard as she could. Warpaint tried to pull her swing but only succeeded in skinning Rockaway's knuckles as the hatchet buried itself in the rifle stock. Before the soldier could pull her weapon free, Rockaway twisted the rifle butt hard, wrenching the hatchet from her enemy's hands. It was a shit way to treat her weapon, but at least it evened the odds somewhat.

Her triumph was short lived, however, as Warpaint used her momentum to deliver a wicked spinning kick, landing a solid shot to Rockaway's gut that knocked her into Gunner. Startled, he swore as she bowled into him, but he stopped her fall enough to keep her feet, and that was all she needed to stay in the fight. Having apparently decided she'd underestimated Rockaway's close quarters skills before, Warpaint struck much more cautiously this time, executing a series of fast slashes and chops that didn't over-commit her weapon to a single swing as she had before.

Rockaway weaved out of the way of some strikes and parried others, moving away from Gunner as she fought, waiting for an opening and wishing she hadn't laughed off the idea of a rigging a bayonet lug on her rifle when Angry Justin suggested it a while back. She quickly gave up trying to trap her attacker's weapon as she had before – Warpaint was too wary for that now. Her combat knife seemed to be calling to her, but it was a siren's song, and she knew it. At this range Warpaint would kill her before she even got it out of its sheath.

"Hit," croaked Gunner, falling back into a sitting position and grabbing at his chest. A small red circle had appeared in the middle of his vest, and even as he tried to unbuckle it to get at the wound, another round struck him in the shoulder and spun him all the way to ground. He was still moving, but there was simply no time to help him. It was all she could do to keep Warpaint distracted enough to prevent her realizing she could be delivering a killing blow to Gunner while he was helpless. "Gunner's down!" Rockaway called out, not sure who might hear her. She could still hear heavy gunfire at Doomsday's end of the trench, and judging from the sound of clashing metal Jimmy was still occupied too.

Confusion crossed Warpaint's features, warring with her bloodlust. "Gunner?" Her words sounded small and choked, like she was wrapping her head around a particularly difficult concept. Her weapon dipped slightly, and she looked at Gunner's weakly struggling body as if she had just realized what it was. "I don't—"

Rockaway didn't hesitate but took the opening and thrust the butt of her rifle straight at Warpaint's face. The soldier snapped out of her momentary reverie and lashed out with her axe, ducking backward and opening a deep cut along Rockaway's left forearm as she tried to bat away the strike. Even distracted, she was fast enough to avoid the brunt of the attack, but Rockaway managed to clip her on the chin and knock her off balance a bit. Her eyelids fluttered and some more lucidity might have returned, but Rockaway couldn't gamble on the control breaking and pressed the attack despite the pain in her arm, swinging for Warpaint's leading knee. Warpaint rocked back on her heels, causing the swing to miss by inches, and then sprang forward, foregoing a hatchet attack to barrel into Rockaway for a takedown.

Rockaway lost her grip on her rifle as she hit the ground but didn't reach for her knife, instead grabbing for Warpaint's throat with her right hand as her attacker came down on top of her, while also delivering a few swift kidney punches with her left. The cut and the angle robbed them of some power, but when Red Ed teaches you to kidney punch, you don't need much to make them count. He'd been known to end a fight with one well-placed shot there in his pit fighting days, and after suffering one too many slaps from Angry Justin she'd been a very good student. Her second punch drew a sharp gasp of pain from Warpaint, which was immediately cut off as Rockaway caught hold of the soldier's throat and pressed hard with her thumb and forefinger. Most people tried to grab with the whole hand, which could work, but those two fingers were surprisingly effective on their own if you knew just how to squeeze.

Warpaint choked and instinctively dropped her hatchet to grab for Rockaway's hand, but the sniper didn't let up, squeezing harder and continuing to pound away at the kidneys. Hands clawed at hers, then fingers scrabbled at her eyes, but Rockaway turned her head from side to side, keeping them from landing any solid hits. Warpaint thrashed and bucked on top of her, desperate to escape the tightening grip, then all at once her eyes rolled back and her body collapsed into dead weight on top of Rockaway. The sniper held on a moment longer, in case Warpaint was playing possum, then rolled her off with a grunt and a shove. She'd live – probably – but she should be out of the fight.

"Kill them! Kill them all!" A high-pitched woman's voice came from somewhere very nearby, carrying over the sound of gunfire and close quarters fighting. The voice sounded ragged and not entirely sane, but also more than a little triumphant, and Rockaway knew that couldn't mean anything good for their little holdout force.

"Fucking try me, bitch!" Jimmy called back, and right after that the sniper heard the distinctive ping-CRACK of a baseball bat breaking bone, followed by an agonized cry and a heavy thud. As Rockaway got Warpaint off of her, she saw Jimmy deliver a wicked backhand swing to the head of the kneeling man whose leg he'd just mangled, laying the attacker out. It was an absolutely brutal hit, though Rockaway knew Jimmy'd pulled it just enough to give the man a decent chance of survival – he could just as easily have caved in the man's skull with a shot like that. He also managed to do it while expertly warding off the other attacker with his shield, keeping it between them and knocking her fire axe aside for swing after swing. Jimmy spared a second to look in Rockaway's direction, a tight smile on his face as he worked.

At the far end of the trench, both Doomsday and Baldy were still up and shooting, though it looked like Doomsday had taken a hit to the leg and Baldy had evidently been peppered by an explosion, another grenade most likely. Neither looked her way but simply kept squeezing off shots, suppressing whatever flanking

125

units were coming their way. Rockaway could see three clips scattered at Doomsday's feet, and knew she'd be running low on ammo soon. If they were lucky, the fight they were putting up might convince the Fort Independence troops to back off and plan another attack; it wouldn't help much, but they could scrounge ammo and bandage up a bit, maybe even pick up some reinforcements if some of the brainwashed soldiers could be brought around.

Rockaway put a foot on her rifle and pulled the hatchet free, then scooped up her weapon and racked the round she hadn't had time to load when Warpaint charged. The balance felt off, but there was nothing she could do about it now. "Ex, you cool?"

"Got this bitch, easy," Jimmy called back, half-singing the words. "You?"

"Bloody Thirteen!" Rockaway said, putting her back against the corner Gunner had been watching. He was still alive, though his movements were getting slower and less frequent; if they didn't get a breather soon, he'd bleed out on them. The sniper took a deep breath, let it out slow and peeked around the corner.

Not fifteen feet away, two Fort Independence soldiers were creeping along the trench wall, having apparently opted for a more cautious advance. Rockaway ducked back as the one in the lead fired on reflex, his trench shotgun taking out a sizable chunk of the corner and spraying tiny fragments into the side of her face as she turned away. Rockaway spat out blood and splinters as the soldier fired again, pulping another section of wall, and when she heard him break open the shotgun she leaned out and fired straight into his chest.

His armor might have had a chance to slow the round at range, but this close it was no match for the high caliber load, and the impact took him clear off his feet. She'd aimed well south of the heart, but at this point she couldn't worry too much about shooting to wound – if they didn't push back this advance, those little acts of kindness wouldn't matter at all. Rockaway heard his partner swearing as the man cried out, but even as she racked her next round, she heard the clang as something bounced off the wall across from her and looked up to see the grenade rolling toward her feet.

"Fuck fuck fuck—" Taking cover wasn't an option, so she lunged for the grenade and grabbed it instead. Before she could try to toss it around the corner, however, the grenade went off in her hand. She heard the explosion distantly, as though it happened somewhere far away, and her hand felt like she'd plunged it into an oilcan fire, but when she looked down her arm her hand was still attached, fingers and all. There was a small blast circle on the ground underneath her hand, and it looked like some shrapnel had scattered nearby, but Gunner didn't even look scratched and he was only a few feet away. Her palm itched madly, and when she turned it over to take a look she could see the scar that Red Hands had left was bleeding freely, soaking a scarlet cross into her gloves. Smoke curled out from under the edges of her gloves as well, and she knew the wound must be smoldering again, the same as it had when she had survived another grenade blast at close range while taking down Big Playboy.

"What the fuck—" Rockaway looked past her singed fingers and saw the second soldier standing there, staring at her in surprise as though he couldn't quite understand what he was looking at. Not that she could have explained it much herself – she'd tried to put the last incident out of her mind, not wanting to think that Red Hands' influence was changing her, but this was proof that the last time was no fluke.

Something about her was definitely unnatural, her hands at least, probably psionic too considering the source. The sniper saw the soldier's expression change from confusion to revulsion, likely because reached the same conclusion about her survival, and he pointed his carbine straight at her head.

"No!" Rockaway extended her hand in a warding gesture and a gout of flame shot from her palm, striking him square in the chest and enveloping his upper body. He shrieked and dropped the rifle, his screams choked by the roar of the flames as he frantically tried to beat them out. It was a losing battle, however, and as Rockaway stared in numb shock he fell to his knees, then toppled over face forward and lay there burning. She felt a sharp pain behind her eyes and suddenly the lights seemed far too bright, the sounds far too loud. Something tickled her lips and even before she tasted copper she knew her nose was bleeding.

"Rock?" Rockaway looked, squinting against the glare, and saw Jimmy staring at her, shield arm low and bloody bat dangling limply from his hand, the two groaning bodies at his feet momentarily forgotten. He had a look of wide-eyed shock on his face, and there was fear in his eyes too, the same sort she'd seen on the faces of the rest of the Dead Heroes whenever Winter used one of her more disturbing gifts. Something in her broke at his expression, and with the utter certainty of a terrible moment she knew that no matter what came after this, things would never be the same between them again.

"I don't know—" Rockaway began to say, when Jimmy went stiff as his body rocked forward from a sudden impact, and the point of a bloodstained blade poked out from the front of his armor, right above his heart.

Chapter Eleven

"Shhh, easy boy," Eve cooed at Jimmy, jerking the knife out of his chest as she stepped out from behind him. Blood ran out of Jimmy's mouth, staining the bandanna tied around his throat, and he fell heavily to his knees, grabbing at the spreading circle of blood on his chest with clumsy hands. His eyes locked with Rockaway's, pained and confused, but when he opened his mouth to speak only more blood came out. Eve put one hand on the side of his head, almost as if she was about to tousle his hair, then gently tipped him over on his side as she walked past.

Eve still cut an imposing figure, but it would have been a serious stretch to call her beautiful in her current state. Her long, strawberry blonde hair was tangled and knotted, and even the heavy kohl designs around her eyes could not disguise the dark circles of too many hard nights. Her skin looked waxy and too-pale in the harsh electric lights, and even her feral grin seemed edged with pain. Most disturbing of all was the hole in her red leather bodysuit, right where Rockaway had put a round a few nights previous. The leather had been crudely cut away from the wound, and a huge square of stained gauze was lashed in place with thick twine. Bloodstains ran down the front of the leathers as well, but mixed in with the blood were long streaks of white, crusted thick in places.

"Get up." Eve looked down at Rockaway contemptuously, Jimmy's blood still dripping from her blade. "Or do you think you've got more of that fire in you?"

Rockaway let her rifle respond for her, scooping it up off the ground where it had fallen while she grabbed the grenade and snapping off a quick shot that should have struck Eve right in the center of her chest. Even without time to aim properly, at this range a novice could've made the shot, and Rockaway was no beginner.

Neither was Eve, however, and she was moving even as Rockaway got the rifle up, avoiding the shot with a neat side-step as casual as making room for someone passing in a hallway. One of her hands twitched and a knife streaked toward Rockaway, glittering in the electric lights. The Yorker flattened as it came at her and watched it slice through the air bare inches above her before clanging off the street.

"Let's do it this way, then," Eve said, ripping the bandage away. The wound underneath was a genuine horror to behold – her flesh was bloated and ripe with corruption, the skin swollen to the point of tearing out stitches, while the act of the tearing off the bandage unleashing a torrent of yellowish-white pus. The odor washed over Rockaway almost instantly, a sickeningly sweet scent like fruit gone bad or flowers left to rot in the sun. She felt her limbs go sluggish, her fingers fumble with the bolt, and even the pain in her head began to recede, as though her mind was filling with a pale, pleasant emptiness. Her whole body sagged, suddenly too heavy to even think of lifting.

"That's right, don't fight it," Eve crooned, stepping closer. Rockaway's knew she had to shoot her, had to put her down before the anesthetic effects of the white lady toxins could put her under, but her body simply wouldn't obey. "It wasn't supposed to be like this, you know. It was supposed to be subtle," Eve nearly bit off the word in her fury, "something that slowly won people over, made them docile, made them mine."

"Too fucking bad," Rockaway tried to say, though her tongue felt too big for her mouth and the words came

130

out slurred and fractured. Eve was almost on top of her now, and if she had been a Yorker the fight would've ended right there. Unless there's a message to deliver, you don't talk to a downed enemy, you talk to his corpse. A lot less can go wrong on you when you do things in that order. But Eve had been a gladiator, an entertainer with knives in hand, and grandstanding is a hard habit to break.

"It worked, too, until you shot me. Now the docs say they can't save me." Eve gestured to the oozing, suppurating wound. "The gland is too toxic, they say. My veins have already greened out, and I'd never even died before. Not once. Not once!" Eve's hands shook with outrage. "They keep draining it, but it's not healing right, won't heal right, and there's no Grave Robber around to take it out properly. I'm going to die, for good, and it's All. Your. Fault!"

Rockaway's vision was going blurry and black around the edges, and her head – too heavy to even lift off the ground anymore – came to rest on the street, lolling over to one side. Eve's boots filled her field of vision, and for a moment all the sniper could think was how insane it was that the last thing she might see in her entire life was a pair of red leather boots. It was so absurd that she might've laughed out loud, if she hadn't looked past them and seen the crumpled form of Jimmy Three Ex sprawled out on the street. It was impossible to make out detail with her eyes so unfocused and her head filling up with gauze, but she imagined she could see the blood pooling around him, staining his beloved work shirt, soaking into his treasured band patches. That was enough for her.

"Fuck this," she mumbled. Despite her injuries, she felt the pain in her mind receding, replaced by a very particular clarity she knew like an old friend. Tourists sometimes mocked Yorkers as hooligans with hair-trigger tempers, but the truth is that while they're easily moved to insults and shouting, that's surface level at best. Most Yorkers have a well deep in their hearts, one that gets filled with all the pain and sorrow and fury that comes with watching their families suffer and their friends die from life in their ruined city. What's down there doesn't come up much, but when they want to Yorkers can reach down deep and draw on all that energy to pull through the hardest, darkest times.

And sometimes it just overflows, and you get one seriously pissed-off Yorker.

Rockaway tapped into that fury and summoned up all the resistance her mind could muster, sweeping the numbing pleasantness from her mind like kicking cans from a stoop. Her scarred palms itched and burned as the numbing receded and the pain rolled back in, but the weight lifted off her limbs and she could move again. She wouldn't have time to get her rifle up for a shot, so she proved it by instead lashing out with a vicious kick to the knee, calculated to dislocate and cripple in a single hit. Even surprised, Eve's reflexes were impressive, and she managed to dodge backward far enough that a surefire crippling shot was reduced to simply a painful strike, but it still staggered her and forced her to back off a few steps.

"Fucking drama queen," Rockaway spat, her voice still not quite right but good enough to deliver that particular message.

"You killed me, you bitch!" Eve shrieked, launching herself at Rockaway with her remaining blade in hand. Gritting her teeth against the pounding in her head, Rockaway rolled away from the leap and back up to her feet. Eve was right on top of her, blade flashing in a series of savage, slashing attacks that Rockaway barely managed to parry with her rifle, the knife scratching the stock and scoring the metal with each strike. "You fucking ignorant bitch! Do you know what you fucking did?"

"Shut up about it already," Rockaway grunted between gritted teeth, giving ground as Eve pressed the assault. The Final Knight's knife work was flashy, probably a holdover from her time as a gladiator in the Roman, but she was fast and she was tricky, layering feints and quick reversals on top of blinding cuts and sweeping slashes. Only the extra reach of Rockaway's rifle and her exposure to so many years of Yorker knife fighting was keeping Eve from landing a serious hit, and those advantages would mean far less when she ran out of room to backpedal. The sniper had managed to rack her next round but couldn't spare even an instant to fire given the whip-crack speed of the strikes coming at her. She wondered if she could call up more fire, but just the thought of it made her head throb so badly she thought her forehead might split under the pressure.

"My gland! My fucking gland!" Eve was ranting as she attacked, her eyes crazed and bloodshot. "You weren't even trying, you fucking Yorker skank! And now I'm fucking septic!" She caught Rockaway's already wounded arm with a backhand that shredded the sleeve and sprayed hot blood on the trench walls. She gave a little cry of triumph and tried to follow with a stab to the guts, but she came in too fast and Rockaway landed a solid shot to the shoulder with the butt of her rifle, knocking Eve back a few steps and giving her a moment to recover. The sniper's eyes fixed on her fallen friend a few paces behind Eve, and she felt a twist in her gut as painful as if she'd been stuck.

"Fucking! Septic!" Eve was still ranting, readying for another attack.

"You killed Jimmy," Rockaway said quietly. Her wounded arm had all but given up, and so she tossed the rifle aside and put a hand on the hilt of her combat knife, popping the button of the restraint strap with her thumb, ready to draw.

"Consider it payback, bitch," Eve sneered. Her eyes flicked to the weapon on the ground and back at Rockaway but she didn't move, as though wary of some trick.

Rockaway pushed aside her pain like a beaded curtain, letting the sound of her pulse thundering in her ears drown her fatigue and her shock, and in the newfound clarity of the moment she realized exactly how she was going to kill Eve. When you've got two skilled fighters, there's one trick to winning a knife fight – accepting that you will get cut. Once you get past that, you can deliver a killing strike while making sure your opponent doesn't land anything but a superficial slash or two. And Eve was really pretty, or at least she had been until zed gunk poisoned her veins. She might have some serious scars under those leathers, but her face and hands were unmarked as far as Rockaway could see, and that said something. Eve was fast and she was deadly, but nobody survives as a knife fighter without taking at least one serious cut to the face along the way. Not unless they're holding back, even if it's just a little bit.

Rockaway pulled her combat knife from its sheath and watched as Eve's smile widened. The Yorker's blade was much heavier than the assassin's thin knife, and Rockaway deliberately turned it over into an inexperienced fighter's grip. "This is gonna hurt," she said simply.

"Oh, I guarantee that," Eve cooed. She danced forward, slashing, but Rockaway didn't take the bait. She knew Eve would expect her to fly into a blind rage and lash out foolishly, but she was well beyond that point, her fury giving her a perfect icy detachment. Rockaway stood as still as she could manage, restraining herself as her body positively vibrated with fury, breathing slowly and calmly, waiting. It was a moment before she realized that she was humming to herself, one of Jimmy's favorite King Bucket songs: "Easy Boy Easy."

She didn't have to wait long. Eve darted in with a feint, slashed low and opened a line across the top of Rockaway's thigh. The sniper tried to parry, a clumsy effort that left her left side wide open, and Eve exploited the gap with a wicked thrust aimed right for one of Rockaway's kidneys. The Yorker felt the blade scratch against her armor before it found purchase and slid through, but her fury overruled the pain, and she clamped down with her wounded arm as hard as she could, driving the knife in deeper but trapping Eve's hand against her body. Eve's look of savage triumph faltered as she tried to jerk her hand free, though she retained enough presence of mind to twist it as hard as she could when it was obvious she wasn't going to break the sniper's grip.

Rockaway let loose a little bit of her fury and hacked downward with her combat knife.

Eve shrieked as the heavy blade bit into her wrist, just past what her leathers protected, severing the hand in one smooth motion. She pulled back the stump, wailing in disbelief, but it was cut short as Rockaway plunged her knife deep into Eve's gut. Normally she would've tried to slip the blade up and under the ribs, take out the heart, but who knows how big that gland was, or for that matter what other horrifying zed parts Eve might have packed in there. As it was, Eve's cry turned to a sickening gurgle as Rockaway wrenched the blade horizontal and dragged it across the Final Knight's torso, disemboweling her with long, ragged cut.

Blood poured from the wound as thick ropes of intestines spilled out, along with a horrifying rotting odor. Rockaway had been around enough gut shots and belly wounds to know that it never smelled pretty, but this was a special kind of horrifying scent, and along with the blood and viscera she saw greenish-white sludge pumping out. Eve hadn't been kidding when she said she was septic; the sniper was actually kind of impressed she had still been standing, truth be told. Puncturing that gland had been turning her insides into a disgusting slurry of rot and melted intestines. Rockaway couldn't exactly say she was too unhappy to see what her bullet had done.

Eve choked on a mouthful of blood and sank to her knees, instinctively clutching at the wound with her good hand as well as her stump as she tried to gather up her ruined guts, but Rockaway wasn't in any mood to grant her any particular mercies. She kicked the Final Knight in the chest, hard, sending her over onto her back, her intestines pooling around her like a nest of snakes. She writhed and twisted, her feet scrabbling weakly for purchase on the blood-slick street, but the movements were clumsy and uncoordinated with pain.

"Stay the fuck down," Rockaway advised Eve, somewhat unnecessarily given her injuries as well as the fact that the Yorker punctuated the sentence with a kick to the head that left Eve lolling and semi-conscious. She tried to protest slightly when Rockaway cut a piece off of her leathers and pressed it down over the infected wound, but it was a weak effort at best, and didn't so much as slow the sniper down.

Not that Rockaway felt much better. Her face was raw from splinters and shrapnel, her arm and leg were soaked with blood from the cuts she'd taken, plus despite the momentary clarity her fury provided she could feel the white lady toxins trying to work on her, trying to bliss her mind and numb her body until she finally succumbed. Even under the bandage, Eve's chest wound was still leaking its septic sludge, and she knew she'd have to deal with that soon or her body would simply quit on her no matter how pissed off she was. And that wasn't even counting the knife still lodged in her side.

It felt like her side was on fire, but after a glance at the wound she ignored her own instinct to pull Eve's blade out of her side – Doc always said never to take out the impaling object if you could help it, especially if the wound wasn't bleeding too heavily – and settled for prying the Final Knight's severed hand off the hilt before the extra weight pulled the blade free on its own. As she walked she could feel things inside her moving and scraping against the blade, but she gritted her teeth and kept going. She tried to spot where Doomsday and Baldy were, but there was no sign of either of them at the far end of the trench, and no time to go looking for them. At least they weren't slumped over dead. That was something.

Jimmy was awfully still when she reached him, and her heart sank as she knelt down to take his pulse, half-wondering why she bothered until he coughed weakly at her touch. His eyelids fluttered for a moment before he finally managed to keep them open and focused on her. If he tried to smile when he recognized her, it was lost as his face contorted in pain. "Hey, Rock," he managed somehow, so faintly she almost couldn't make it out. "You OK?"

The idea that he'd ask after her when he had taken a knife to the heart was so unexpected and so ludicrous that Rockaway actually laughed, though she also noticed the mixed effects of her fury and the white lady toxin in the fact that her laugh sounded more than a little unbalanced, just a little too shrill to be entirely right in the head. At least she hoped that was why it sounded that way. "Me? Fuck yeah, I'm great." She pulled a length of clean cloth from a thigh pocket, wrapped it around her hand three times to get the right thickness and then pressed it down on his wound. "There, that should help. Though honestly I'm not sure why I fucking bother, mostly."

"What?" Jimmy asked, eyes as wide as he could manage.

"I mean, what kind of a fucking ace bat man lets some overhyped gladiator bitch get the drop on him like that?" Rockaway continued, as if she hadn't heard him. She took his right hand and placed it on top of the bandage. "Press down, hard as you can. You've lost a lot but looks like the fucker missed your heart, so this should keep you from bleeding out. Least until I find you a real doc, anyway. Unless you're feeling up to a little faith healing?"

"Kings, I wish," he said, gritting his teeth at the pressure, "but I'm pretty fucking tapped, sorry."

"Fuck. That would've helped." The sniper shook her head as if lamenting one of the world's great tragedies. "I swear, a guy gets one fucking three way and his fundamentals just go all to shit."

"Yeah," Jimmy said, coughing then smiling with bloodied teeth. "Fuck that guy. I mean seriously. That's some fucked up bullshit right there."

"No joke. You see what happened to Doomsday?" Rockaway tried to look around, but couldn't manage much. "She's supposed to be the medic in this damn outfit."

Jimmy tried to shake his head but couldn't manage more than a twitch. "Thought I heard her shouting, but no, didn't see nothing. She gone?"

138

"Looks like. Baldy too. Kings, what a fucking mess."

"Hey, you're calling on the Kings now? Awesome." Jimmy patted her arm, then noticed the knife sticking out of her side. "Holy shit, Rock! What the fuck?"

"It's not so bad," Rockaway lied. "Bitch lost her hand to do it, so I'd say I won that round." She glanced over at Eve, who seemed to be coming around again despite the wide pool spreading around her of blood, viscera and worse. It figured. Assholes never died easy. "Speaking of, I gotta learn some shit from her before she checks out." Rockaway brushed his hair off his forehead with her fingertips. "You ain't gonna fucking punk out on me before I can be back to do more medical shit, are you?"

"Fuck no," Jimmy said, coughing up a bit more blood. "I don't need to come back from some dead time with your rifle pointed at my fucking face. I'll be here. Promise."

"Cool." She rapped her knuckles gently on his shoulder. "Hang in. I'm gonna go get us a key and some fucking answers. Got it?" Jimmy nodded and rested his head on the street. He closed his eyes but began to hum, faintly at first but gaining strength. King Bucket, as usual – "Gonna Take Some Killin'", an old favorite. "Wiseass," Rockaway said, standing up and walking over to where Eve was still twitching. Most of the time the infection was something of a blessing, at least to the living – being able to bounce back relatively quickly from broken bones, gunshots and worse wasn't such a bad thing, especially with fully trained doctors being such a rarity. But sometimes, it kept people alive when it would really have been a blessing for them to simply die, and Eve was a solid case in point.

Not that Rockaway minded at the moment. "Hey.

Fucker." The sniper knelt down, ignoring the pain in her side as best she could, and slapped Eve's cheek until the Final Knight's eyes stayed open and focused, two points of pure hatred directed right at her. "You're dying, but it's ugly. I can help you out, maybe even make sure you don't get back up as one of them later, but you're gonna answer a few questions first. Waste my time, lie to me, I'll draw this out a long fucking time. First up, where's your fucking key?"

"Tossed it off the bridge," Eve spat.

Rockaway didn't reply; she just reached down, grabbed a length of intestine and tugged. Eve hissed like a scalded cat before she grayed out from the pain and the Yorker had to patiently slap her back to consciousness. "Try again."

"In my chest wrap." Eve's voice was pained. When Rockaway didn't move to follow up, Eve gave a cough that might have been intended to be a laugh. "What's wrong? Don't like girls?"

"You think I'm rummaging around in your tits when you're stuffed full of zed parts, you best think again, bitch. Now get it, slow and easy. And don't move that fucking bandage either, or I'll make this a hundred times fucking uglier, believe that." Eve kept glaring but reached into her jacket and emerged with a bloody chain dangling from her fingers. Rockaway took it and examined it as best she could with weary eyes, but the key looked identical. She wiped the blood off on Eve's leathers and put it around her neck. It jangled against her other necklaces and then fell silent. The sniper supposed she should feel triumphant to finally have it in hand, but all she felt was tired.

"You don't get it," Eve hissed. "You're just delaying it. York is going to burn, and there's nothing—" Her ranting trailed off into a high yowl as Rockaway took hold of her exposed intestine again, this time pulling slowly rather than giving it a sharp tug.

"I gotta tell you, I'm fucking sick of this conspiracy bullshit, I really am," Rockaway said conversationally, taking care to pull just hard enough to keep Eve from talking but not so hard that she'd pass out again. "You're a Final Knight. You're fucked in the brain and want to burn everything down. I fucking get it." She eased up on the pressure, took Eve's chin and forced her to look her in the eyes. "All I want to know now is, who's the goddamn traitor in Domino?"

"Fuck yourself, Yorker trash. You'll just have to find that out on your own." Eve managed a ghastly smile. "What's wrong? You're looking a little tired. Sure you don't want to just lie down for a minute?"

"Last time," Rockaway repeated, though to be honest she was feeling a bit dizzy. The last of her rage was ebbing from her system, the adrenaline going with it, and she could see her vision getting blurry at the edges once more. "Who's the traitor?"

Eve didn't answer, but just reached over and tried to pull away the bandage. Rockaway caught her hand and held it in place over the wound. "You know what? Fuck you. We'll find your asshole partners without you. In the meantime, I picked up some shit from recently. Fucking freaky, but it has its uses. Like this." With that Rockaway focused on the scar on her palm, on the pain and burning she was feeling, letting those thoughts flow like propane past the open flame that was the psionic presence in her mind, igniting with the sheer force of her concentration.

Fire flowed out of her palm, controlled this time, charring Eve's hand and incinerating the bandage. Rockaway kept concentrating, directing the fire into the wound, sending it throughout Eve's body, burning up the white lady toxins and everything else along with it.

Eve opened her mouth to scream but only fire came out, her skin smoking and blackening like meat on a grill as fire coursed throughout her body. Her hands swatted at Rockaway, clawing mindlessly as the flames cooked her from the inside out, but the Yorker didn't flinch, just held on and willed her fury into flame. Only when little was left but greasy ashes and blackened bones did Rockaway finally pull her hand back, scar bleeding and smoking.

Distantly part of her was horrified and amazed at how easy it was once she concentrated on it, as though the ability to call flame with her mind had been in front of her for her whole life and she'd simply missed it somehow. It reminded her of learning her numbers from the Doc when she was thirteen – the first time she'd put together two and two and understood why they made four, something so simple that it seemed amazing she'd never figured it out before, so simple it was frustrating when someone else hadn't figured it out yet. Was that why psions always seemed so impatient and superior? Because they couldn't understand why nobody else had figured out what they knew?

Rockaway shook her head. Philosophical bullshit could wait for some time when she and Jimmy weren't bleeding out. Her rage seemed to have burned up right along with Eve's body, and now she just felt heavy, her thoughts sluggish. She limped back to Jimmy, one hand holding the blade in as she walked, and half-sat, half-collapsed next to him. He was unconscious at first, but she bumped into him as she sat and he stirred, groaning weakly. The bandage was ominously dark but his hand still held it in place, and when his eyes finally opened they were clear, if pained. "You get the bitch?"

"Yeah," Rockaway said thickly. Something trickled down her chin and when she wiped it the back of her hand came away bloody. "Shit, I'm stuck good."

Suddenly lying down in the bloody ground of the trenchworks seemed like a decent enough idea, just for a moment. She slid down, pillowed her head on his shoulder, and together they stared up into the night.

"Too bright," Rockaway managed, squinting at the lights.

"I see stars," Jimmy said, looking past them.

"Fucking knives." Rockaway tried to raise her head to look at the wound, thought better of it. "'m a fucking sniper. Fuck business do I have fighting toe to toe like an asshole?"

"Mrh," Jimmy grunted in agreement, but his attempt at a squeeze just made him cough and then go still. Rockaway couldn't tell if he had just died, hoped he'd just passed out, but the lights were in her eyes and she found it harder and harder to avoid closing her eyes to block them out. Before she realized she'd even done it, she was already unconscious.

Chapter Twelve

Rockaway didn't wake up so much as fly from the bed and up to her feet, her body tingling and bursting with energy. She caught a quick glimpse of a room with wood floors and peeling white paint, as well Jimmy Three Ex reaching out to catch hold of her with an expression of comical surprise on his face, then her senses flooded with information to the point where she had to close her eyes to avoid a total sensory overload. Jimmy wrapped his arms around her, pinning her arms to her side, and her fingertips tingled and she kept curling and uncurling her fingers, the callouses on her fingertips rubbing through her frayed gloves against the raised ridges of the crosses cut into her palms.

Beyond the familiar smell of the greasy junk Jimmy used to spike his hair and the earthy tang of the tar he used on the grip of his bat, she smelled lamp oil and gun smoke, damp fabric and old leather. There were voices around too, at least a dozen, most of them unfamiliar except for one that had a faintly familiar ring she couldn't quite place.

"What. The Fuck. Was That?" Rockaway asked, speaking slowly as she tried to sort of the rapidly whirling thoughts spinning in her head. The experience reminded her of a hit of rush she'd done when she was younger, which had seemed like a great idea until she tried to steady her rifle and missed a nearby bottle on six tries.

"New trick," Jimmy said, sounding almost embarrassed. The bat man gave her a little extra squeeze. He smelled like fresh sweat and dried blood, but underneath it he smelled like Jimmy, and right now that went a long way. He pushed a hand through her hair, clumsily trying to straighten it out a bit. "Seems I got a bit more of the touch than I thought."

"You're a natural!" An unfamiliar but infectiously energetic voice spoke from a few steps away. Rockaway pulled back from Jimmy a little and opened her eyes to see one of the most unusual figures she'd ever seen in her life. He was a man of average height with dirty blonde hair that fell straight to his shoulders beneath a brown hat so old and battered as to be nearly shapeless. He wore a long brown coat, equally ragged, and festooned with so many old buttons that in places it was hard to see the color of the fabric underneath. Most of them were old and dented, a few had their paint worn or chipped off from years of wear and exposure, and of the ones left it was a mix of strange symbols and bizarre words that didn't make any sense to her, though she imagined there were quite a few Jones and other salvagers of old world relics out there who'd give a lot to get their hands on them.

Most striking of all, though, were his eyes, or lack thereof. Though he had a pair of scratched sunglasses, they had slid down to the end of his nose, revealing empty sockets, black hollows that nevertheless seemed to stare right into her, made somehow even more unsettling as it was accompanied by a broad smile. "Welcome back, hero!"

"You know my gang?" Rockaway asked, suddenly wary. "I know you?"

"Everyone knows you!" The man clapped his hands together excitedly. "You're the hero, brought back from the brink of death to right great wrongs and beat the bad guys!"

"Don't mind the Rev," came a laconic voice from the hall. "He's a Telling Vision. He sees everything as one of his damn scriptures come to life." Though they shared common roots with the King's Court in their veneration of pre-Fall culture, the Telling Vision differed sharply in just about every other way. They pointed to the altars found in almost every pre-Fall home, central places of worship and community where the people of the past had gathered to witness comedies and dramas, the adventures of great heroes and the downfall of great villains. While some fortunate temples such as the great Thirty Rock Monastery in York still had working sets, most Telling Visionaries had to make do with hunting down paper copies of their sacred scriptures, studying the abbreviated versions found in the Telling Vision Guide, or simply passing down the great scenes and memorable quotes from one generation to the next.

Like the King's Court, most Telling Visionaries dedicated themselves to a particular genre of scripture, or sometimes even a single icon or tale. This made them notoriously unpredictable, and caused Rockaway to give them a wide berth as a rule. Some of them could be pretty chill, and they knew some cool stories, no question, but when some members just seek to bring the light-hearted joy of ancient comedies back to the world and others emulate the faceless killers of the great terror epics, it's hard it know exactly what to expect. And in her experience, unpredictable was always a risk best avoided.

Her whole run being a case in fucking point, in fact.

The speaker stepped into the room, and Rockaway knew him for a Yorker at a glance. The Old York caravan plates on his pauldrons were a giveaway, of course, but there were other, more subtle signs as well. He had the lean, muscular build of a climber rather than the thicker muscle flatlanders tended to develop, combined with a bit of unconscious swagger in the way he carried his old carbine that immediately screamed York to her practiced eye. While his old brown ball cap and battered armor might have been scavenged from any battlefield, the many scarves and tied bandannas bore the signs of a half-dozen Yorker gangs, marking him as a diplomat and granting him safe passage through their territory. He took off his dark glasses and smiled at her, not a generic greeting but an easy smile of familiarity, and then it clicked.

"Sloan? Shit, that you?" Rockaway said, sliding out of Jimmy's arms to grab Sloan's forearm and pull him in for a shoulder bump. "Good to fucking see you!"

"Told you she'd remember," Jimmy said. He reached out and shook Sloan's hand warmly. He jerked a thumb at the Rev, who was still standing there beaming, as if the whole scene had been orchestrated solely for his amusement. "Thanks for the introduction, man. I mean, Kings, this sure beats the record for the most fucking miracles I've seen in a day."

"No worries, brother, no fucking worries at all." Sloan turned and called out to the hallway. "It's cool, they're up. You can come in."

"So what the fuck are you doing down here?" Rockaway asked.

"Yeah, I knew you'd ditched York, but I never thought you'd go traitor for a dump like this town," Jimmy teased. The Yorkers laughed, while the Rev moved his sightless seeming gaze back and forth between them like a stray dog watching meat passed from hand to hand.

"Long story," Sloan shrugged. "Went all over, man, you wouldn't fucking believe. No fucking luck, though, so I settled in this little town up north. Fucked up burg, no lie, but I just couldn't go home, you know?

Not after." Rockaway nodded. Sloan's story wasn't a unique one in the history of York, but it was still a sad one, his whole family killed by someone he never saw, only heard was called Mr. Black. She'd heard the whole thing from Ricky the Babe, a mutual friend who ran with the Lonely Street gang, and hadn't faulted the poor bastard when she heard he took off not long after the killing. "Got a fresh lead a few weeks ago, though, figured I'd see if I could track it down, you know?"

"Anything?" Rockaway asked, though she was pretty sure from his expression that she already knew the answer.

"Nah," Sloan said, looking away quickly. "But you can't stop trying, you know?"

"Don't let the bastards grind you down," Jimmy half-spoke, half-sang the old prayer, capping it with a hopeful smile. Sloan nodded, and a quiet moment stretched out between them. "Where's Doomsday?" Jimmy asked.

"Your girl is downstairs with the Major," Sloan said.

"Cool," Rockaway said, relieved. "Where the fuck did she go? She just kinda vanished during that fight. I thought she—" Rockaway swallowed fucking ditched us before it could do any harm, feeling guilty it ever occurred to her, and chose instead to say "—got shot up or something."

"That chick is hard as hell, man," Sloan said, shaking his head in admiring disbelief. "Wily as shit, too. Way I heard, she took out like, five of their guys without killing any of them, found a way into the fort like some kind of fucking ghost and talked the Major down from killing all three of you. Because the Major, she's pissed as fuck right now. They've been on lockdown for days and all of a sudden some Yorkers

148

crash the trenches and her people are shooting each other? She's the kind to burn people the fuck down and scatter the ashes just to be sure, you know?" Sloan glanced at the door. "Shit, they've been real polite about it and all, but I've been a fucking prisoner for a few days now. Was bunking here when the shit started up, and they ain't been too inclined to let me out."

"The Signal brought you all here for a reason," the Rev announced, causing Rockaway to jump a little. Somehow she'd managed to forget that he was there, which was a feat, considering his appearance. He pointed to Rockaway. "The wounded hero!" Now to Jimmy. "The miracle worker!" Over to Sloan. "The surprise twist!"

"Fuck you calling a twist?" Rockaway asked sharply, but Sloan held up a hand.

"S'cool, he's just, you know … like that. Before you came he was hanging all over me, babbling about how my story was on high-ate-us while a midseason replacement came along." Sloan saw their blank looks and turned to the Rev for explanation, but the rumpled preacher simply shrugged unhelpfully, still grinning. "Fucked if I know what that means, but I gotta admit, he was right about there being a surprise I didn't see coming." He slid another glance at the Rev. "Somehow that just makes it more creepy, though. Fuck."

"What surprise? Us?"

"Shit yeah, what else did you think it'd be?" Sloan snorted. "No disrespect to your girl downstairs and her mad diplomacy skills, but if I hadn't been here to vouch for you with the Major too, things might still have stepped off ugly."

"I told you! The audience hates an early cancellation!" The Rev wagged his finger at Sloan. "And it's sweeps, so all bets are off!" He threw his hands in air triumphantly, and seemed oblivious to the fact that no one else was celebrating with him.

"What the fuck are sweeps?" Rockaway asked.

"I don't know," Sloan said, "but apparently they're important. It's probably a Telling Vision holiday, like their Battle of the Bands or something."

"Time to break out the big guns! Really pull out the stops!" The Rev continued.

"I know he sounds fucking crazy as shit," Sloan said, "but he was dead on about me being in the right place at the right fucking time."

"Not just you either. He knew we were coming, Rock," Jimmy said, nodding at the Rev. "No shit. They said I was nearly dead when they dragged me in, but that he was waiting right where they were going to lay me down. Didn't even have to move, that's how exact he was. Then he laid on hands and called the fucking almighty and bam, just like that, I'm back on my feet." He spread his arms wide, inviting her to say otherwise. "Fucking amazing."

"I take it that's where you picked up this new fucking trick?" Rockaway gestured down at her bloodstained gear but unmarked skin. "Because I gotta say, I fucking approve."

"Yeah," Jimmy said, a little distantly. "I saw how bad you were – they said the surgeon hadn't been able to do anything, that you were on your way out – and I thought about how I felt, what the Rev had just fucking done for me, and shit, it just clicked, you know?" He shook his head, smiling but looking a little dazed. "It makes no goddamn sense, I know."

"Fuck it," Rockaway said. "Like any of us really know how the Kings work, or the Telling Visions, or anything else, right? What matters is that it fucking works. End of story." She rolled her shoulder, found it still a little tingly. "Would've been nice to have some of this before, though, I don't mind fucking saying," she teased.

"I wouldn't count on it any time soon," Jimmy admitted, missing the humor. "Maybe it's cause it was my first time, but fuck, it felt like that took a lot out of me. I mean, I'm not bleeding from the eyes or shit, but still." He held up a hand and waggled it back and forth in a so-so gesture. "So give me a while before you nearly get yourself fucking killed again, OK?"

"Done." Rockaway looked back over the Rev, who was still beaming in their general direction, though not quite pointed directly at any of them. "And what do we owe you for these miracles, Rev? I gotta imagine quality holy work don't come cheap."

"Price?" The Rev pulled away, aghast. "Never! All I ask for is heart, hero!"

"Yeah, well, thanks, but I don't like owing anyone, so – wait, I got just the fucking thing." Rockaway snapped her fingers, picked up her pack from the floor next to where she'd been laid down and rummaged through it.

"Oh, you're not," Jimmy said, looking disgusted, but Rockaway pulled out the bag she'd placed Big Playboy's freaky zed heart in after she'd cut it out back in the Pine Barrens. It still glowed a faint green, and she couldn't say for certain, but it seemed like she felt it beat weakly, though that could just have been it shifting in the bag.

"Here you go," Rockaway said, placing the bag gently in the Rev's hands. "One heart." She looked up and saw Sloan looked puzzled and Jimmy just shaking his head. What? I didn't want to carry the damn thing anymore! she mouthed at Jimmy. He rolled his eyes in response but, she noted, didn't make a move to stop her either.

"Oh, I like you, hero!" The Rev weighed the bag solemnly, nodding and whispering something to himself, squeezing it slightly in his hands. "The audience loves a sense of humor! Always makes it easier to relate! And the Sponsors—"

They were spared further thoughts on what the sponsors might or might not want by the arrival of a pair of armed guards in dented metal and dirty combat fatigues. "The Major wants to see you two," one of them said, pointing at Rockaway and Jimmy. Her tone gave no indication of how friendly she thought this meeting might be, though they didn't move to disarm either of the Yorkers, which was always a good start.

"What about me?" Sloan asked, but the other guard just shrugged disinterestedly.

"Time for a commercial break," the Rev said, taking hold of the young man's arm and gently tugging him in the direction of the bunks at the far end of the room. Reluctantly the young Yorker allowed the preacher to lead him away.

"See you soon, man," Rockaway said as they gathered their things.

"The Major's pretty cool," Sloan answered. "Just don't say any stupid shit and you should be OK. You feel me?"

"Yeah, that should be no fucking problem," Jimmy muttered as they guards led them down the old wooden stairs and into the Fort Independence staging area. "She's a model of goddamn restraint."

"Oh, fuck you," Rockaway said. "I'm not an idiot. Long as she doesn't set me off, everything'll be just fucking fine."

Chapter Thirteen

"So, these are the other crazy assholes who like taking shots at my people." The woman's voice was mild, with just a touch of dry humor, but there was no mistaking the effect her presence had on the other people in the room – it had to be the Major that Sloan and the others had mentioned as the one running the show around here.

She was younger than Rockaway had expected, late twenties at most, dressed in blue jeans and a sharp olive drab military jacket that looked like a better-preserved cousin of Rockaway's own battered relic, with a drab military cap and shoulder length blonde hair neatly tucked behind her ears. A polished pistol in a hip holster was her only obvious weapon, but the ease with which she wore it suggested that it might be enough regardless. She looked up from a large map spread across the table in front of her, obviously sizing up Rockaway and Jimmy.

"That gonna be a problem?" Rockaway said, hearing Jimmy sigh as the guards tensed. Around the room other locals in various types of military gear looked up from their discussions around wall-mounted maps and stacks of supplies, waiting to see how this would go. In the far corner, an ancient generator clanged softly as it kept spinning.

"Well," the Major said diplomatically, "on the one hand, normally I kill anyone who lays a hand on my people, no questions asked." For a moment violence hung in the air, thick as smoke from a dirty campfire, then the Major cracked the faintest of smiles. "On the other hand, you people hit what you shoot at and you took down a psion who'd mindfucked a score of my people, and I can respect that." She came around the table and put out her hand. "They call me the Major."

"Tribeca Rockaway, of the Dead Heroes." Rockaway shook the Major's hand, and they only squeezed a little bit. Nice grip. She nodded at Jimmy. "My boy there is Jimmy Three Ex, Dead Hero and the best damn bat man in the Heights."

"Thanks for taking us in," Jimmy said respectfully, shaking hands as well.

"Well, it just happened that there was another Yorker around who'd done some patrols for us and could vouch for you, not to mention you landed in my lap after days of this Rev lunatic chewing my ear off about us getting our own spin-off if we played our cards right during sweeps." The Major looked around suddenly, as if speaking his name might somehow conjure up the strange priest. She turned her attention to one of the guards on the door. "Bradley, where is our fascinating visitor?"

"He is, ah, resting upstairs, Major." The guard shuffled uneasily. "He lay down, put a big bag on his chest, stuck these strange wires into his ears, and just … lay there."

"He did what?" The Major arched an eyebrow.

"I—I'm sorry, I don't know. I got out of there in a hurry, sir." His voice dropped to nearly a whisper. "He freaks me out a bit, sir."

"Well, if it's not dangerous, I suppose I can deal with not listening to more Telling Vision ranting for a few hours. Don't worry, Bradley." The Major turned back to the trio of outsiders in her war room. "So, here we are. A couple of gang members from York – no offense—"

"None taken," Rockaway said evenly. "'S how we do."

154

"—and an agent of the Federal Bonded Inquisition." The Major reached into a pocket, handed back Doomsday's credentials. "Your superiors are very interested to hear that you're still up and about, agent. Very interested."

Doomsday looked surprised. "You checked up on me? How?"

"Agent Anderson, do you really think that the Inquisition could have an outpost in my city and keep it a secret? Especially with a host of Purebloods trying to climb up my ass on a regular basis?" The Major snorted. "Think again. They're pretty good at covering their tracks about their headquarters location, I'll give them that, but we've had radio contact with them for years. Mostly just to make sure we keep out of each other's way, which suits me fine." Her eyes glittered darkly. "They had some interesting things to say about you, too."

"Hold on!" Doomsday said, putting up a placating hand. "I can explain!"

"Your agent," said the Major calmly, ignoring Doomsday and addressing the two Yorkers instead, "isn't an agent. Not anymore, anyway."

"Wait, what?" Jimmy said, mock-outraged.

"Is this about your undercover thing?" Rockaway asked. Doomsday nodded, not quite sure if that was the right response but hoping it would suffice. Rockaway looked back at the Major and gave an elaborate shrug. "Yeah, we know all about that shit. So?"

"I see," the Major said, clearly not expecting that response. "Interesting. When we made contact and identified your friend here, the Inquisitors on the other end were quite specific about the fact that she was no longer one of them, and that we were to keep her detained until they could come to collect her."

"You're not an agent anymore?" Rockaway said, catching Doomsday's eye. "I thought it was, you know, fake bullshit to fool the Darwinists. Was that a lie?"

"Yes and no. They had to make it convincing," Doomsday said, holding eye contact. "Wouldn't be much of a cover if they didn't, right?" Rockaway searched her friend for any sign of deception and couldn't find any – but then, that was the point of her whole job. For her part, Doomsday kept the conversation moving. "But what's this about being collected?"

"I told them we were preparing for another round of assaults from the Duponts, and that I couldn't spare soldiers to play jailor for a couple of strays that wandered into my territory until they decided to come pick them up." The Major's lips quirked in a momentary smile. "They were not pleased."

"That was fucking kind of you," Rockaway said.

"Look, I have no disagreement with the Inquisition as such," the Major said. "They want to re-establish a strong federal government, and I can get behind that, but the fact remains that they haven't exactly been much help in the past. Sure, they'll hire out some of ours to escort engineers to work on the rails heading out of the city, but when Johnny Rockets sends his Retrograde thugs over from the Markets on a raid, they don't even answer our request for assistance. And let's not even get started on the Duponts. Why they haven't helped the other Purebloods clamp down on those lunatics, I'll never understand." She gave Doomsday a pointed look. "Isn't that point of the Inquisition? Putting the Purebloods to work rebuilding instead of fighting over the wreckage?"

"I don't have an answer," Doomsday admitted. "I wish I did, Major."

"Not your fault," the Major answered. "The question is, did I make the right call?"

"I fucking hope so," Rockaway said. "Things really that bad about the Duponts, or was that bullshit to put them off?"

"I wish it was," the Major sighed. "Fact is we've been getting hit hard for nearly a month straight. We even had to reach a cease-fire with the Markets gangs – they're getting hit as hard as us, and if they go down we'll have enemy on two sides, the river to another and only the burned zones to the north to retreat into. Not good options."

"With respect, Major," Doomsday said carefully, "if you give me access to your radio setup to contact the Inquisition, not only can I prove I am still an agent, but I think I can earn you a lot of goodwill in your fight against the Duponts. If I may?"

"By all means," the Major said with a sweep of her hand. "Just keep it at a social volume, if you don't mind." She raised her voice to be heard by one of her radio operators. "Lockwell? Can you clear a set for the agent here?"

"Yes, Major." The young woman nodded smartly. "Just finished confirming our latest shipment from Bravo."

"Good. Hedon knows we need that brass. Is it on schedule?"

"Yes ma'am. After that I was scheduled to contact Boulder Run about the ore they're supposed to be – it can wait," the operator stood up as the Major cleared her throat, saluted and nodded at Doomsday. "All yours, agent."

"Thanks." Doomsday walked over to one of the stacks of dented-looking equipment, leaned in and appraised the machine with a practiced eye and asked a question of the operator. The agent made a few adjustments, took a deep breath and let it out slowly before speaking.

"Clocktower, I'm running late. I need the time."

The radio buzzed for a moment before a young male voice came back clearly. "This is Clocktower. Sounds like your watch is broken. Model and serial number?"

"It's a Ripley, serial number: eff you are why one six one," Doomsday said calmly. "How copy, Clocktower?"

It was hard to judge something like inflection with just a voice through a tiny speaker, but Rockaway thought she detected a bit of hesitation in the reply. "Clocktower has a solid copy. Let me look that model up. This may take a moment." The line went dead again.

"Yeah, no kidding," Doomsday muttered.

It was a few minutes before the radio flared to life again, and this time it was a different male voice – older and confident, with a definite air of authority – that spoke. Rockaway frowned; it sounded familiar, but she couldn't quite place it. "Clocktower verifies model. Now, Ripley, please confirm my identity to proceed."

Doomsday's mouth fell open, and it took her a moment to collect herself enough to reply. "Bishop, ell vee four two six." She hesitated another moment, then blurted out: "It's good to hear from you, sir."

"Verification complete." There was a little chuckle on the other end. "Not the best radio protocol, but forgivable considering the circumstances. Report?"

Doomsday looked at the others before replying. "Knockout is a success, sir. Say again, Knockout is a success. How copy?"

"Solid copy. Do you have the gloves in hand?"

Doomsday looked surprised, and a little puzzled. "Ah, yes, gloves are affirmative, sir. How did—"

"Bishop confirms solid copy on gloves. Stand by for further instructions."

"Gloves?" Jimmy asked. In response Rockaway simply tugged on her necklaces, where the launch keys were tucked in among her many other jewelry pieces. Recognition flickered in his eyes and he nodded. For her part, Rockaway just shook her head. She'd be real glad when they could be done with all this secret agent bullshit.

The radio came back to life. "Well done. Are the Dead Heroes with you?" Just like that, Rockaway remembered where she'd heard the voice before – it had only been once, but it had been a memorable meeting. Agent Freeman, the G-Man who'd stopped her back in York and strong-armed her into sending a confirmation of her delivery to Big Playboy back in Aysea.

Doomsday only looked more confused, but kept it out of her voice. "Yes, sir. Confirm on the Dead Heroes."

"Tell them the Inquisition will make good on its promises. Also, please pass along my apologies to the Major as well. As it did not contain verification code, our radio operators mistakenly did not pass on the details of the earlier transmission to their superiors." A slight pause. "They have been disciplined for this operational oversight. How copy?"

"Solid copy, Bishop." Something obviously still wasn't sitting right with Doomsday, but Rockaway assumed that she was used to not knowing all the details. That was the problem with a crew like the G-Men; she could understand taking orders, that was just plain necessary sometimes, but too many secrets eventually wound up burning a crew. In the Dead

Heroes, one of the gang might not agree with what Boss Tone said – in fact it was pretty fucking common – but the crew was too small to keep many secrets. "Bishop, may I request advisement on the disposition of the gloves?"

"Preparations are underway for collection, Ripley. Is the Major there with you?"

"Affirmative on that, Bishop." Doomsday turned a dial and the volume of the radio increased significantly. "Send traffic."

"Major, I'd like to personally thank you for taking in my agent and her … deputies, especially considering the mistakes of our subordinates. You have helped a crucial mission succeed, and the Inquisition will not forget this assistance, rest assured."

"With all due respect, 'Bishop'," the Major said, "gratitude is fine, but what we really need is more bodies on the ground around here. As I'm sure you're already aware, the Duponts have no trouble finding mercenaries to throw at us, and plenty of cred to purchase high-end weapons. We've even taking artillery fire. We need relief and resupply, and soon. How copy?"

"Solid copy, Major," Agent Freeman replied, a little archly. "As my agent can testify, I hold considerable clout in the Inquisition. I will see to it that the League allocates considerable resources to support your efforts, with priority. Is that more acceptable?"

"Thank you."

"Major, I will require one more thing. We will be sending two units for aerial retrieval, so I need you to escort my agent and her deputies to the cleared plain at St. Peter's memorial and hold that position until they are safely aboard and away. How copy?"

"Aerial retrieval? What the fuck does that mean?"

Rockaway asked. She remembered the sounds they'd heard in the woods a few nights back, like huge caravans cutting through the sky. Of course, there was also the feeling that came with them, the sense that Red Hands had been along for the ride as well. "Do they really have fucking aircraft?"

"I guess we'll find out," Doomsday replied.

"Solid copy, but that's a no-go plan," the Major responded grimly as they spoke. If the concept of aircraft thrilled her, she hid it well. "St. Peter's is too close to the hot line. Besides, it's taken heavy shelling the past few days. I doubt you're going to find clear ground for an extraction, and frankly I can't spare the soldiers for an escort. Our scouts have reported that we could be looking at another push any time now. How copy?"

"Solid copy." Agent Freeman sounded like each word was swallowing a bitter pill, and the radio was silent for a moment. "What is the status of Love's Graveyard?"

The Major looked surprised. "There's been some horde activity in that area over the past couple of weeks, but no enemy contact. Should be intact. Are you calling this the location for the extraction?"

"Confirmed, extraction will take place at Love's Graveyard." Agent Freeman's tone seemed to soften very slightly. "Ripley, are you ready to move out?"

"Affirmative, sir. Within the hour. What about the Dead Heroes?"

"Secure whatever local support you can and head to the extraction point immediately." There was another brief, almost undetectable pause. "As for your deputies, please extend my invitation for them to join you. We have arrangements to make regarding their return to York and compensation for their efforts. How copy?"

"Solid copy, Bishop." Doomsday said. Rockaway saw Jimmy frowning, his expression echoing her own feeling. Maybe it was just natural Yorker suspicion, but getting paid and rewarded for a job well done felt too good to be true. "We will gather the gloves and other necessaries and depart for the rendezvous immediately."

"Bishop copies all. Welcome home, agent. Bishop out."

"Well then," the Major said as the activity of the room began to return to normal. "It seems that sometimes it pays to listen to strangers and lunatics, even when they tell you not to put a bullet in those that did yours harm. I'm not sure how comforting that is, to be honest, but there you have it." She shook her head, as if still unconvinced about what had just transpired. "And now the Inquisition is offering to ride to our rescue. Incredible."

"Fuckin' weird life, ain't it?" Rockaway asked, not feeling particularly philosophical. "Any chance you can spare some folks to lead us to this Love's Graveyard place?" The Major shook her head. "Fuck. Well, got any ammo you can spare, at least? 'Cause I'm damn near tapped." Doomsday agreed with that assessment.

"That I can help you with, as well as directions to get you through the trenchworks. Love's Graveyard isn't far, so it shouldn't be too much of a problem. I hope you don't mind that we don't draw you a map, though – never know what might fall into enemy hands."

"We know how that goes," Jimmy said ruefully.

"Bradley here will show you to the armorer, with my permission to draw ammunition and basic foodstores if you need them." The Major gestured to the war room. "Meet back here when you're ready and I'll have your guide prep you. Sound fair?"

"Thank you, Major," Doomsday said, shaking her hand. "For the help now, and for having faith in us earlier. Saints watch over you and your soldiers."

"Kings sing your praises," Jimmy added, nodding respectfully.

"And may we be the fuck out of here before you know it," Rockaway said, snapping a hasty salute. "Because just between us, York is looking fucking better by the minute."

Chapter Fourteen

"You sure you're ready?" Sloan asked, looking down the trench corridor. "I mean, it's pretty cold of the Major, not giving you an escort or shit."

"What a shock, after how gracious you were as we were leaving," Doomsday said sarcastically.

"The fuck can we do about it now? Nah, we're cool." Rockaway shrugged, though to be honest it still rankled her a little. Judging from the way Doomsday tugged at her harness, she was also pretty pissed, but doing her best to hide it. "Never gonna get used to spending so much time down at street level, but yeah, we're cool." Rockaway flashed him a smile she didn't quite feel. "Hey, you stood for us. That's fucking solid."

"No joke," Jimmy added, spinning his bat in his hands. "We owe you."

"Fuck it," Sloan said dismissively. "Least I could fucking do, right? It's good to see some real Yorkers. Been down here too long, all they've got is this watered down Delphian bullshit."

"Hey!" Doomsday said, mock-offended. The Yorkers laughed.

"Just sorry I can't go with you. But you know how it is. I gotta keep running things down till I find that Mr. Black and even up the fucking score, knowumsayin'?"

"Too fucking right." Rockaway grabbed Sloan's hand and pulled him in for a chest bump. "Get some for us when you find him, motherfucker."

"Just don't finish it too fast," Jimmy added, clapping him hard on the pauldron.

"Take care," Doomsday said, shaking Sloan's hand solemnly As if on cue, they heard the distant thump of far-off artillery as the Duponts started the latest round of hostilities, the explosions following a moment later, far enough away to be little more than thumps themselves but close enough for the impacts to briefly light the sky. Rockaway could hear gunfire as well, the high crack of sharpshooters' rifles and the sporadic barking of close quarters firefights starting up along the line.

The all-hands siren started a moment later from the Fort Independence clock tower, soft at first but rapidly winding up into a full-on banshee wail. It seemed a foolish sort of thing, bound to attract zed for miles, but apparently it was a traditional call to arms and the mere suggestion that they not use it had earned her icy stares from all the natives in the room.

In any event – time to get moving.

Rockaway threw Sloan a last nod by way of salute and took off down the trench corridor at something just under a run, Jimmy following a few steps behind and Doomsday bringing up the rear. With the trench lights out they had just a bit of moonlight to go by, but fortunately a lifetime without much paper or things to write on it breeds a killer memory, and Rockaway had the trench layout burned into her memory from their exit briefing with the Major.

They reached the first corner and fell in up against the trench wall, Doomsday covering as Rockaway peeked around. Clear. She signaled as much with a quick thumbs up and they were on the move again.

The Major had routed patrols out of their area for the next hour to avoid any friendly fire incidents – even when Eve's mind control had been revealed and Doomsday had flashed her badge, the locals weren't exactly trusting. She didn't blame them. Back in York if anyone had crashed Dead Heroes territory and shot up some of the crew, it wouldn't have mattered if they'd had psions mind-riding them the whole way, Boss Tone would've put bullets in their heads and dumped them to the scavengers. This was getting off light, as far as she was concerned.

"You know this is a fucking trap, right?" Jimmy grunted as they picked up the pace to cover a particularly long corridor. Rockaway loved and hated long avenues for the same reason – they were a sniper's dream. And while the Major had stressed that neither the Duponts or Johnny Rockets' crew had made it this far into their territory, all she could think of what a sweet target they'd make to any shooter with an eye on that nice long trench.

"We don't know that for sure," Doomsday said, but her tone was grim.

"The Final Knights have a fucking double agent somewhere in Domino," Rockaway said. "Big Playboy had the fucking note in his pocket, Eve damn near spelled it all out. What more do you fucking want?."

"I know," Doomsday conceded. "But I've been thinking about that. What if there is no traitor? What if the Knights just found out about the facility some other way? It's not impossible they came across it on their own."

"Still not fucking good for your fucking security," Jimmy growled, signaling for them to pass him around the corner. At least here the trenchworks had more switchbacks – slowed down progress some, but the lack of long straightaways made them a bit less exposed at any one time.

"No, it isn't." Doomsday said. "But I'm just saying we can't automatically assume the worst."

"Have you been fucking paying attention on this trip?" Rockaway hissed, sweeping the corridor as they moved. She caught sight of a guard stand up ahead, one of a couple the Major told them they'd be passing, and she took out the signal whistle for when they were closer.

It would fucking suck to get this far just to be shot by some jumpy kid on guard duty.

"She's got a point," Jimmy agreed. "Things have been thoroughly fucked."

"I'm not saying I disagree!" Doomsday said, exasperated. "I'm just saying we can't assume that's the case and just go in shooting, that's all." They reached the intersection approaching the guard stand, and Rockaway blew two short blasts on the whistle, followed by three long ones. A moment later there was an answering double blast: all clear, proceed.

"I'm still fucking curious what could get the Final Knights and the Iron Cross in bed together," Jimmy muttered, waving up at the two huddled figures up in the makeshift guard tower. One of them waved back as they passed. "That's some crazy bullshit right there."

"Got a theory on that," Doomsday said. "I think it's the Duponts."

"Fuck would they be interested in with some Yorker mercenaries and gangers?" Rockaway asked, catching a sparkle of light in a nearby window. She made a sign and the others froze, but after scoping it moment she realized it was just light catching on what was left of some glass.

"Maybe not just them," Doomsday admitted. "But I think they're the driving force."

"Zed, hold up." Rockaway pulled back around the corner so that she was just barely peeking. Ahead the trenchworks seemed to be cutting across and old roadway, but part of the barricade wall had been forced, and a half-dozen shamblers were shuffling through the gap, heading in the general direction of the artillery fire. Noise like that would be drawing zed for miles; they probably had dozens of these breaches wherever the shamblers accumulated in enough numbers to knock a gap in the trench walls. "Was six, now eight. I say wait it out."

"We should be getting close to the Shooting Gallery tunnel cut," Doomsday said. "If we can make it to there we can do a couple of blocks underground, if the trenches are too crowded."

"Fucking great," Jimmy grumbled. He hated anything to do with the underground.

"Soon as this group passes, we'll make for it." Rockaway leaned back against the trench wall, taking a breather and watching her breath steam in the cool air. "So what's this about the Duponts?"

"They're the only ones who fit all the clues," Doomsday said, taking a swig from her canteen. "Think about it. First of all, they have the money to hire the Iron Cross. Second, Big Playboy and Eve both said that the plan was to use this bomb to nuke York, right?" Rockaway nodded. "Which happens to be the seat of the Lineage League and all its records. They wipe that out, suddenly a whole lot of their rivals are gone, as is anyone who tries to say different when they make their claim as legitimate Purebloods."

"Makes sense," Jimmy said, nodding.

"Yeah, but what about Eve and Big Playboy? They're not Duponts, and I don't think they were taking anyone's money." Rockaway ducked out and saw another pair of shamblers staggering through the gap. "Fuck, they're still coming."

"I can't quite explain that," Doomsday admitted. "Maybe the Final Knights found out and decided to help spread some massive chaos and destruction. That fits, right?" Rockaway allowed that it was, as far as she knew. "Or maybe there are some Final Knights actually in the family, pulling the strings, and they reached out to some other followers in Aysea. You think it's coincidence everything's led here, the city the Duponts are after?"

"Oh, shit," Jimmy cut in quietly as Rockaway was about to answer, the urgency in his voice making both of his companions immediately snap around to see what had provoked that response.

It wasn't hard to spot. Not forty yards behind them the trench wall was starting to bulge inward, and they could see pale, rotted hands pushing through the gaps. "Horde," Doomsday said tightly. "Those guards—"

"On it." Rockaway blew the whistle, a long high note. The guards stirred to life in their outpost, giving them a chance to retreat maybe, but she'd also just alerted every zed in range to fresh meat a lot closer than the front. "Move move move!" Rockaway said, as the wall they were watching gave way and the horde began streaming through. It wasn't just shamblers that poured through, though; a few of the corpses were smoldering, leaving sparks in their wake like fireflies.

"Cinders! Fuck!" Jimmy exclaimed, his face pale. Cinders had a mutated form of the infection that caused parts of their body to produce a sort of sticky gel that burst into flame in contact with a lot of ordinary materials. Some of them could expel gobs of the stuff, spitting it on targets that often burned down trying in vain to scrape it off. Anyone who relied on hand weapons had extra hate for those zed, as their bodies were coated in those oils and tended to melt weapons that came in contact with them.

"Push through!" Rockaway turned around the corner and found two shamblers staggering in her direction through the gap she'd been observing, arms reaching out from only a few yards away. She put her shoulder down and bulled into them, trying not to gag on the smell of rotted flesh as she used her rifle to cross-body them away from her up against the far trench wall. She didn't press the attack, trusting Jimmy to take care of them on the rebound so she could keep moving. It was an old gang tactic for moving through a horde, but it worked.

Well, so long as you could keep moving, anyway. When she turned the next corner, the sound of Jimmy's bat pulping skulls no far behind, she saw the trail of sparks in time to pull up short as two shamblers and a cinder hobbled toward her. The cinder made a horrible coughing sound deep in its throat, its eyeless head jerking spasmodically as if in the throes of a tremendous fit, and Rockaway had just enough time to drag Doomsday against the trench wall before it vomited a thick oily mass past them. The glob struck the wall at the corner and immediately began melting the metal of the barricade.

"Gonna have to shoot," Doomsday said, raising his pistol.

"Fuck it," Rockaway said, firing and taking the top of the cinder's head off. Flames jetted out of its empty skull as the mixture inside caught fire, putting eerie flames in the creature's empty sockets, and it kept staggering forward. Rockaway fired another round, this time blowing out the cinder's neck, more flames flaring up from the stump as the head rolled toward them, blazing like a jack-o-lantern. The body continued for another two steps before it collapsed, twitching, a spreading pool of sticky flaming liquid spreading around it.

Next to her, Doomsday fired three quick shots at the first shambler, pulping its head above the jaw; not nearly as resilient as its more mutated friend, the corpse toppled over immediately in a sprawl of rotted skirt. The hem drifted into the burning pool and caught, and suddenly the trench corridor got a lot narrower as the second zombie went up as well. Doomsday didn't react – three more shots put down the other shambler in almost identical fashion, leaving its body slumped in the corner of the trench almost as though it was sitting down for a nap.

"Jimmy! Let's go!" Rockaway called out, sparing a look back for the bat man. He delivered a last skull-crushing strike to one of the downed shamblers, just to be sure, and bounded after them. The sniper moved to the next corner, already hating this game – it was like every turn was competing to be worse than the last.

Sure enough, the next stretch was a bit wider, but also had maybe a dozen or more zed shambling toward them. "Fucking horde!" she swore. "No way to just push through that."

"We keep shooting it'll just get worse," Doomsday said, loading a fresh clip just as Rockaway put in a fresh magazine. Always better to swap out a partial if you had the chance, at least in a situation like this. "The entrance to the Shooting Gallery should be off the trench spur ahead to the right. If we go quickly—"

"Got it. You shoot your side, I'll shoot mine. Clear?" Rockaway said. She glanced at Jimmy. "You got sweeper?"

"Fuckin' right," Jimmy said, breathing hard with adrenaline. Somewhere not too far behind them, there was a tremendous sound of metal scraping on concrete as something larger than a shambler pushed its way through one of the gaps. "Go!"

Rockaway and Doomsday took the corner wide, standing next to each other and unloading on the mob of shamblers heading their way, working their sides. Rockaway swore as she realized she'd miscounted; there were more than a dozen zombies here, more like half again that number at least. She gritted her teeth and did her best to take her time on the trigger, make each round count – headshot/down, headshot/down, headshot/

down, headshot/down. On her side Doomsday stood in a shooter's posture as if she was shooting cans on a rooftop, sometimes needing a second bullet to put down a particularly stubborn zed but never missing a shot regardless.

Then the shamblers parted as if directed by unseen force, and one of the corpses from the middle of the pack surged forward. Rockaway had never seen anything like it before – it had on the gore-encrusted remains of a medic's smock or butcher's apron, and large, jagged blades instead of hands. Strike that – the hands had grown around the blades, like a splinter left in the body, until it was hard to tell where one ended and the other began.

Whatever it was, it gave a weird howl and charged with a burster's speed, covering the ground in the space of a few seconds. Rockaway and Doomsday both fired as it came on, but neither could land a decisive headshot, and the body shots barely altered its stride. It fixed Rockaway with filmy eyes that nonetheless seemed to still contain a spark of real, intelligent malice. No, more than that – purpose. It didn't just want to rend and tear, it wanted to agonize her. As sure as she was standing there, she knew it.

"Bloody Thirteen!" Jimmy hollered, barreling toward it with his shield. The zed saw him coming and changed its path to intercept, and the two collided with terrible crunch of metal and flesh. Jimmy tried to get his weight under it and push the zed over on its back, but it rolled around the edge of his shield and lunged forward with one of its cleaver hands, straight at his heart. Jimmy knocked the strike aside with his bat and actually head-butted the zed as it pressed into him, the move doing little aside from gaining him a few feet as the impact pushed the zombie back. That was enough, and when it

172

slashed at him again he easily deflected the blows on his shield.

"Keep shooting!" Rockaway called out. It might be too risky to shoot into that melee, much as she wanted to help Jimmy, but the shamblers behind them weren't about to respect a duel in progress. Doomsday nodded as she changed clips and the two of them started picking off the shamblers at the fringes of the pack, trying to time their fire to make sure they wouldn't hit Jimmy. One after another they put the shamblers down, until the trench floor started to pile with them.

Not that Jimmy even seemed to notice. He and the zed, having recognized capable opponents in each other, shifted to much more cautious attacks, the zombie testing his speed with the shield, Jimmy trying to break one of its blades and bring himself some relief from the relentless slashing attacks. He got a lucky hit in, knocking its knee hard enough to give it a limp and take away some of its lunging power. Rockaway thought he had it then, but his backswing missed its head by inches as the creatures ducked back.

With a roar, the zed delivered an overhead chop straight down into the rim of shield; Jimmy caught it easily, but the blade actually bit several inches into the metal, getting stuck fast in the process. Before Jimmy could capitalize on it, the zed hooked its other awkward hand around the edge of the shield and pulled with all its might, shrilling a high hunting cry as it tore the shield nearly in half. If Jimmy hadn't modified the strap into a breakaway, he might have lost his arm too, or at least badly dislocated it as the zed ripped it away. As he pulled free of the wreckage of his shield, though, Jimmy struck back, landing a shot that broke several ribs with a sickening crack.

"Come and have a go!" Jimmy sang, face bright

with fury as he spun his bat in his hands, shifting to a two-handed grip. No, not just bright with fury – she heard phantom music and his bat seemed to glow with swirling white light. The remaining shamblers froze, and even the blade-handed zed staggered back a moment. Jimmy waited, humming and seemingly oblivious to what was going on, and after a moment the zed came at him, slashing and hacking.

Jimmy knocked one swing aside and blocked the other straight on, letting go of the bat with one hand and grabbing the zed's arm, jerking it toward him. It tried to pull away but the knee he'd injured earlier wouldn't hold up and it stumbled forward onto its knees. Before it could rise, Jimmy brought the bat up and then crashing down on its skull three times, so fast it seemed like a blur, each hit accompanied by a thunderous phantom drumbeat. By the second hit the zombie's head was already mostly a few splinters of bone held together by leathery skin; by the third he had pulped its spine as well.

Doomsday dropped the last of the shamblers – not a dangerous exercise, exactly, but already putting a hurt on their ammo count – and Jimmy turned back to face them as the glow from his bat faded. He had a wide grin and actually winked at Rockaway. "Did you fucking see that? Did you fucking hear that?"

"Fucking sweet," Rockaway said quickly, "but we gotta run. All that shooting will draw more of the horde in a fucking hurry." Jimmy nodded good humoredly and the three of them raced down the trench. Rockaway felt a flood of relief as they turned down the spur path and she spotted the Shooting Gallery stairwell up ahead. Once they got inside they could go the next few blocks were all underground, a path through an old complex that had been dug out before the Fall. Supposedly the first Delphians had sheltered there during the worst of the violence, but abandoned it when it was safe to go topside. Now the Fort Independence forces used it as a cut-through when the trenches got too hot at street level, and they'd been assured they'd re-emerge only a few blocks from the rendezvous.

They spun the wheel on the massive steel door, pulled the lever as the Major had instructed and the door swung open neatly and quietly despite its battered appearance. Beyond was just a yawning stretch of pure blackness. Doomsday and Jimmy fished out their new hand crank lights while Rockaway covered the top of the stairwell. The new lights were a bonus – the Major had ground her teeth a little at the thought of giving up the precious gear, but Doomsday had stretched the authority of her badge as far as it would go and wrung them out of her.

"Come on, let's go," Doomsday said, gesturing the others inside. Inside the air was stale and musty, but there was none of the scent of rot that would warn them of zed or fresh refuse that would indicate other survivors. Not yet, anyway. "I don't want to stick around and find out whatever else is running with this horde.

"Too fucking right," Rockaway said, wishing she had a free hand for a light of her own, or maybe some of the light sticks she'd lost back in York. The fight with the fisher seemed like a thousand years ago now. Her body certainly agreed – she'd been beat up, shot, stabbed and put back together a few times since then, and holy powers aside, there was only so much of that a body could take, especially as they'd been on the run more or less continuously the entire time.

"Can't believe the fucker trashed my shield," Jimmy grumbled as they sealed up the door, though Rockaway suspected he was simply looking for something to talk about other than the fact that he was heading underground. For someone who got along well with Lascarians and other tunnel folk, Jimmy hated visiting them at home.

"Better it than you," Rockaway countered, and he grunted in grudging agreement. "The fuck was that, anyway? I've never heard of zed with fucking bullshit knife hands, have you?" Jimmy shook his head, looking particularly grim in the light of the hand cranks. "You?"

"Not me," Doomsday said. If Jimmy looked grim, the pale-skinned Doomsday looked ghostly. "Butchers must be a local treat."

"Butchers," said Jimmy, sounding it out speculatively. "I like it. Fits."

"Hooray for fucking us," Rockaway said. "We discovered another breed of horrible goddamn monsters. We'll have to tell the Doc all about it when we get home, so he can put it in his book." Jimmy snickered and Doomsday smiled. "C'mon, let's keep moving." She pointed further down into the Shooting Gallery and they headed out cautiously, Doomsday on point and Jimmy bringing up the rear, Rockaway hating every second of not having her own light the deeper they went.

Whatever the original function had been, the place had held up well. There were two levels Rockaway could make out in the dim, shifting glow of the flashlights; the upper one they were on seemed better preserved, with rows of fortified gates marking different storage areas on either side. The lower level was more of a mystery, though that had as much to do with the fact that they didn't have much light to spare to investigate it. From what little Rockaway could make out, it looked like it was similarly designed, with rows of spaces running side by side, but while the upper level was a series of neat gates, the lower level was more chaotic, with boxes scattered across the floor some of the spaces open while others had been heavily barricaded.

"This place is fucking creepy," Jimmy said, jumping a little at the sound of his own echo. "I can see why they don't use it much," he added, much more quietly.

"Yeah, but it's quiet," Doomsday said softly. "I approve of quiet right now." Neither Jimmy or Rockaway could say much to that, so they moved on, sweeping with their lights. Once Rockaway could've sworn that she saw something scuttling out of the edge of Jimmy's light, but they didn't hear anything, and her fears of another ambush eventually faded.

When they reached the other end of the Shooting Gallery, Rockaway called an injury and ammo break. Somewhat miraculously, they'd managed to break through the horde without picking up more than a few scrapes and bruises, not even anything Doomsday wanted to waste gauze on as most of them were already knitting back together. Rockaway and Doomsday refilled their empty and partial clips and magazines; no sense in not topping those off while they had a chance.

"I can't believe we didn't get fucking jumped down here," Jimmy said, sipping from his canteen. "Seriously. Forget how much the Kings love me, that's the real fucking miracle right there."

"You're really gonna fucking jinx it like that?" Rockaway teased.

"C'mon, we're at the damn door!" Jimmy said. "Two locks and we're out."

"How far to Love's Graveyard?" Rockaway asked Doomsday.

The agent did some quick reckoning in her head, tracing in the air with her finger. "Not too far. Four blocks, I think." The others drew in sharp breaths at that. "I didn't say it was right outside. I said it wasn't far."

"Well, let's not keep your boss waiting," Rockaway

said. "We all good?" The other two nodded, and they opened the massive steel doors. Rockaway signaled that she'd head up first and scout around, but she had just reached street level when she hurried back down the steps. "Nevermind. He can fucking wait."

"What is it?" Doomsday asked, though she looked like she'd already guessed.

"More fucking horde movement. The trench was thick with them, more than we could push through by far." Rockaway shook her head. "Good news is they seem to be moving at a pretty good fucking pace toward all that shelling south of us. Bad news is we're going to be stuck down here for a fucking while."

"You're shitting me," Jimmy breathed, what little color he'd regained at approaching topside again already draining from his face. He gulped his water hard and looked nervously over his shoulder at the darkness of the Shooting Gallery.

"Relax," Rockaway said. "We'll check every couple of minutes, go as soon as it's clear."

"Promise?" Jimmy asked.

"I promise," Rockaway replied. She slung her rifle, found his hand and squeezed it. The sniper looked over at Doomsday. "You should catch a nap. I feel fucking great after getting the big miracle – well, like I've slept in the last day anyway – and I'm sure he does too, but you've been running flat out for too long. Get some sleep, we'll cover."

"Don't have to tell me twice," Doomsday said, laying down on one of the steps with her pack as a pillow, one hand curled her holster like a child holding a toy. In less than a minute the sound of her faint snores echoed off the stone.

"Unfuckingbelievable," Jimmy said, looking down at the sleeping agent. "The shit some people can do, right?"

"Too fucking right," Rockaway said, thinking of the phantom music and the shining light that had accompanied his swings as he took down that butcher. That was one of the most frustrating yet endearing traits about Jimmy – he always seemed to overlook himself when he was taking account of the incredible things in the world. "You gonna be OK down here when I go topside to check?"

"Fuck no, I'll be a fucking mess," Jimmy said, but before she could say anything he pointed to the sleeping agent and added, "but to look out for her? Yeah, I'll be cool. Do what you gotta." He looked out at the darkness again, his jaw set. "I got this."

Contrary to Jimmy's expectations, nothing came lunging out of the darkness for them; contrary to Rockaway's, the horde never caught sight of her and gave chase. Later on she'd look back and think that it was almost like the world was holding its breath, waiting to see what happened next.

Not that it would be disappointed.

Chapter Fifteen

"You're late." Agent Freeman stared at them as they approached, impassive behind his sunglasses. He looked exactly the same as the last time Rockaway had seen him – dark suit, white shirt, dark hat, his posture casual and slightly bored despite being in the middle of a city under siege with an active horde in the area. His only concession to the situation was the sleek pistol in one hand, and even that was held rather listlessly at his side, as if he hadn't wanted to draw it at all and been convinced otherwise.

Of course, his relaxed attitude might also have had something to do with the fact that he was standing in the middle of a flat plain of badly poured concrete, with two strange looking machines perched behind him like weird insects. They had wide metal blades on top and a smaller set on their tails, with bodies like awkwardly shaped caravans attached underneath. They reminded her of something the Doc had taught her about once, pre-Fall flying machines called helicopters. Not that anyone had seen one in ages, of course, but some of his books had pictures, and she remembered them because they reminded her of the dragonflies that buzzed the pools in the Brokelands in the summer.

"You've gotta be shitting me," Jimmy breathing, eyes wide like a little kid at their first Bottle Rocket Day. Even Doomsday looked a little awestruck, though she hid it better. The bat man elbowed Rockaway. "You see these fucking things?"

"Kinda hard to fucking miss it," Rockaway replied, though she had to admit she was having trouble keeping her own reaction in check. To have not just one but two of these machines, and in working condition? The sniper felt a sinking feeling in her gut as she realized she had seriously underestimated the power of the G-Men and the Lineage League. Not to mention what she was carrying was worth to them, if just to meet her they were willing to risk flying them here and revealing their existence to anyone with eyes.

Living in the Heights, the Dead Heroes still found landing pads for the machines on top of some of the bigger buildings, and it looked like someone had filled in and paved over this park to make exactly such a thing sometime in the past. The only sign of what it must have been before was a weird old sculpture, battered and corroded red letters that spelled the word "LOVE." What remained of it was partially submerged in the concrete, sticking out like an old tombstone in a long-neglected graveyard.

If that had been the purpose for the park, it had long since been adapted for other uses. Both of the helicopters had their side doors open and Rockaway could see the grim figure of Agent Torv sitting in the far machine, her long rifle across her lap, eyes focused on the group as they approached. Just for good measure, there were other black-suited figures waiting in both machines, G-Men by the look of them but more heavily armed and armored than Freeman and Torv, with polished shooters and vicious-looking hand weapons at the ready.

"Real fucking friendly," Rockaway said, eyes narrowed.

"Don't shoot anyone yet," Doomsday whispered.

"Got a feeling it won't be fucking long now," Rockaway muttered, and then they were close enough for Agent Freeman to hear. The sniper slid one hand off her rifle as though to wipe it on her pants, made two quick gestures with her middle finger toward the nearest thug and then tapped her knee while she rolled her head at the far machine: You get these two, I got them. Jimmy clicked his tongue twice to let her know he'd seen it. She couldn't pass anything to Doomsday, but the agent had good instincts, Rockaway knew she'd fall in.

Well, she hoped anyway.

"Sorry sir. We were delayed by horde activity, had to hole up in a bunker for almost an hour until they passed." Doomsday stopped up short and came to something like attention. Jimmy stood at her left side to be closer to the soldiers he could meet at close range, Rockaway standing to her right and a short ways away to give her a good angle on Agent Torv and the others in the far machine. "If I may? It's good to see you again, sir."

"You too, Agent Anderson." Agent Freeman's smile was there and gone so fast Rockaway wondered if she'd only imagined it. "I can imagine you're eager to be formally reinstated – no more of this undercover work. Am I correct?"

"It would be nice to finally be a real agent, sir." Doomsday smiled back, the expression not quite reaching her eyes. Too much time around real Yorkers, Rockaway supposed. Tended to mute the sentimental stuff a bit. "Much as I, ah, enjoyed this assignment, it would be nice to be agency recognized."

"I'm sure that won't be a problem. First, however, we need to verify what you've obtained." Agent Freeman turned and signaled to Agent Torv, who walked about halfway between the two of them and stopped, waiting. "If you would?"

"Sir?" Doomsday hesitated. "With respect, wouldn't it be best to verify in more secure location?" As if to punctuate her sentence, a fresh round of artillery strikes sounded off in the distance, accompanied by flashes and slight ground tremors as they impacted.

"Noted, agent," Agent Freeman said coolly, "but you have been off-book for some time, shall we say. Certain precautions are warranted." He put his palm out. Doomsday looked at Rockaway, who held it for a moment before she shrugged and fished the key from around her neck. She passed it to Doomsday, who paired it with hers and handed it to the senior lawman. Agent Freeman turned them over in his hands, a thoughtful look on his face, then turned and lobbed the pair over to Agent Torv. The blonde caught them one-handed and spun on her heel, walking back to the other machine and climbing aboard.

"What's she doing?" Rockaway asked, feeling the hair on the back of her neck begin to stand up. "'Cause it looks like she just walked off with the only fucking reason we have to believe you'll play ball with us."

"Promises were fucking made," Jimmy said. "No offense."

"So I keep hearing," Agent Freeman replied, shifting his gaze back to Doomsday even as he replied to Jimmy. "I'm not sure exactly what my agent promised you, but if these keys check out, the Inquisition will do its best to honor those assurances." He reached into his coat and produced a heavy envelope emblazoned with the symbol of the Inquisition, handed it over to Doomsday. "A personal guarantee, if my promise doesn't interest you."

"That'll do for now," Rockaway said curtly, as Doomsday tucked the envelope into her pack. "Thanks."

"Sir, I have other concerns." Doomsday stepped forward, leaned in to speak confidentially. "I have strong evidence that Domino has been compromised."

"Oh?" Agent Freeman's relaxed manner tensed notably, and Rockaway saw a reflection of it in the soldiers seated in the helicopter behind him. "What is that?"

"We took down a Final Knight who had the name of your base on him," Rockaway said. "And his partner – the bitch who had the other key we just handed over – was headed right for this fucking town like she knew she had friends waiting."

"You got any Iron Cross on your payroll?" Jimmy added, just low enough so the mercenaries couldn't hear.

"As a matter of fact, yes." Agent Freeman shrugged. "We've used them often in the past, when a simple military presence was desirable."

"Are you kidding?" Rockaway took a step forward, feeling anger flare up.

"Rockaway," Doomsday said, a cautionary note in her voice, but the Yorker bulled past it with an impatient wave of her hand.

"No, fuck that. Some of those assholes came with you, right?" The sniper asked, and was rewarded with a look of genuine surprise that cracked the senior agent's poker face. "Shit. They fucking did, didn't they? Are you fucking serious? You really think those psycho mercs are gonna just back your play when there's a nuke at stake?"

"How did you know that?" Agent Freeman asked.

"Answer her fucking question," Jimmy said quietly.

"Call it a fucking hunch," Rockaway said. She studied the G-Man's face, which was rapidly regaining its composure. "You brought Red Hands. And you don't even know it, do you? Fuck. Fuck fuck fuck!"

"Having this 'Red Hands' along would be quite impressive, as I understand you killed the man yourself when you left York," Agent Freeman said calmly. "That was actually a useful bonus, as we figured with him gone, it would be less of a problem to involve the Iron Cross in this – hold on." Suddenly the senior agent cocked his head to one side as if listening to something, then brought his wrist up to his face and started speaking into a thick bracelet. "This is Bishop. Go for traffic." Rockaway opened her mouth to ask who he was talking to, but caught Doomsday shaking her head and bit back her words.

"Confirm." Agent Freeman lowered his hand. "Looks like the keys are good." Behind him the other helicopter's blades began turning, slowly at first but rapidly gaining speed. "We are returning t—say again?" He brought his wrist up abruptly. "Say again, all after unauthorized."

"Sir, I don't think it's safe to take open channel traffic—" Doomsday began, but Agent Freeman raised his hand, evidently listening again.

"Bishop copies all." The senior agent lowered his wrist, his face very still, the color slowly draining from it. "There was an unauthorized train departure, northbound, right after we left. Our Iron Cross mercenaries were the only ones onboard." A pause followed that couldn't have been more than one or two heartbeats, but felt more like minutes. "And they have the Domino with them."

Rockaway saw the two G-Men soldiers behind him exchange a look, and whatever the signal was, she knew it one had just been given. The long blades started spinning on the other helicopter and there was the unmistakable sound of an engine coming to life.

"Ambush!" Rockaway called out, raising her rifle

and dropping to one knee as Jimmy jumped forward to take on the two soldiers at hand. A shotgun went off and she heard a gurgling moan, followed by five pistol shots in rapid succession, but she trusted Jimmy and Doomsday to get her back while she found her shot.

Agent Torv was outlined in the window of the helicopter, a tempting target, but the two soldiers actively firing shooters in the open door were a more immediate threat. The blades were kicking up a hell of a downdraft now too, forcing her to squint behind her shades and causing her to duck down reflexively against the force of the wind.

The traitorous G-Men were firing rapidly, but didn't seem to be aiming for live targets as much as they were blasting away at the helicopter. She could hear the impacts and saw fluid start trickling from the underside of the helicopter, not to bits of glass from the cockpit window. Rockaway swore and put a round in the throat of one, causing him to jerk and tumble out of the doorway, but her perfect matching shot was ruined as the other helicopter abruptly lifted off, and she caught him in the leg instead.

It was flying. It was really flying.

In her life, Rockaway had been through floods, horde attacks, gang wars and even an inferno that burned down almost two blocks of Dead Heroes territory, but the sight of the machine actually leaving the ground struck her motionless for several precious seconds. Everything around her seemed to fade into the background for a moment, and she got that strange feeling she sometimes had when she looked out at the York skyline, or when Mercy turned up a particularly intact novelty during her digs. She'd never really been able to put it in words, but if she could, it probably would have been a sense of amazement at what people had been capable of, before it all got flushed away.

Then all the noise and shouting snapped back, like surfacing from a lake, and Rockaway realized she had just moments left before the machine vanished. The sniper fired twice as the helicopter flew off, both shots striking but not causing any immediate visible effect, and then it was out of range. "Fuck!" Rockaway swore.

"Freeman!" Doomsday called out, and Rockaway turned to see Doomsday kneeling over her fallen superior, whose chest had been pulped by the shotgun of a G-Man that was now slumped half-out of the helicopter, a bullet hole perfectly centered in her forehead. At a glance the Yorker could tell that Agent Freeman was dead, but Doomsday was trying to render medical assistance anyway.

Behind her Jimmy was engaged with the Iron Cross with a large sword; Jimmy had a cut on his cheek but the mercenary had one mangled arm dangling uselessly against his side and had been pushed back against the helicopter, struggling to parry swing after swing as Jimmy rained down attacks. Rockaway thought about taking out the Iron Cross but before she could even make the decision Jimmy feinted high, drawing the merc's sword up for a cross block, but committed to a vicious side swing that caved in the side of the man's head with a dull crack. Jimmy gave it another swing, just to be sure, and then turned back to Rockaway, spattered with blood and one cheek entirely red below the cut, as if he'd painted his face. "Fucker's down," he spat, touching his cheek gingerly and wincing as he found the edges of wound.

"Got one of the assholes for sure in the other helicopter, tagged another but don't think it brought him down. Check the – what the fuck do you call someone who operates one of these fucking things?"

"Pilot," Doomsday said automatically, not looking up.

"The pilot, yeah, see if they got hit." Rockaway was already second-guessing her decision not to take the shot at Torv, but there was no fixing it now. Instead she walked over to Agent Freeman's body, where Doomsday had darkened both sleeves with blood almost to the elbow. "Hey. Hey! He's fucking gone."

"I know," Doomsday said, sitting back on her haunches. "I know."

"We'll bring him with us, you can be there for him when he comes back." Rockaway leaned down and tapped Doomsday on the temple, lightly but enough to get her to look up in surprise. "Next time don't go all medic while one of us is still in a fucking fight six feet away, got it?" She said the words quietly, to make sure Jimmy didn't overhear, but there was no mistaking the intensity she put in it either.

Doomsday seemed to snap back to herself and nodded. "Sorry. It's just—" Doomsday pointed to Agent Freeman's neck, where the veins were already turning a dark, sickly green. "It doesn't look like he's coming back."

"Shit." Rockaway was no doc, but she had to agree – she'd never seen green that bad and had someone came back thinking and talking when it ran its course. Leaving him would be certain death if he came back whole, but bringing him with them might mean having him come back as a zed right in their midst. "Looks like we should just fucking finish it."

"Pilot's alive, just loves to fucking stay in cover," Jimmy announced, pulling a thin young man in a work jumpsuit out with him. The pilot looked ashen when he saw the bodies, particularly Agent Freeman's, but to his credit he didn't get sick or lose his shit.

"This bitch's been shot the hell up," Rockaway asked bluntly, gesturing at the helicopter with her rifle. "Think it still works?"

"This bitch? This bi-" The pilot started angrily, then seemed to remember that he was outnumbered and unarmed and backed down. "I'll—I'll have to take a look," he said, hopping down and walking around the vehicle. "Can you believe it? They actually shot at this beautiful machine? Do you know how insane that is? How much this thing is worth?"

"Best get to it or the shooting will fucking start again," Rockaway growled. The pilot flinched as though she'd slapped him and scurried away to survey the damage.

"What's his story?" Jimmy said, nodding at Agent Freeman. "He coming back?"

"Doesn't look too fucking likely," Rockaway said.

Doomsday flinched. "I know. And I'll do what has to be done. But without him—"

"Worry about that later," Rockaway insisted. "We've gotta stop these assholes. We'll figure out who owes what later, if there is a fucking later." She saw the pilot come back around. "Well? What's the fucking word?"

"It'll take some time, but yeah, I think we should be able to get airborne." The pilot chewed his lip nervously, not wanting to ask what followed but asking it anyway. "Question is, on whose authority?" Jimmy went to step up, but Doomsday held the big man back.

"I'm Agent Dana Anderson," she said, handing the pilot her identification. "Agent Freeman is down, and along with these others Agent Torv appears to have broken her vows with the Inquisition and conspired with rogue elements for nefarious purposes. I'm officially requesting pursuit."

"That fucking good enough?" Rockaway added.

"Who are these people?" The pilot asked, though Rockaway noted that he stepped back when he caught Jimmy still giving him a hard look.

"They're officially deputized, and besides they saved your life less than a minute ago – so does it really fucking matter? Get this damn thing working again!" Doomsday barked. The pilot went wide-eyed and snapped a hasty salute, then grabbed a toolkit from inside the vehicle and got to work on some of the bigger holes. "What?" Doomsday said, looking at the two Yorkers. "Something wrong?"

"Nothing," Rockaway replied.

"Are we really gonna be flying in this thing?" Jimmy asked, looking at the helicopter. Despite the fresh cut on his cheek, not to mention the splashes of blood and sweat and grime of the last few hours, he managed to show a little of that same wonder as before.

"You heard the man," Rockaway said, looking down at Agent Freeman's body. "We've got a fucking train to catch."

Chapter Sixteen

"Holy shit," Rockaway kept repeating under her breath, watching the countryside race past below as the helicopter roared along above the tracks. She kept telling herself it was just like being on a rooftop, but her eyes called bullshit on that and her body agreed. It had been a little thrilling at first, when the blades started whirling and the machine started vibrating and then there was that lurching feeling as they left the ground, but as the ground fell away and the buildings started flashing by she got a dose of something she'd rarely felt since she was small: vertigo. It was all she could do to keep from being sick, and to keep her mind distracted she tried to focus on the landscape instead.

At first she'd been impressed by how long the city'd gone on as they headed out of the town proper – the Delphian Wastes weren't tall like York, but they did sprawl pretty impressively – even if most of it was burned out houses and crumbled buildings. Then as they got further north the towns gave way to woods again as the forests slowly moved back in to reclaim the blasted suburbs. Street after street of collapsed, overgrown houses continued on for miles it seemed like.

She saw a few zed, heads rolling up to stare at them as they flashed past overhead, but didn't spot any live individuals. Probably hiding from the sound, which didn't strike her as such a bad idea – back in the Pine Barrens, when they'd heard these things coming overhead they'd felt like hiding too. Even now she felt fucking miserable and a little scared of the thing, to be honest, and she was riding in it. Growing up in the Heights, she was no stranger to tall places, but those

191

heights didn't usually move like this. It made her grip the armrests on her seat until her fingers hurt, just to fight the feeling as though the world was going to drop out from under her at any second.

"You know we can hear you, right?" Doomsday's voice came over her headset, small and mechanical-sounding. The agent was a little paler than normal and seemed to be breathing quickly, but was otherwise managing to hold it together with little visible strain. Her tone was teasing, but there was a warning note underneath it: don't lose your shit on me.

"Yeah, yeah, g'fuck yourself." Rockaway forced her fingers to let go of the armrests, flexed them. The ache in her palms was back, and though they'd wound her hands up with clean linen she could tell they'd soon be soaked through. If nothing else, Red Hands owed her for a lot of goddamn medical supplies. She swallowed another surge of nausea. "This ain't fuckin' natural, that's all."

"Easy, Rock! It can't be much longer." Miserably enough, Jimmy actually appeared to be enjoying himself, which only made Rockaway feel even more sick and embarrassed. He kept looking out the window too, a smile on his face like a kid watching his first striptease, tapping his bat against the side of his boot with restless energy. It was one of his pre-fight tics, and normally it drove her up the fucking wall, but right now it was downright comforting.

"How much further?" Doomsday asked their pilot.

"We should be coming up on the train soon," he called back, and there was no mistaking the anxious note in his voice even with the noise of the rotors and the hum of the headphones. "It can't be that much further, these tracks may be new but they don't exactly look factory standard, so I doubt they can push it much faster." There was a significant pause. "Are you sure you want to do this?"

"Do we look like we're kidding, asshole?" Rockaway growled, relieved to have something to be mad at instead of simply sitting there being queasy. "This plan goes off, motherfucker is going to blow up half of goddamn York."

"Not to mention touch off a Pureblood power struggle that'll make the Delphian siege look like a fireworks show," Doomsday added.

"Fuck that noise!" Jimmy said, still smiling.

"No, no, I get that," the pilot said hastily, "I mean trying to drop down on it from here. You know that's goddamn insane, right?"

"You got a better idea?" Rockaway asked, half hoping he might.

"Yes, actually," the pilot responded, as if reading her mind. "We can fly ahead, maybe down some trees on the tracks, get him to stop the engine that way. How's that sound?"

"Not bad, actually," Doomsday admitted. She turned in her seat to look back at Rockaway with a quizzical eyebrow raised. The Yorker grunted. It was a half-decent suggestion, but only half. As much as she preferred it to dropping a line out of this machine and fast-roping down, there were a few logistical problems.

"You got a fucking axe stashed in here somewhere?" Rockaway said curtly. "Because his bat and our knives ain't gonna cut shit down."

"Just a thought," the pilot replied, a bit defensively.

"He's gonna hear us fucking miles away," Jimmy pointed out, gesturing up at the helicopter rotors. "Surprise is fucked."

"I dunno," Rockaway said. "I saw this shit coming, I don't know what the fuck I'd do, give me all the

warning you fucking want. Besides," she held up
her hands so he could see the blood seeping into the
wraps, "I think he's gonna fucking know when I get
close." What she didn't mention was that ever since
they're started off in the helicopter, she'd been hearing
whispers just like she had the last time she'd been in her
dead place. And if she concentrated for a moment it was
almost like her vision blurred out and another image
took its place, like seeing from another pair of eyes. She
shook her head to clear it. "Don't mean we won't still
fucking grease the asshole."

"What's the plan?" Doomsday asked.

"Kill every motherfucker on that train," Jimmy
offered.

"Yeah," Rockaway agreed. "Doomsday, go for the
driver."

"Engineer." The pilot cut in. Rockaway looked
over at Jimmy and he rolled his eyes.

"Whatever his fucking job title is, find him and
fucking end him fast. Got it?" Doomsday gave her a
thumbs up in response. "And you," Rockaway pointed
at Jimmy, "fucking kill everything you find, but don't
break shit. We don't know how this fucking bomb
works, so try not to set it off early, got me?"

"I ain't no Darwinist," Jimmy huffed. "I got no
need to see a nuke go off up close."

"Can you imagine?" Doomsday asked, looking
equal parts excited and terrified at the thought. Most
survivors probably would have been struck with
almost superstitious awe at the thought of something
so complex and so destructive, but Rockaway figured
the agent's assignment to the Nuclear Division of the
Federal Bonded Inquisition probably put her a little bit
ahead of most everyone else in terms of handling the
thought. "An actual nuke. It's amazing one survived

this long. I can't even believe it."

"I'm trying not to think about it too hard," Rockaway said, and meant it. "I'll take care of fucking Red Hands." She saw the other two exchange a look. "Hey. I got that asshole. But you gotta trust me. And don't fucking drop him, not unless I say so. He gets popped and I'm not ready, it's gonna be fucking rough, you feel me?"

"But –" Jimmy said, but Rockaway held up her hand.

"And you gotta promise me, if he goes down and I'm not... not me, you'll put me the fuck down before that asshole gets away with my body."

"What?" Doomsday asked, eyes wide. Even the pilot twitched a little, as though he wanted to turn to look at her but thought better of it.

"No doubt," Jimmy said, his cheer fading as his mouth set in a resolute line. Only a crinkling at the corners of his eyes betrayed the emotions he must have been feeling, but he didn't let it surface. Rockaway let out a breath she didn't realize she'd been holding in – she'd worried he was going to fight her on it, but then again, was it so different from putting down one of their own when they came back zed? She reached out a hand and he clasped it in his own, somewhere between a soldier's grip and a lover's clasp. She didn't mind the ambiguity.

After just another moment, she extended her other hand to Doomsday. The agent took it and held it, not speaking, the three of them just holding on – to each other, to the moment, against everything coming. Impossible to put it into words, so they didn't, just let it ride, Jimmy humming into the headset. When they let go, Rockaway breathed in and breathed out, just like she did before taking a tricky shot, and the world

195

195

seemed to settle just a bit.

"OK," Doomsday leaned forward and tapped one of the circles on the counter in front of the pilot. "How are we doing?"

"We've got maybe another 30 minutes before I need to turn back," the pilot said. "That's the comfort zone, anyway. I could push it, but I'd rather not."

"You ain't turning back til we find the fucking train," Jimmy said.

"I am precisely the last person in this aircraft that you want to threaten," the pilot replied evenly, not even bothering to turn around. "So I suggest you knock that shit off right the hell now. I listen to her because she's got the badge, but even then that loyalty only goes so far. My first and only job is returning this aircraft intact. Understood?"

"You'd really let York fucking burn to save this thing?" Rockaway asked.

"Miss, do you know how many of these are still working?" The pilot didn't wait for her to answer. "Maybe six, in this whole country. So yes, that's my priority. Clear?"

"Fucking crystal," Rockaway muttered, looking out the window again. A small town slipped by below, houses half-collapsed from years of wind and snow, caravans rusted into little hills in the streets. A few shamblers lolled their heads in her direction, started staggering in the direction of a sound that would already be long gone by the time they'd gone thirty yards. She thought she caught other shapes in the trees as well, moving a little faster, hunters maybe, the outrunners of the horde. It was easy to see how a town like that died – no barriers, no high places to hole up, not enough open space to grow food. Hell, she could take it apart at a glance and she was flying by overhead.

Not for the first time she wondered what the hell everyone had been thinking before the Fall, living like that.

Must have been nice to walk around like carefree assholes all the time.

"There, up ahead." Rockaway craned her head to see what Doomsday was talking about, Jimmy doing likewise. Around a bend ahead they could see a thick plume of smoke over the trees as the train's engine chugged along. Doomsday looked back at the two Yorkers and gave a thumbs-up sign – if her hand was shaking slightly it was hard to tell against the background vibration of the helicopter. "Go time!"

"Easy boy, easy boy, take your time," Jimmy sang into the headset, and from the looks of it he was still singing even as he took off the headphones and unbuckled his flight harness. Rockaway fumbled at her straps, swearing at the sweat on her hand, but Doomsday appeared and patiently worked the clasps until she was free, giving a smile as she hauled her to her feet. The Yorker couldn't hear what the agent was saying, but she could read lips well enough: You good?

"Let's fuckin' finish this," Rockaway shouted in response, slinging her rifle as Jimmy pulled open the helicopter's side door. The cold wind ripped at them like the gust through a forty story window and she grabbed an overhead rail for support, gritting her teeth and trying to block out the scenery whipping past them as the pilot dropped down lower, the trees seemingly only inches from the tips of the rotors. She didn't know what would happen if they actually touched, but had to figure it would be a bad scene.

Jimmy passed her the cable and she clicked the carabiner in place on the hand rail. The rail was bolted to the interior and didn't give when she tugged on it, hard, so it would have to do. There was no safety harness or other failsafe, but that didn't bother her – most of the climbing they did in the Heights didn't have any such insurance policies either. You learned to check the gear you had and live with the risk – it's not like worrying would do much good. In a way the familiarity of it helped steady her stomach. She'd rope dropped before, and from higher up than this. The fact that she'd never done it from a flying caravan was something she tried not to focus on.

Nobody spoke, not that they could easily hear each other over the roar of the blades and the wind rushing past, but when Rockaway moved to be first down the line, neither of them stopped her. She wondered how close the pilot could get them, how much line she'd need, but the concern was almost academic.

Besides, with a crew of who knew how many Iron Cross mercenaries onboard, falling was the least of their worries.

Chapter Seventeen

When the helicopter rounded the bend, Rockaway finally caught sight of the train. It was only four cars long and a mismatched abomination of a thing besides, a huge smoke-belching engine pulling it along with an open car of coal behind it, wheels shrieking on the tracks as it went. Two burly men were feeding coal into the engine by the shovelful, both stripped to the waist and gleaming with sweat from the exertion of keeping the massive old beast underway at speed.

Just behind the engine and its feeder car that was another open car that had something large and irregularly shaped placed right in the middle it, a ragged blue weatherproof tarp lashed across it making it impossible to say exactly what might be concealed underneath, though Rockaway could certainly guess. Bringing up the rear was a small enclosed car, an old freight hauler from the look of it, the remnants of painted designs flaked off of the sides and replaced with so much rust and wear she was amazed that it was still holding together. Especially with the light helicopter perched on top of it, balanced precariously on the rusting freight car. It looked empty, which meant the keys had already been delivered.

Domino was hot.

That wasn't the only threat, either. Armed Iron Cross members were everywhere on the train. Three of them were gathered on the open car, two with pistols and another with a rifle while another, sword-wielding mercenary had emerged from the rear car. The two with pistols began firing, causing Rockaway to duck back inside. Trying to avoid the worst of it, the pilot swerved the helicopter back and forth, and Rockaway heard the muted thumps as a few shots thudded into the bodywork. She had no idea how delicate something like this was, but she was betting bullets didn't do it much good, and as they cleared the last car Rockaway knew he wouldn't hang around for much more punishment.

"Slow the fuck down!" Jimmy yelled over the roar, but if the pilot heard him he didn't listen. Instead he ramped up the speed and they soared over the middle car, passing dangerously close to the other helicopter's rotors in the process. In a few seconds they might overshoot the train entirely, and if he did that Rockaway wasn't sure he'd have the nerve for another pass, not with so many shooters blasting away. Sooner or later they were bound to hit something vital, crew included, and that would end the ride even faster.

Fuck it. Time to go.

"I fucking hated birthdays anyway," Rockaway muttered to herself, flashing a tight smile at Jimmy and Rockaway before stepping out the door as the train raced by beneath her. The downdraft from the rotors and the rush of the wind nearly tore the rope from her hands, but she gritted her teeth and held on, riding the rope down with skill born of years of practice. She angled for a fast landing in the midst of the Iron Cross by on the central car, see if she could try to take away their ability to use their shooters for a moment or two at least. It was a desperate move and more than a little foolish, but she didn't figure too many sane, reasonable plans were born of hanging out of flying machines.

One of the Iron Cross snapped off a shot as she swung past him only a few yards away, but he had to squint hard against the downdraft and the shot went wide. She had an instant to feel triumphant before she realized that despite her speed down the rope the helicopter had overshot her chosen spot, and she found

200

herself dangling above the coal car. There was no time to hope for a correction – she caught a glimpse of Jimmy in the door above her, ready to the ride the line right behind her – and Rockaway let go, tumbling the last few feet into a pile of loose coal. The landing raised a cloud of black dust but the pile was loose enough that it gave nicely under her weight and helped spread out some of the impact.

Too nicely, in fact – Rockaway tried to get to scramble to her feet only to have the pile slide beneath her feet, spilling her onto her back in a tumble of loose black rocks. Her yelp of surprise earned her a lungful of thick black dust and she trailed off into a hacking cough, struggling to sit up as she unslung her rifle. At least the slide had also taken her below the lip of the coal car, otherwise she'd be an easy target flopping about in this mess.

Lying on her back, she looked up and saw the helicopter slow down suddenly, leaving just an instant to see Jimmy halfway down the rope and Doomsday leaning out the door firing her pistol before they passed out of her line of sight. She thought she heard a heavy impact a second later, maybe even singing, but that might just have been some wishful thinking. Either way she wouldn't be doing anyone any good lying down here in the coal, not when their first priority was stopping the damn train.

Rockaway got into a crouch, rifle loose and low, found the most sure footing she could and rose up cautiously, popping her head above the lip of the coal car to take a glimpse in the direction of the engine. Ahead of her, she saw the two coal tenders had apparently been waiting for her to pop back up, and cut loose with pistols as soon as she appeared. Rockaway ducked down immediately, a couple of the shots striking the coal pile in front of her and sending puffs of dust into the air, another striking the side of the car about six inches from her head and making her wince. She didn't know what was going on behind her, but she could hear the helicopter and had to trust that they had her back.

The first rule of sniping is never show up where you've been spotted. Rockaway shifted sideways a couple of feet, trying to keep as much of the pile for cover as she could. As trained as the Iron Cross were, she figured they'd have shifted position too, but there was only so much room for the two of them to move without getting in each other's way. She took an educated guess on where their positions might have moved to and popped up, rifle up and ready this time. She was off by a hair, but they'd missed her spot too, and rifle or not she was a helluva faster shot. Rockaway pulled the trigger as the mercenary shouted a battle cry, the high power round catching him right in his open mouth and blasting the back of his head off like a fist punching through rotted plaster. His pistol jerked in suddenly aimless hands, firing once before he fell out of sight.

His partner was steadier, though, and if she hadn't already been ducking back down he probably would've done the same right back to her. As it was, the round creased the side of her head, causing a bloom of white in her field of vision and knocking her back against the side of the coal car hard. Rockaway pushed aside the initial panic of a head wound – if it was worse than she thought, she'd find out in a moment when she pitched forward on her face, and if it wasn't she had fucking work to do. She could feel blood running down the side of her head and shook it to clear the spots from her vision, fighting a swell of nausea as she did so.

Rockaway could definitely hear more gunfire nearby, and even over the roar of the helicopter she was sure she heard the high crack of Doomsday's sidearm in the mix. The sniper had just enough time to get her bearings when she saw the Iron Cross emerge from cover at the far end of the coal car, and managed to launch herself to the side as he put three shots right where her chest had been seconds earlier. The pile offered her a little cover, but so long as he kept her scrambling she'd never get a good return shot. Unless he jumped into the car with her, but that was a rookie move, not something an Iron Cross would do. He'd keep her off-balance until he could line up a good shot, and then lights out.

She'd done it enough times herself. She knew how it worked.

Rockaway tried a feint, lifting her rifle up a little out of cover behind the pile, but he didn't bite. Careful. She went to lean out a little in the other direction, see if she could catch a glimpse of his position, but had to jerk her head back almost immediately as another shot went by, striking the back of the car with a resonant clang. Shit. He had her zeroed. As a sniper, she was fucking screwed.

As a psion, though, she had options.

Rockaway focused on the scar on her right hand, called up the feelings she'd felt when she was burning Eve down, saw her glove start to smolder, felt that tingling spread from her palm up to the tips of her fingers, saw the flames begin to coalesce just beyond her nails. She fixed that image in her mind and watched the flames grow to match it, until she had a small ball of flame hovering just above her palm. It took her a moment to realize the sound she was hearing was her own laughter. "I'm a fuckin' pyro. Who knew?"

Rockaway muttered, then she leaned out and chucked the ball of flame at the coal on the far side of the car.

Another shot grazed her arm as she did, but when the superheated psionic flames hit the coal it instantly vaporized a chunk of it and ignited a large portion of what remained. A thick plume of smoke rose up immediately, dense black clouds that obscured the far end of the coal car even as they flowed back over her. As distractions went, it would only last a moment or so, but that would be all she needed.

Rockaway scrambled to the top of the coal pile as fast as she could, climbing out of the cloud of smoke with her rifle leveled. The Iron Cross had stepped back from the rail, one hand up against the smoke in his eyes; he caught sight of her as she emerged from the billowing blackness and swung his pistol up to track her, but Rockaway was faster. At this range you hardly needed to aim, and she fired a shot from the hip that struck the mercenary in the middle of his bare chest. To his credit he grunted in pain but stayed on his feet for a moment, trying to aim with the grim determination of the mortally wounded.

"Fuck!" Rockaway tried to juke to the side and wound up sliding down the coal pile towards him instead. The mercenary's face twisted in an angry snarl of triumph and he fired, once, twice; Rockaway felt the impacts like sledgehammer shots to the gut and hoped her armor held. Broken ribs and bruising she could handle, but being poisoned by her own guts was another story.

"Fucking die! Fucking die!" The sniper squeezed off her second shot as the mercenary fired his third, her round tearing out the side of the mercenary's throat and sending his final shot inches wide into the coal. He staggered to the side and collapsed out of sight, but Rockaway had no time to enjoy the victory – somewhere behind her she heard a small bang and what sounded like metal groaning against metal, followed almost instantly by a massive explosion that rattled her teeth and made her innards shudder.

Bits of shrapnel winged past, and she cried out as a jagged piece stuck itself into her shoulder. Another piece the size of her leg landed in the burning coal next to her, showering her with sparks and burning debris. The entire car shook, jumping an inch or so in the air as something truly huge struck behind her, and there was a wrenching feeling followed by the scream of metal against metal, incredibly loud but quickly fading. Rockaway could hear screams behind her too, including one hopeless, drawn-out scream that could only be someone burning to death. It didn't sound lie Jimmy or Doomsday, which was good, but it might well be her in a moment if she didn't get out of the burning coal car.

The Yorker staggered to the edge of the car and pulled herself over the side, landing heavily on the open metal of the engine car. The two Iron Cross she'd shot were sprawled next to her, the headshot one staring blankly at the sky, the other one on his stomach in a pool of blood. As she watched, his blood flowed down to the gap where the cars were connected, dripping down on the tracks clacking by underneath. There was a small enclosed car at the front of the engine, presumably where the operator sat, but the door was closed and before she could investigate there was another lurching crash.

Rockaway got unsteadily to her feet and looked in the direction of the sound. It was hard to make out through the smoke from the burning coal car, but she could see the car with the covered cargo receding into the distance behind them, the small figures of Jimmy and Doomsday moving amid the flames, the shapes of a few Iron Cross engaging them. Off to the side of the tracks, one of the helicopters was a twisted heap of burning debris, while another large piece of flaming helicopter wreckage lay on the tracks between the two halves of the train, still smoldering in the spot where it had fallen and severed the connection between the cargo car and the coal carrier.

"Fuck," Rockaway managed, her head still ringing from the explosions and the grazing shot. She had to figure out a way to stop the train and get back there, before she left Jimmy and Doomsday behind out here, much less facing down those Iron Cross assholes without her.

Unfortunately, she didn't realize her time had already run out.

Chapter Eighteen

"Hello, Rockaway." Red Hands' voice was calm, almost friendly, but she felt her muscles freezing up as he was speaking. He was putting a body lock on her, just like he'd tried before, but when she tried to focus on breaking free it felt like the paralysis anticipated her intentions, flooding numbness and rigidity into her limbs wherever she tried to focus her will to break free. One hand was trapped against her gut where it had been checking her armor, while the other held her rifle locked in frozen fingers. She tried to speak, to curse, to say something, but her jaw was locked shut.

Red Hands made a little tsk tsk sound from somewhere a few feet behind her. "Oh, give me some credit. As though I hadn't noticed your mind's resistance was getting stronger. No, no, we're going to have a little chat, and you're going to stand there and behave. Understood?"

Like that, the pressure on her jaw released. Rockaway gulped down a few deep breaths before she responded. "You talk too fucking much."

Red Hands appeared at her right side, stepped slightly ahead of her and waved a hand over the burning coal car. Frost followed the arc of his arm, a wave of chilled air that fell on the coal and extinguished it as surely as if a colossal bucket of water had been tipped over the entire blaze. There was a blast of steam and thin grey smoke, and just like that the fire was out.

"You've picked up a few tricks, I've noticed." Red Hands turned to face her, different features than she'd seen last but the same triumphant smile on his face. He was slightly taller than last time and older too, stocky, with brown hair under a plain black military cap and a dark goatee peppered with gray. He was simply dressed, in the fashion of the Iron Cross, black boots and combat pants with a dark tactical vest sporting a simple black cross emblazoned on a white field on the back. He might have been just another mercenary, except for the bleeding red crosses cut into his hands. That, and the undisguised malice in his eyes. He gestured back at the now-extinguished coal car. "I'm better. Remember that."

"Missing something, asshole?" Rockaway flicked her eyes to what was left of the other cars, now gradually disappearing into the distance, oily smoke rising from the wreckage of the tangled helicopters off to the side of the tracks. "A bomb, maybe?"

Red Hands shrugged. "Annoying, but that's all. If a little trauma could prematurely detonate that device, it would've blown long ago." He smiled that wolfish smile of his. "Of course, if that pretty Inquisitor of yours managed to survive the helicopter explosion, I imagine she's trying rather frantically to figure out how to stop the reaction I initiated."

"You already set the fucking thing to blow? Kings, that's fucked up." Rockaway lost sight of the other cars as they turned a bend, leaving her staring at a screen of trees.

Red Hands laughed and stepped back to the front of the engine, out of her sight. "What can I say? I couldn't resist. With me managing it, of course, the reaction wouldn't get out of control until it was time, but without me?" There was a loud grinding sound and the engine ground to a painful halt, metal screeching on metal the entire time. "Who knows?"

Rockaway tested the paralysis again, straining her muscles trying to push against it in several different places instead of focusing on one or two in particular, but the power mirrored her efforts, and she was no closer to moving than before. The Yorker swore quietly. Red Hands was an egotistical asshole, but he wasn't an idiot. He wouldn't toy with her for long. Then, just like that a memory rattled up from a few years back, and she knew how she was getting out.

It had been a gang summit, the Dead Heroes along with the MPYRE Dogs, Grip Set, the Lonely Street Gang, the Green-Eyed Angels and a half-dozen other crews, all talking trade routes and other business shit. She'd been security for Boss Tone and Red Ed, half-listening to the arguing that was passing for a meeting, when all of a sudden Jeter's voice cut through the fighting. "Lissen up, muthabitches! Ya don't win every fight with a shooter, so try usin' ya goddamn brains! Ya fuckin' feel me?"

Rockaway couldn't use her shooter, but she could use her brains.

And thanks to her captor, she had one powerful, fucked up, psionic brain.

Red Hands was still talking, of course. "It had to change. This country is broken, and the League doesn't want to fix it. Not really. They just like fighting over the scraps. I thought the Iron Cross might be able to muscle them out, storm the League directly, but they fell in love with the credits being offered, the fools."

"Yeah, fuck them for making a living," Rockaway agreed mockingly. She was fighting down the panic, forcing her mind to clear to where she could concentrate again. "Assholes."

"Credits don't fucking matter!" Red Hands shouted, furious. "Do you have any idea how humiliating it is to be forced to stoop down to working with traitors, devil worshippers and wannabe kings? To smile and pretend to let them lead the dance while you're doing all the real work? Fixing the rails, buying the guns, finding idiots who just happen to be sitting on a fucking nuke?" He spat angrily. "You have no idea how long I've been planning this."

"Do fucking tell."

"Sixteen." Red Hands leaned in close behind her, so close she could feel his breath on her ear. "This body makes sixteen. But this will do it, I promise you. This will be the wakeup call that—"

Rockaway took a deep breath and concentrated on the hand frozen against her chest, willing the fire to manifest at her fingertips like it had before. The Yorker felt the heat start to build up, ignoring her body's warnings as she called up the flame. She saw her armor start to smolder, then cried out through clenched teeth as the ball of pyrokinetic energy manifested right against her chest, superheating her armor and searing her chest.

The flame only lasted for an instant, but that was enough – her limbs snapped back under her control as the pain overrode his psionic controls, just as it did when she saw Winter put a body lock on someone. Rockaway knew she had a few seconds at most before he dropped another bout of paralysis on her, though, and she didn't think he'd spend so long talking this time. Then again, Angry Justin liked to say a real fight only took about six seconds to decide, maybe less. So she made them count.

One thing a lot of people overlook about snipers is that they're versed in pretty much every use of their rifle you can imagine. Sure, scoring headshots from down the block is the main idea, and at close quarters Rockaway generally preferred her combat knife, but to draw that would take a couple more seconds than she had.

And her best friend was the best bat man in York.

So instead she reversed the rifle in her grip and swung the butt like a baseball bat as she turned, aiming for Red Hand's jaw and putting all the power behind it a lifetime of climbing in the Heights had given her.

The mercenary reflexively threw up a hand to block, exactly the response she'd hoped for as it kept him from focusing on his psionic powers for another crucial second. The butt caught him right on the wrist and broke it cleanly, leaving it to dangle painfully at the end of his arm. He clutched instinctively at his wounded wrist, hollering something she couldn't hear over the pounding of her pulse in her ears.

Rather than pressing the attack straight on, the sniper stepped just to his side, planted a foot behind his leading foot and hip-checked him. Caught off-balance, Red Hands tripped over her trapping foot and toppled over on his back, landing hard on the metal of the engine platform. Rockaway followed him down, using the fall to land a wicked elbow drop on his throat that left him gasping and pinning him partially beneath. She felt his broken wrist trapped under her and ground her weight on it as she hooked her legs around his to trap them.

Red Hands recovered enough to lash out with his good hand, pointing it at her across his body as the scar on his palm ignited, but Rockaway grabbed his wrist and pointed it high so that the blast of flame passed a few feet above her instead of engulfing her upper body. Blood dripped from the scar and it looked like Red Hands was readying another blast, so she kept hold of his wrist with one hand, grabbed his elbow with the other, braced her shoulder against his and put all her strength into a single, sharp tug. Red Hands howled curses as his shoulder popped out, but the light in his palm immediately died.

It wasn't over yet, and Rockaway knew it. She wedged herself partially under Red Hands and shifted her arms to apply a rear naked choke. The mercenary kicked, trying to find leverage to break the hold, but with both arms disabled and her legs hooking him it was a futile effort. "Anything else to say, motherfucker? Huh?" Rockaway hissed, tightening her grip while he struggled weakly in her arms. "C'mon, you chatty bitch!" She hauled back with all her strength, listening to him gurgle and wheeze. "Fuckin' talk to me!"

"Kill … this … body…" Red Hands gasped, "I'll … just … take … yours." What followed was a horrible, wheezing, gurgling sound that might have been his attempt at a laugh. It trailed off a moment later and he went limp, unconscious, but the longer she held on, the more her scars began to itch, and her head began to swim.

"Shit!" Rockaway fumed, breaking the hold and rolling out from under Red Hands. The throbbing in her scars began to fade almost immediately, and her head began to clear. Much as she hated to admit it, it didn't look like the fucker had been bluffing when he said he'd gotten inside her head and built some sort of emergency shelter there for his consciousness.

"Fuck!" Rockaway got to her feet, adrenaline still coursing through her system, and stared down at the unconscious mercenary in frustration. If she killed him now, it seemed too fucking likely that he'd take over her body, or at least he'd try, and she wasn't sure what might be left of her mind or body even if she won that battle. At the same time, she wasn't about to leave him here to recover and keep fucking with her in the future; even if he didn't chase her down, she didn't like waiting around for the day when he'd get killed by somebody else and suddenly show up in her brain, looking for a new home.

"Son of a bitch!" Rockaway kicked Red Hands but he didn't wake up, just groaned and shifted slightly. She could take him as a prisoner, but she didn't have any rope, much less any manacles, and besides he was a psion. Who knew what crazy shit he could do, even tied up? Unless she cut his hands his hands off to keep him from using those crazy scars, it wasn't like she could – wait.

Just like that, Rockaway had an idea.

It was kind of a shit idea, she had to admit, and it depended in part on her being able to figure out how to use her psionic powers for a healing jolt like she'd seen Winter do in the past, but it was also kind of a brilliant one. If nothing else, it would make him sorely fucking regret rigging that nuke to blow, and if that wound up burning her, well at least she could say she fucking tried. Sometimes that's the best you can do, at the end of a hard road.

Checking carefully to make sure Red Hands wasn't waking up or playing possum, Rockaway rummaged through her pack and pulled out a few old belting straps she sometimes used for carrying extra gear, as well as some bloody gauze a thick handful of scrap fabric. She placed each of these next to Red Hands, humming "Easy Boy Easy" as she worked, feeling her head clear bit by bit in the execution of simple tasks.

Only when everything was in place and she thought she was focused enough to call on her psionic ability again did she finally unsheathe her combat knife and get to work. Red Hands did finally wake up at that, of course, but by then it was far, far too late.

Chapter Nineteen

In the end, Rockaway met Doomsday and Jimmy halfway, after walking along the tracks for what felt like days but couldn't have been more than an hour or two. By the time they saw her, the weight on her back had begun to stagger her, and she was having some serious second thoughts about her plan. Jimmy noticed her first and gave a shout, breaking into a run with Doomsday on his heels.

"You fucker! You fucker!" Jimmy chanted over and over as he got close, his voice somewhere between fury and relief. He didn't slow as he closed the distance either, and bowled into Rockaway at nearly full speed, causing her to drop her package and yelp in alarm as the big bat man enveloped her in a massive hug, lifting her entirely off the ground and spinning around twice, kissing her the entire time before she managed to push back enough for him to let go. "What the fuck happened? Did you kill Red Hands?"

"Doesn't look like it," Doomsday said, before Rockaway could answer. Now that she was closer, Rockaway could see the agent had a nasty bruise on one cheek, and one hand kept clutching at her ribs as she walked. For that matter, Jimmy had several nasty cuts on his right arm, and a whole section of his chest armor had been removed, for reasons Rockaway wasn't sure she wanted to know. Judging from the expressions on their faces, she probably didn't look too much better. The agent nudged the package on the tracks, and it moaned faintly. "Nice work on the tourniquets."

"Yeah, well, learned from the fucking best, right?" Rockaway said weakly. Jimmy offered her a canteen with the Iron Cross symbol stamped on the side and the sniper drank deeply, then splashed a little on her matted hair.

"Besides, I actually gave him a little jolt, healed those cuts right up. Doesn't bring back the fucking limbs, but I think it stabilized the blood loss. Figured he'd have fucking kicked by now otherwise, tourniquets or not." She took another long pull on the canteen. "Thanks."

"Drink it all if you want. We've got plenty." Jimmy hefted his pack, which rattled and bulged with freshly liberated gear. "Kings, did you carry this asshole all this way?"

"Well, he didn't fucking walk, did he?" Rockaway said. "What happened with the nuke? He told me he'd armed it, that it couldn't be disarmed"

"Sounds like he told you true. It's armed, I can tell that much," Doomsday said unhappily. "I mean … what do you even do with something like that? I couldn't figure out how to disarm it. I risked removing the keys—" she held up the two necklaces that had caused all the trouble, "—but it didn't seem to do anything. It looks like there's some kind of buildup going on, it sounds like there's some kind of buildup at work, but it's not like there's a clock counting down to tell me how much more time we've got." She looked away sheepishly. "Sorry."

"What the fuck for?" Rockaway said. "'Cause you didn't know how to disarm a fucking nuke no one's seen since for-fucking-ever? That some psycho fuck rigged to blow unless he was personally there to babysit it? Fuck, I didn't even think you could disarm that shit. Wouldn't even have thought to fucking try."

"No joke," Jimmy added. "You ask me to disarm it, I'd have probably just tried to break that shit with my bat and got us all blown the fuck up. Truth."

"Thanks." Doomsday managed a shaky smile.

"What about Torv?" Rockaway asked.

"Dealt with," Doomsday said darkly, smile erased as if it had never been there, and Rockaway nearly took a step back at the look that passed across the agent's features. "Don't worry about her. But that brings up the point that we should probably be getting the fuck out of here, right the hell now." The agent looked at the two Yorkers. "What? You're starting to fucking rub off on me."

"Promised this asshole he'd have a front row seat for the nuke going off, if it was going to go off anyway." Rockaway spat, saw it flecked with red. Something to worry about later, assuming the bomb didn't go off first. "Figured I'd come check on you two while I was at it."

"Like we needed fucking help," Jimmy scoffed. "We had those assholes cold. Even after the fucking helicopters exploded."

"Inquisition's going to be fucking pissed about that," Rockaway said.

"Two things," Doomsday said, stepping up and reaching out for Rockaway's face with her good hand. The sniper assumed she was going to look at one of the cuts, but the agent just pulled her in close and gave her a long, gentle kiss.

"Damn," Jimmy teased when they broke the kiss a minute later.

"Oh, shut up," Rockaway said, and gave him a shorter one, though it was no less passionate for its duration. "It's been a fucking day."

"Two things," Doomsday repeated. "One, thanks for not getting yourself killed. Two, I appreciate the whole macho thing about carrying him to the bomb, and I think I love you a little bit just for thinking of that, but at this range? We're still in the front row seats."

"No shit?" Rockaway asked. "From that little thing?"

"No shit," Doomsday answered. "Trust me, they pack a lot more punch than you'd think. From the look of it that was a late pre-Fall model, and the holes punched in York can tell you how bad those could be. We need to get moving, and quickly. I don't know what exactly that one's capable of, but I'd start feeling comfortable around the five mile mark, and we're still well-inside that boundary."

"What about fallout?" Rockaway said. "Don't nukes, like poison everything for miles even beyond what gets blown the fuck up?"

"We're Yorkers," Doomsday said patiently. "We grew up in a whole city that counts as a hot zone. As long as we don't stick around too long after it goes off, I figure we should be OK."

"We're Yorkers," Rockaway said, pointing to Jimmy and herself. "You're a tourist."

"Speaking of, where the fuck are we going?" Jimmy asked before Doomsday could respond to the teasing. He gestured down the line at the tracks. "I mean, do these really go all the way to York, you think?"

"Probably," Doomsday said, wincing as she probed her ribs, "but we're going to need to find some kind of shelter soon. We've got no tents and no caravan, and I don't know about you, but I don't know how far it is to home, and I don't plan on sleeping on the tracks every night until we get there. We need to get our bearings, learn the local hotspots, and hopefully pick up some fresh gear, if not transportation."

"Well, we've got a train, for starters. An engine and some coal anyway, but that'll help, right? Plus there was a sign, train had just passed it when we stopped," Rockaway said, jerking her thumb back down the tracks in the direction she'd come. "Whole buncha towns listed on it, arrows pointing all over the fucking place, distances." She ticked them off on her fingers, remembering. "Hayven, Ripton Falls, Bravo, Boulder Run, Gatorland— "

"Gatorland?" Doomsday asked incredulously. "Where the hell are there alligators around here?"

"—Cascadia Rendezvous, and El Dorado."

217

217

Rockaway finished as if she hadn't heard, "They might not be much out here in the fucking sticks, but fuck it, better than nothing, right?"

"What's the nearest one?" Jimmy asked, opening another canteen and sipping from it.

"Hayven," Rockaway recalled. "'Bout 15 miles, if the sign was right."

Doomsday looked up at the sky, calculating. "If we get the engine going again we should be able to make that not long after dark, as long as we get underway soon and keep a good rhythm on loading the coal." She paused. "And if the tracks are fine, of course."

"You sure you can keep that pace?" Jimmy asked gently. "Shoveling coal and shit? 'Cause the way I'm feeling now I couldn't do any more laying on hands, much less calling on the Kings, and it'll be hard to treat your own ribs if we're on the move."

"You've done plenty," Doomsday said, smiling. "I can manage."

"Me too, in case anyone's fucking interested," Rockaway said, managing a slight smile to show she wasn't actually pissed. In truth she felt like she'd been run over by the train rather than ridden on it, but it seemed like everything still worked, and that was good enough for now. "Besides, leaving now suits me just fucking fine. I was tired of carrying this asshole already." Rockaway leaned down and rolled Red Hands over. His eyes fluttered but didn't quite open, not until she'd given him a few slaps anyway. "Hey. Fucker. Wake up."

"Grrrrpf." When the mercenary's eyes did finally open, they immediately narrowed to furious slits and he did his best to vocalize, but between the gag and his missing tongue all that came out was a low moaning noise. What remained of his limbs twitched weakly, but ultimately was of no greater use than his ruined tongue.

"Grrrrpf!"

"I'm not you, OK? I don't get off on speeches. So this will be fucking short." Rockaway pulled up the words she'd been working on as she carried the mercenary for the last hour, dealt them out slowly and deliberately as a dealer starting the final hand of the night. "You came at us with the Iron Cross, and Final Knights, and traitorous fucking G-Men, and you still lost. You thought you were clever with your psion bullshit, making me like you and shit, but in the end all it did was help me fucking kick your fucking ass."

"Too fucking right," Jimmy muttered darkly. Doomsday said nothing, but Red Hand's continuing struggles only proved that looks really couldn't kill.

"We're the Dead Heroes, motherfucker, the hardest gang in the Heights." Rockaway leaned in close to Red Hand's face, saw the fear creeping in behind the hate, felt a smile cross her face. "We're not just gonna kill you, we're gonna fucking nuke you. See if you can outrun that with your fancy fucking psion brain, bitch." The last she said so low and so close it was meant only for him. "'Cause I'm betting this sorry life is going to be your fucking last."

Rockaway rose up and turned back to the others as Red Hands thrashed wildly, eyes wide with terror and malice. "Let's go. I left my pack back at the engine, we can get it on the way." Without so much as a backward glance they headed down the tracks, feet crunching in the gravel, leaving the maimed mercenary to wait for the detonation alone.

Asshole.

Chapter Twenty

They walked in silence for a few minutes before Doomsday spoke. She didn't look at either of them, just kept walking with her eyes down, the words starting off slowly but gradually gaining speed as she spoke. "So, I've been thinking. I'm not sure what I'm going to be coming back to, when we get back to York. And that's kind of a big fucking problem."

"What do you mean?" Jimmy asked.

"I mean, ever since I was a kid, all I wanted to be is a G-Man. This was my first assignment, and I ... I don't know if I can go back. I really don't."

"You're no fucking quitter," Rockaway said, but Doomsday shook her head.

"That's not what I meant. I believe in this country – what it was, what it could be again. I'd die for it. I know that. But there's a problem." Doomsday took a deep breath, exhaled slowly. "Agent Freeman was the only one who knew that I was really undercover, and hadn't actually washed out of the Inquisition." She made a face. "Well, Agent Torv knew too, but—"

"She don't fucking count," Jimmy said, with finality. "'Specially now."

"I see the fucking problem." Rockaway chewed on it for a moment. "No chance that Agent Freeman told anyone else?"

"I don't know, but I don't think so," Doomsday said miserably. "He was famous for keeping secrets. It was kind of his job, really. And for an operation like mine? It depended on me being an agency washout. If he told too many people about it, sooner or later it would get out." She pulled her hair aside, revealing the brand of the Darwinist symbol on the nape of her neck. "Saints, they branded me and sent me packing in disgrace just to help sell my cover. They were serious about this operation."

"Well, they picked the right fucking chick to get results," Jimmy said, trying to raise her spirits. It got a tiny smile from Doomsday, which was something.

"What about your folks? What do they know?" Rockaway asked.

"I haven't talked to them in years. The Inquisition promised nothing would blowback on them from my fake washout, but I couldn't get in touch." She looked hopeful. "They're probably still with Mister Blackthorn, I guess."

"What about that guarantee he slipped us?" Rockaway asked. "That help?"

"Let's see," Doomsday said, fishing the envelope out of her pack. She opened it and scanned the papers inside, but judging from the way the look of hope on her face quickly died it didn't seem encouraging. "It's all about the Dead Heroes, and the Inquisition recognizing their service to the country and the Lineage League. Should keep your gang from suffering any pushback from all this, which is good, but there's nothing here for me."

"So what are you gonna do?" Jimmy said, giving Rockaway a look. The sniper made a little come on gesture but Jimmy just pointed at Doomsday and shook his head.

"I don't know. I can't go back to being a G-Man. I guess I could see if Mister Blackthorn has a place in his household…" Doomsday trailed off, not looking at either of them. Jimmy gave Rockaway another look, a little more pleading, and the sniper sighed.

"Girl, you know I got your back, but if you're waiting for us to ask, you're going to be waiting a long-ass time. You got something you want, fucking speak up." Rockaway gave the agent a level stare, waiting.

Doomsday swallowed. After watching her gun

down zed at point blank range, bar fight a bunch of burly Mericans and cross a hundred miles of bad terrain, it was oddly adorable to see her nervous like this. "Do you think I could jo—"

"Yes," Jimmy cut her off with utter finality.

"Absofuckinglutely," Rockaway concurred.

"Thanks." Doomsday beamed at them both gratefully, Jimmy returning it full force, Rockaway allowing herself a small tired smile after just the slightest of pauses.

The three walked along in quiet for a while after that, the sight of the engine in the distance making the walk a little easier, hearing just the sounds of three pairs of tired boots crunching in the gravel along the railroad tracks, their breath steaming in the chill. As they walked, Jimmy cleaned his bat with a rag from his pack, Doomsday thumbed bullets into her clips from an ammo pouch on her belt, and Rockaway worked on her detached scope with a clean rag soaked with water from a stolen canteen, trying to work out all the coal dust without scratching her lens. Birds called here and there in the trees, and the clouds moved slowly by overhead, unconcerned with the damaged world below.

It was a nice walk, though it probably would've been more relaxing if they weren't waiting for a nuke to go off at any minute. As it was though, compared to the hours and the days before it, it wasn't so bad.

"This place is pretty and all," Jimmy began at last, speaking slowly and with great solemnity, "but you know what? Fuck it." He gestured at the trees stretching as far as they could see on either side of the tracks and the green hills rising beyond them. "Fuck every one of these trees, and fuck every fucking tweety bird in them. I want a fucking building with cracked concrete, I want broken fucking windows, and I want fucking mean-ass dogs on rusted-ass chains, and I want fucking ladders, and I want

222

–" he gestured wildly "I want evil-eyed fucking pigeons!"

"Evil-eyed pigeons?" Doomsday raised an eyebrow.

"Don't ask him, he'll only fucking tell you." Rockaway rolled her neck wearily, hearing it crack while Jimmy and Doomsday laughed at his rant. "But you know what I want? I'd fucking kill for some proper cans. Franks 'n beans, shit like that. Real fucking food. Ever since we hit Aysea it's been nonstop hillbilly fruits 'n preserves bullshit."

"Franks and beans," Jimmy said dreamily. "Fuck, now I'm hungry."

"Me too," Rockaway agreed. "Toilet sangria, too. And it's gotta be Uncle Chuck's. First thing I do, I'm raiding the fucking stores."

"I never thought I'd say this," Doomsday said at last, "but I can't wait to get off the ground, sleep somewhere high and secure. This ground level shit is making me fucking paranoid, you know?"

"Kings, I was just thinking that!" Rockaway exclaimed. They reached the engine and pulled off the Iron Cross corpses, putting an extra bullet in each body for good measure before tossing their own packs onto the platform. "Assholes," Rockaway muttered, rolling the bodies into the trees while Jimmy shoveled the first few loads of coal into the furnace. Despite her injured ribs, Doomsday offered a hand to Rockaway and helped her up on the train. "Seriously, though, I can't fucking wait to be in a nice high perch again."

"How do people fucking live like this?" Jimmy said, eyeing the blue skies and green trees with deep suspicion as the train began chugging forward once more.

"Fucking savages." Doomsday agreed, giggling a little at her own profanity.

"Fuck it all," Rockaway said simply, patting Doomsday on the shoulder before picking up a coal shovel and taking a place next to Jimmy as he worked.

"Let's go home."

Epilogue

So. Yeah. That's how it all went down.

Sure, there was some more excitement on the way home – a town names itself something like Hayven, it's just asking for trouble in a world like this, knowumsayin' – but after what they'd been through in York, Aysea, the Pine Barrens and the Delphian Wastes, it wasn't no big thing. Well, except for the nuke going off, of course, but there wasn't shit they could do about that, right? Sometimes there's just a limit to all the thrilling fucking heroics even a Yorker can pull off, and all things being even, anyone who doesn't think they still did pretty damn great is a fucking asshole.

Besides, it also proved that Red Hands couldn't outrun a nuke. So, fuck him.

Not long after the three got back to York, a Postwalker delivered this big package to the Federal Bonded Inquisition. I bet they just about shit bats when they opened it, too. It was a ton of scraps of paper talking about Operation Knockout, the main point being how the Final Knights, the Iron Cross and the Dupont family tried set off a nuke in the middle of York. Supposedly the Lineage League got a copy too, just to make sure a fucking fire got lit. And shit, you should've seen the retaliation from the Purebloods and their G-Men. They tore the balls off the Iron Cross and hired every other merc who could hold a shooter or a blade and sent them down to the Delphian Wastes to fucking stomp on the Duponts. The fight ain't over, but way I hear it, I wouldn't want to be a fake-ass Pureblood any time soon.

Broadway Jack hadn't run nearly far enough,

'case you were wondering. The G-Men caught him hiding out up north, some little backwoods town called Ripton Falls, where he'd tried to set up some quack medicine practice. They dragged his ass back to York and dropped him at the edge of Dead Heroes territory. They say he had a bow on him but I call bullshit on that; the G-Men don't do cute, you know? Supposedly you could hear him screaming all the way down in the Plunge when they worked on him. And anyone who thinks Rockaway's got a mean streak obviously never saw her sister Gramercy with a blade, so I guess it was his bad luck they took turns. Good fucking riddance, the prick.

Of course, it wasn't all good news. That packet the G-Men got also had Dana Anderson's badge. Seems she put together the evidence and sent to them right before getting killed trying to disarm the nuke. Her parents took it hard, like you'd expect – their Pureblood boss actually gave a shit, too, if you can believe that. He lets them weekend in the Heights now; it seems to help them grieve to go see the people who were with her right up until the end. I heard they even got the G-Men to put their daughter's name up on a memorial wall at Inquisition headquarters, which sounds about right, because when Dana Anderson died Doomsday became a Dead Hero for real.

She did pretty well for a tourist, too, made her colors fast and wore them proud like a real Yorker should. Sure, Doomsday got a lot of shit for not coming by the gang natural like most of them did, of course, but she gave it back as good as she got it, and that's what matters. Plus she's a damn good field medic, it's hard to really look down on somebody who's put your guts back in after you were careless enough to let them slip out. She even played up the good parts of the outsider thing to become a speaker for the gang after a while, a damn good one, and believe me, I love York but there are too few emissaries and too many fucking shooters in this town. Rumor has it she was the one that got Mercy and Rockaway to talk like sisters again too, though I like my teeth too much to ask anyone involved if that's true.

Jimmy Three Ex? What do you expect? He fell right back into life with the Dead Heroes, moving up to Angry Justin's second in command when the gang was in the field. Learned the holy rites from Boss Tone, too, and helped convert some more of the Heroes. Even Rockaway, who seemed to figure she owed the Kings for getting her through the whole bullshit trip. Anyway, that wasn't the weirdest thing that happened. No, the crazy thing was that as word started getting out about what happened, kids started coming to him, one or two at first, then more, asking if he'd teach them to be bat men. To the surprise of no one but himself, Jimmy turned out to be a pretty good teacher too. If you wanna learn the trade, he's on the short fucking list to talk to about it, no question.

For a little while things were sticky when they finally got home, in part because Doomsday and Jimmy Three Ex were obviously a thing and didn't care who knew it. I think half of the Dead Heroes waited for Rockaway to snap and kick the shit out of both of them, and the other half waited for her to break down and join them out in the open. It was that kinda deal. I mean, the three of them spent so much time together it pretty much didn't matter, so gives a fuck, right? Besides, everyone knew that when Boss Tone said the words over Jimmy and Doomsday to make 'em official, he was talking to Rockaway too. She didn't hang around them any less because after they got the words, that's for sure.

Didn't even move out of their room, in fact.

Rockaway … even when she got home, it took her a long time to come back, you know? She spent a lot of time with Winter and the Doc, having conversations nobody was supposed to hear; while nobody tried to pry, there's only so much shit you can hide in a small gang. Nobody gave her shit about the psion thing, not after One-Way Kev lost two teeth making a bad joke about it, but except for Mercy and Ex and Doomsday, there was always a little more distance between her and the rest of the crew than there was before. And sniper is a lonely goddamn job in a gang to start with, so that's saying a lot.

Not that you would know, though, not most nights. She bullshitted with the crew, she picked fights when she felt like, drank too much hooch sometimes and never gave Angry Justin a moment's peace. What? You expected she'd be all gloomy and shit? All this time and you really don't know fucking Yorkers, then. Even after all that crazy bullshit, Rockaway did her part just like she ever did, shooting motherfuckers that needed it and looking after her own.

But damn, you know? I mean, god DAMN.

Sometimes, just sometimes, Rockaway's mind would go a tug on some of the loose ends, wondering if any of what happened would come back on her and her people. The letter from Agent Freeman worked its magic with the Inquisition, of course, and it wasn't like the Iron Cross was going to send so much as a hard look in their direction, but some nights she'd wonder if the Final Knights were going to come calling. Or if she'd see them coming if they did, or if they'd fight like the cowardly pussies they were, knives in the dark and all that shit.

And some really long nights, she'd wonder who Red Hands had meant when he talked about 'the professor' way back on the docks, and she'd wonder just how big the conspiracy was that they'd stumbled into. If his talk of sixteen bodies and who knows how long had been more than bullshit, and if not, just what that might have meant. Those nights she tended to have nightmares about him showing up on a dead gray beach, hands outstretched and coming for her. But when she woke up he was dead and she was not, he was ash on the breeze and she had her boy and her girl with her, and she'd just smile a sleepy smile and mutter something that might've been "bring it on" before going back to sleep.

If this 'professor' thought about revenge, she reconsidered real goddamn quick, let me tell you.

Anyway, talk about one hell of a fucking trip, right? And it all started with a simple fucking delivery run. But that's how this shit goes, sometimes. Just like you never see the bullet that kills you, destiny likes to sneak in and wreck your entire goddamn life. If it works out in the end, well, it all happened for a reason, you know? And if it doesn't, it's just another goddamn day in this fucked up world. Fortunately, when destiny needs shit done, it gets a Yorker for the job.

And Rockaway was the greatest goddamn Yorker I ever knew.

About the Author
Peter Woodworth

Peter Woodworth was introduced to role-playing games at the age of 5, when he and his brother discovered some oddly shaped dice while walking home from school. He's been gaming in one form or another ever since. He started writing professionally at 15, before anyone could tell him how unlikely it was that game companies would hire anyone his age with no previous credits.

Despite his embarrassingly naïve submissions, a series of kindly editors took pity on him, and since then he has worked as a writer for several companies including West End Games, Eschaton Media, White Wolf Game Studio, and Evil Hat Games. In that time he's worked for a variety of live-action and tabletop game lines, including Changeling: The Lost, Mind's Eye Theatre, Vampire: The Masquerade, Fiasco, Changeling: The Dreaming, Ravenloft, Hunter: The Reckoning, Spirit of the Century and (naturally) Dystopia Rising.

Outside of games and game writing Peter found his other calling in life as an English professor at a small college in southern New Jersey. When he's not meeting deadlines or grading term papers, he tends to be burning music mixes, watching cheesy paranormal television shows, debating literature with his far more scholarly wife, or just gaming with the best group of friends a geek could ever ask for.

After the dead arose...

Dystopia followed.

DYSTOPIA RISING

Original Concept Michael Pucci Executive Producer Ashley Zieb Writers Sean Jaffe Michael Pucci
Reviews and Editing Megan Jaffe Clifton Richards Design and Layout Joshua Brain Jaffe Matthew Volk
Artists Joyce Cheung Richard Sole Zachary Horchberger Peter Moschel Johnson Jennifer Lazaroff
Liz Lehman Andrew J. Scott

**Available in stores
and through online retailers
www.DystopiaRising.com**

www.ingramcontent.com/pod-product-compliance
Lightning Source LLC
Chambersburg PA
CBHW071902220626
47052CB00002B/173